Franz Kafka was born in Prague in 1883, the son of
a prosperous Jewish Czech merchant. He trained in
law and worked for a Prague insurance company.
He began to keep a diary in which he relentlessly
analysed his inner life. In 1912 he met a young
woman from Berlin, Felicie (Felice) Bauer, and was
twice briefly engaged to her. His unsatisfactory
love-affairs, his relationship with his father, and his
own inflexible intellectual honesty and almost
psychopathic sensitivity, combined to weaken his
health and in 1917 he discovered he was suffering
from tuberculosis. He resigned his appointment a
short while later and stayed in various sanatoria. In
1920 he met Milena Jesenka-Pollak, with whom he
later corresponded. In 1923 he met Dora Dymant
and lived with her for a time in Berlin. His
progressive illness drove him back to Prague before
he entered a sanatorium near Vienna. He died in
1924.

Kafka published a few works in his lifetime and left
directions that his unpublished writings should be
destroyed. These instructions were disregarded by
his friend and executor Max Brod. *The Trial*
appeared in 1925, followed by *The Castle* in 1926,
America in 1927 and *The Great Wall of China*, a
selection of his shorter fiction in 1931.

One critic described Kafka as the 'symptom and
product of his age, depicting with frightening
exactitude the dilemma of modern man in search of
a soul.'

Franz Kafka

Wedding Preparations
in the Country

and Other Stories

Penguin Books

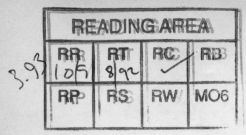

PENGUIN BOOKS

Published by the Penguin Group
Penguin Books Ltd, 27 Wrights Lane, London W8 5TZ, England
Viking Penguin, a division of Penguin Books USA Inc.
375 Hudson Street, New York, New York 10014, USA
Penguin Books Australia Ltd, Ringwood, Victoria, Australia
Penguin Books Canada Ltd, 2801 John Street, Markham, Ontario, Canada L3R 1B4
Penguin Books (NZ) Ltd, 182–190 Wairau Road, Auckland 10, New Zealand

Penguin Books Ltd, Registered Offices: Harmondsworth, Middlesex, England

Wedding Preparations in the Country (*Hochzeitsvorbereitungen auf dem Lande*, New York, 1953) and *Letter to His Father* (*Brief an den Vater*, New York, 1953) translated by Ernst Kaiser and Eithne Wilkins and first published in Great Britain by Martin Secker & Warburg, Ltd 1954

Two Dialogues (Munich, 1909), *Meditation* (*Betrachtung*, Leipzig, 1913), *The Judgement* (*Das Urteil*, Leipzig, 1913), *A Country Doctor* (*Ein Landarzt*, Leipzig, 1919) and *A Hunger Artist* (*Ein Hungerkunstler*, Berlin, 1924) translated by Willa and Edwin Muir and first published in Great Britain by Martin Secker & Warburg, Ltd 1949

This selection first published in Penguin Books 1978
10 9 8 7 6

Printed in England by Clays Ltd, St Ives plc
Set in Linotype Lectura

Contents

Wedding Preparations in the Country

[First Manuscript (A)]

I

When Eduard Raban, coming along the passage, walked into the open doorway, he saw that it was raining. It was not raining much.

On the pavement straight in front of him there were many people walking in various rhythms. Every now and again one would step forward and cross the road. A little girl was holding a tired little dog in her outstretched hands. Two gentlemen were exchanging information. The one held his hands palm-upward, raising and lowering them in regular motion, as though he were balancing a load. Then one caught sight of a lady whose hat was heavily laden with ribbons, buckles, and flowers. And hurrying past was a young man with a thin walking-stick, his left hand, as though paralysed, flat on his chest. Now and then there came men who were smoking, bearing small upright elongated clouds along ahead of them. Three gentlemen — two holding light-weight overcoats on their crooked fore-arms — several times walked forward from the front of the buildings to the edge of the pavement, surveyed what was going on there, and then withdrew again, talking.

Through the gaps between the passers-by one could see the regularly laid stones of the carriage-way. There carriages on delicate high wheels were drawn along by horses with craning necks. The people who sat at ease on the upholstered seats gazed in silence at the pedestrians, the shops, the balconies, and the sky. If it happened that one carriage overtook another, then the horses would press against each other, and the harness-straps hung dangling. The animals tugged at the shafts, the carriage bowled along, swaying as it gathered speed, until the swerve round the carriage ahead was completed and the horses moved apart again, only their narrow quiet heads inclined towards each other.

Some people came quickly towards the front entrance, stopped on the dry mosaic paving, and, turning round slowly, stood gazing out into the rain, which, wedged in by this narrow street, fell confusedly.

Raban felt tired. His lips were as pale as the faded red of his thick tie, which had a Moorish pattern. The lady by the doorstep over there, who had up to now been contemplating her shoes, which were quite visible under her tightly drawn skirt, now looked at him. She did so indifferently, and she was perhaps in any case only looking at the falling rain in front of him or at the small name-plates of firms that were fixed to the door over his head. Raban thought she looked amazed. 'Well,' he thought, 'if I could tell her the whole story, she would cease to be astonished. One works so feverishly at the office that afterwards one is too tired even to enjoy one's holidays properly. But even all that work does not give one a claim to be treated lovingly by everyone; on the contrary, one is alone, a total stranger and only an object of curiosity. And so long as you say "one" instead of "I", there's nothing in it and you can easily tell the story, but as soon as you admit to yourself that it is you yourself, you feel as though transfixed and are horrified.'

He put down the suit-case with the check cloth cover, bending his knees in doing so. The rain-water was already running along the edge of the carriage-way in streaks that almost extended to the lower-lying gutters.

'But if I myself distinguish between "one" and "I", how then dare I complain about the others? Probably they're not unjust, but I'm too tired to realize all this. I'm even too tired to walk all the way to the station without an effort, and it's only a short distance. So why don't I remain in town over these short holidays, in order to recuperate? How unreasonable I'm being! The journey will make me ill, I know that quite well. My room won't be comfortable enough, it can't be otherwise in the country. And we're hardly in the first half of June, the air in the country is often still very cool. Of course, I've taken precautions in my clothing, but I shall have to join with people who go for walks late in the evening. There are pools there, one will go for a walk the length of these pools. That is when I'm sure to catch cold. On the other hand I shall make but little showing in conversation. I shan't be able to compare the pool with other pools in some remote country, for I've never travelled, and talking about the moon and feeling bliss and rapturously climbing up on heaps of rubble is, after all, something I'm too old to do without being laughed to scorn.'

People were going past with slightly bent heads, above which they carried their dark umbrellas in a loose grip. A dray also went by, on the driver's seat, which was stuffed with straw, a man whose legs were stretched out so negligently that one foot was almost touching the ground, while the other rested safely on straw and rags. It looked as though he were sitting in a field in fine weather. Yet he was holding the reins attentively, so that the dray, on which iron bars were clanging against one another, made its way safely through the dense traffic. On the wet surface of the road one could see the reflection of the iron meanderingly and slowly gliding from one row of cobbles to the next. The little boy beside the lady opposite was dressed like an old vintner. His pleated dress formed a great circle at the hem and was only held in, almost under the very arm-pits, by a leather strap. His hemispherical cap came down to his eyebrows, and from the top a tassel hung down as far as the left ear. He was pleased by the rain. He ran out of the doorway and looked up wide-eyed into the sky, in order to catch more of the rain. Often he jumped high into the air, so that the water splashed a great deal and passers-by admonished him severely. Then the lady called him and henceforth held him by the hand; yet he did not cry.

Raban started. Had it not grown late? Since he wore his top-coat and jacket open, he quickly pulled out his watch. It was not going. Irritably he asked a neighbour, who was standing a little further back in the entrance, what the time was. This man was in conversation, and, while still laughing together with his companion, said: 'Certainly. Past four o'clock,' and turned away.

Raban quickly put up his umbrella and picked up his suit-case. But when he was about to step into the street, his way was blocked by several women in a hurry and these he therefore let pass first.

In doing so he looked down on a little girl's hat, which was made of plaited red straw and had a little green wreath on the wavy brim.

He went on remembering this even when he was in the street, which went slightly uphill in the direction he wished to follow. Then he forgot it, for now he had to exert himself a little; his small suit-case was none too light and the wind was blowing straight against him, making his coat flutter and bending the front spokes of his umbrella.

He had to breathe more deeply. A clock in a near-by square down below struck a quarter to five; under the umbrella he saw the light short steps of the people coming towards him; carriage-wheels squeaked with the brakes on, turning more slowly; the horses stretched their thin fore-legs, daring as chamois in the mountains.

Then it seemed to Raban he would get through the long bad time of the next fortnight too. For it was only a fortnight, that was to say, a limited period, and even if the annoyances grew ever greater, still, the time during which one had to endure them would be growing shorter and shorter. Thus undoubtedly courage would increase. 'All the people who try to torment me, and who have now occupied the entire space around me, will quite gradually be thrust back by the beneficent passage of these days, without my having to help them even in the very least. And, as it will come about quite naturally, I can be weak and quiet and let everything happen to me, and yet everything must turn out well, through the sheer fact of the passing of the days.

'And besides, can't I do it the way I always used to as a child in matters that were dangerous? I don't even need to go to the country myself, it isn't necessary. I'll send my clothed body. If it staggers out of the door of my room, the staggering will nòt indicate fear, but its nothingness. Nor is it a sign of excitement if it stumbles on the stairs, if it travels into the country, sobbing as it goes, and there eats its supper in tears. For I myself am meanwhile lying in my bed, smoothly covered over with the yellow-brown blanket, exposed to the breeze that is wafted through that seldom-aired room. The carriages and people in the street move and walk hesitantly on shining ground, for I am still dreaming. Coachmen and pedestrians are shy, and every step they want to advance they ask as a favour from me, by looking at me. I encourage them and they encounter no obstacle.

'As I lie in bed I assume the shape of a big beetle, a stag-beetle or a cock-chafer, I think.'

In front of a shop window, in which, behind a wet glass pane, little hats for men were displayed on small pegs, he stopped and looked in, his lips pursed. 'Well, my hat will still do for the holidays,' he thought and walked on, 'and if nobody can stand me because of my hat, then all the better.

'The form of a large beetle, yes. Then I would pretend it was a matter of hibernating, and I would press my little legs to my bulging belly. And I whisper a small number of words, instructions to my sad body, which stands close beside me, bent. Soon I have done – it bows, it goes swiftly, and it will manage everything efficiently while I rest.'

He came to a domed arch at the top of the steep street, leading on to a small square all round which there were many shops, already lit up. In the middle of the square, somewhat obscured by the light round the edge, was a low monument, the seated, meditative figure of a man. The people moved across the lights like narrow shutters, and since the puddles spread all the brilliance far and wide, the sight that the square presented was ceaselessly changing.

Raban pressed far on into the square, but jerkily, dodging the drifting carriages, jumping from one dry cobble to further dry cobbles, and holding the open umbrella high in his hand in order to see everything all around. Finally, by a lamp-post – a place where the electric tram stopped – which was set up on a small square concrete base, he halted.

'But they're expecting me in the country. Won't they be wondering about me by this time? Still, I didn't write to her all the week since she's been in the country, only this morning. So they'll end up by imagining even my appearance quite different. They may be thinking that I burst forward when I address a person, yet that isn't my way at all, or that I embrace people when I arrive, and that's something I don't do either. I shall make them angry if I try to pacify them. Oh, if I could only make them thoroughly angry in the attempt to pacify them.'

At that moment an open carriage drove past, not quickly; behind its two lighted lamps two ladies could be seen sitting on dark leather seats. One was leaning back, her face hidden by a veil and the shadow of her hat. But the other lady was sitting bolt upright; her hat was small, it was edged with thin feathers. Everyone could see her. Her lower lip was drawn slightly into her mouth.

As soon as the carriage had passed Raban, some bar blocked the view of the near horse drawing the carriage, then some coachman – wearing a big top-hat – on an unusually high box was moved across in front of the ladies – this was now much farther on – then their carriage drove round the corner of a small house that now became strikingly noticeable, and disappeared from sight.

Raban followed it with his gaze, his head lowered, resting the handle of his umbrella on his shoulder in order to see better. He had put his right thumb into his mouth and was rubbing his teeth on it. His suit-case lay beside him, one of its sides on the ground.

Carriages hastened from street to street across the square, the horses' bodies flew along horizontally as though they were flung through the air, but the nodding of the head and the neck revealed the rhythm and effort of the movement.

Round about, on the edges of the pavements of all the three streets converging here, there were many idlers standing about, tapping the cobbles with little sticks. Among the groups they formed there were little towers in which girls were pouring out lemonade, then heavy street-clocks on thin bars, then men wearing before and behind them big placards announcing entertainments in multi-coloured letters, then messengers ... [*two pages missing*] ... a little social gathering. Two elegant private carriages, driving diagonally across the square into the street leading downhill, got in the way of some gentlemen from this party, but after the second carriage – even after the first they had timidly tried to do so – these gentlemen formed into a group again with the others, with whom they then stepped on to the pavement in a long cavalcade and pushed their way through the door of a café, overwhelmed by the light of the incandescent lamps hanging over the entrance.

Electric tram-cars moved past, huge and very close; others, vaguely visible, stood motionless far away in the streets.

'How bent she is,' Raban thought when he looked at the photograph now. 'She's never really upright and perhaps her back is round. I shall have to pay much attention to this. And her mouth is so wide, and here, beyond doubt, the lower lip protrudes, yes, now I remember that too. And what a dress! Of course, I don't know anything about clothes, but these very tight-sewn sleeves are ugly, I am sure, they look like a bandage. And the hat, the brim at every point turned up from the face in a different curve. But her eyes are beautiful, they're brown, if I'm not mistaken. Everyone says her eyes are beautiful.'

Now an electric tram-car stopped in front of Raban and many people round him pushed towards the steps, with slightly open, pointed umbrellas, which they held upright with their hands pressed to their shoulders. Raban, who was holding his suit-case under his arm, was dragged off the pavement and stepped hard into an invisible puddle. Inside the tram there was a child kneeling on the seat, pressing the finger-tips of both hands to its lips as though it were saying good-bye to someone who was now going away. Some passengers got out and had to walk some paces along the tram in order to work their way out of the crowd. Then a lady climbed on to the first step, her long skirt, which she hitched with both hands, stretched tightly round her legs. A gentleman held on to a brass rod and, with lifted head, recounted something to the lady. All the people who wanted to get in were impatient. The conductor shouted.

Raban, who now stood on the edge of the waiting group, turned round, for someone had called out his name.

'Ah, Lement,' he said slowly and held out to a young man coming towards him the little finger of the hand in which he was holding the umbrella.

'So this is the fiancé on his way to his betrothed. He looks frightfully in love,' Lement said and then smiled with his mouth shut.

'Yes, you must forgive my going today,' Raban said. 'I wrote to you this afternoon, anyway. I should, of course, have liked very much to travel with you tomorrow, but tomorrow is Saturday, everything'll be so crowded, it's a long journey.'

'Oh, that doesn't matter. You did promise, but when one's in love ... I shall just have to travel alone.' Lement had set one foot on the pavement and the other on the cobbles, supporting his body

now on one leg, now on the other. 'You were going to get into the
tram. There it goes. Come, we'll walk, I'll go with you. There's still
plenty of time.'

'Isn't it rather late, please tell me?'

'It's no wonder you're nervous, but you really have got plenty
of time. I'm not so nervous, and that's why I've missed Gillemann
now.'

'Gillemann? Won't he be staying out there too?'

'Yes, with his wife, it's next week they mean to go, and that's
just why I promised Gillemann I'd meet him today when he leaves
the office. He wanted to give me some instructions regarding the
furnishing of their house, that's why I was supposed to meet him.
But now somehow I'm late, I had some errands to do. And just as
I was wondering whether I shouldn't go to their apartment, I saw
you, was at first astonished at the suit-case, and spoke to you. But
now the evening's too far gone for paying calls, it's fairly impossible
to go to Gillemann now.'

'Of course. And so I shall meet people I know there after all. Not
that I have ever seen Frau Gillemann, though.'

'And very beautiful she is. She's fair, and pale now after her
illness. She has the most beautiful eyes I've ever seen.'

'Do please tell me, what do beautiful eyes look like? Is it the
glance? I've never found eyes beautiful.'

'All right, perhaps I was exaggerating slightly. Still, she's a pretty
woman.'

Through the window-pane of a ground-floor café, close to the
window, gentlemen could be seen sitting, reading and eating, round
a three-sided table; one had lowered a newspaper to the table,
held a little cup raised, and was looking into the street out of the
corners of his eyes. Beyond these window-tables all the furniture
and equipment in the large restaurant were hidden by the customers, who sat side by side in little circles. [*Two pages missing.*]
... 'As it happens, however, it's not such an unpleasant business, is
it? Many people would take on such a burden, I think.'

They came into a fairly dark square, which began first on their
side of the street, for the opposite side extended farther. On the
side of the square along which they went walking there was an
uninterrupted row of houses, from the corners of which two – at

first widely distant – rows of houses extended into the indiscernible distance in which they seemed to unite. The pavement was narrow by the houses, which were mostly small, there were no shops to be seen, here no carriage passed. An iron post near the end of the street out of which they came had several lamps on it, which were fixed in two rings hanging horizontally, one over the other. The trapeze-shaped flame between conjoined sheets of glass burned in this tower-like wide darkness as in a little room, letting darkness assert itself a few steps farther on.

'But now I am sure it is too late, you have kept it a secret from me, and I shall miss the train. Why?' [*Four pages missing.*]

... 'Yes, at most Pirkershofer – well, for what *he's* worth.'

'The name's mentioned, I think, in Betty's letters, he's an assistant railway-clerk, isn't he?'

'Yes, an assistant railway-clerk and an unpleasant person. You'll see I'm right as soon as you've got a glimpse of that small thick nose. I tell you, walking through the dreary fields with that fellow ... Anyway, he's been transferred now and he goes away from there, as I believe and hope, next week.'

'Wait, you just said now you advised me to stay here over tonight. I've thought it over, it couldn't very well be managed. I've written to say I'm coming this evening, they'll be expecting me.'

'That's quite easy, send a telegram.'

'Yes, that could be done – but it wouldn't be very nice if I didn't go – and I'm tired, yes, I'll go all right. If a telegram came, they'd get a fright, into the bargain. – And what for, where would we go, anyway?'

'Then it's really better for you to go. I was only thinking ... Anyway I couldn't go with you today, as I'm sleepy, I forgot to tell you that. And now I shall say good-bye, for I don't want to go through the wet park with you, as I should like to drop in at Gillemann's after all. It's a quarter to six, so not too late after all for paying calls on people you know fairly well. Addio. Well, a good journey, and remember me to everyone!'

Lement turned to the right and held out his right hand to say good-bye, so that for a moment Raban was walking against Lement's outstretched arm.

'Adieu,' Raban said.

From a little distance then Lement called back: 'I say, Eduard, can you hear me? Do shut your umbrella, it stopped raining ages ago. I didn't have a chance to tell you.'

Raban did not answer, shut his umbrella, and the sky closed over him in pallid darkness.

'If at least,' Raban thought, 'I were to get into a wrong train. Then it would at any rate seem to me that the whole enterprise had begun, and if later, after the mistake had been cleared up, I were to arrive in this station again on my way back, then I should certainly feel much better. If the scenery does turn out to be boring, as Lement says, that need not be a disadvantage at all. One will spend more time in the rooms and really never know for certain where all the others are, for if there is a ruin in the district, there will probably be a walk all together to that ruin, as will certainly have been agreed some time before. Then, however, one must look forward to it, for that very reason one mustn't miss it. But if there is no such sight to be seen, then there will be no discussion beforehand either, for all will be expected to get together quite easily if suddenly, against all the usual practice, a larger expedition is considered right, for one only has to send the maid into the others' apartments, where they are sitting over a letter or books and are delighted by this news. Well, it is not difficult to protect oneself against such invitations. And yet I don't know whether I shall be able to, for it is not so easy as I imagine it now when I am still alone and can still do everything, can still go back if I want to, for I shall have no one there whom I could pay calls on whenever I like, and no one with whom I could make more strenuous expeditions, no one there who could show me how his crops are doing or show me a quarry he is working there. For one isn't at all sure even of acquaintances of long standing. Wasn't Lement nice to me today? – he explained some things to me, didn't he, and described everything as it will appear to me. He came up and spoke to me and then walked with me, in spite of the fact that there was nothing he wanted to find out from me and that he himself still had something else to do. But now all of a sudden he has gone away, and yet I can't have offended him even with a single word. I did refuse to spend the evening in town, but that was only natural, that can't have offended him, for he is a sensible person.'

The station clock struck, it was a quarter to six. Raban stopped, because he had palpitations, then he walked quickly along the park pool, went along a narrow, badly lighted path between large shrubs, rushed into an open place with many empty benches leaning against little trees, then went more slowly through an opening in the railings into the street, crossed it, leapt through the station entrance, after a while found the booking-office and had to knock for a while on the iron shutter. Then the booking-clerk looked out, said it was really high time, took the bank-note and slammed down on the counter the ticket he had been asked for and the change. Now Raban tried to count his change quickly, thinking he ought to be getting more, but a porter who was walking near by hurried him through a glass door on to the platform. There Raban looked round, while calling out, 'Thank you, thank you!' to the porter, and since he found no guard, he climbed up the steps of the nearest coach by himself, each time putting the suit-case on the step above and then following himself, supporting himself on his umbrella with one hand, and on the handle of the suit-case with the other. The coach that he entered was brightly illuminated by the great amount of light from the main hall of the station, in which it was standing; in front of many a window-pane – all were shut right up to the top – a hissing arc-lamp hung at about eye-level, and the many rain-drops on the glass were white, often single ones would move. Raban could hear the noise from the platform even when he had shut the carriage door and sat down on the last little free bit of a light-brown wooden seat. He saw many people's backs, and the backs of their heads, and between them the upturned faces of people on the seat opposite. In some places smoke was curling up from pipes and cigars, in one place drifting limply past the face of a girl. Often the passengers would change places, discussing these changes with each other, or they would transfer their luggage, which lay in a narrow blue net over a seat, to another one. If a stick or the metal-covered corner of a suit-case were sticking out, then the owner would have his attention drawn to this. He would then go over and put things straight again. Raban also bethought himself and pushed his suit-case under his seat.

On his left, at the window, two gentlemen were sitting opposite each other, talking about the price of goods. 'They're commercial travellers,' Raban thought, and, breathing regularly, he gazed at them. 'The merchant sends them into the country, they obey, they travel by train, and in every village they go from shop to shop. Sometimes they travel by carriage between the villages. They must not stay long anywhere, for everything must be done fast, and they must always talk only about their goods. With what pleasure, then, one can exert oneself in an occupation that is so agreeable!'

The younger man had jerked a note-book out of the hip-pocket of his trousers, rapidly flicked the leaves over with a forefinger moistened on his tongue, and then read through a page, drawing the back of his finger-nail down it as he went. He looked at Raban as he glanced up and indeed, when he now began talking about thread prices, did not turn his face away from Raban, as one gazes steadily at a point in order not to forget anything of what one wants to say. At the same time he drew his brows tightly down over his eyes. He held the half-closed note-book in his left hand, with his thumb on the page he had been reading, in order to be able to refer to it easily if he should need to. And the note-book trembled for he was not supporting his arm on anything, and the coach, which was now in motion, beat on the rails like a hammer.

The other traveller sat leaning back, listening, and nodding at regular intervals. It was evident that he was far from agreeing with everything and later would give his own opinion.

Raban laid his curved hands palm-down on his knees and, leaning forward, between the travellers' heads he saw the window and through the window lights flitting past and others flitting away into the distance. He did not understand anything of what the traveller was talking about, nor would he understand the other's answer. Much preparation would first be required, for here were people who had been concerned with goods since their youth. But if one has held a spool of thread in one's hand so often and handed it to one's customer so often, then one knows the price and can talk about it, while villages come towards us and flash past, while at the same time they turn away into the depths of the country, where for us they must disappear. And yet these villages are inhabited, and there perhaps travellers go from shop to shop.

In a corner at the far end of the coach a tall man stood up, holding playing-cards in his hand, and called out:

'I say, Marie, did you pack the zephyr shirts?'

'Of course I did,' said the woman, who was sitting opposite Raban. She had been dozing, and now when the question waked her she answered as though she were talking to herself or to Raban. 'You're going to market at Jungbunzlau, eh?' the vivacious traveller asked her. 'Jungbunzlau, that's right.' 'It's a big market this time, isn't it?' 'A big market, that's right.' She was sleepy, she rested her left elbow on a blue bundle, and her head drooped heavily against her hand, which pressed through the flesh of the cheek to the cheek-bone. 'How young she is,' the traveller said.

Raban took the money that he had received from the cashier out of his waistcoat pocket and counted it over. He held up each coin firmly between thumb and forefinger for a long time, and also twisted it this way and that on the inner surface of his thumb with the tip of his forefinger. He looked for a long time at the Emperor's image, then he was struck by the laurel-wreath and the way it was fastened with knots and bows of ribbon at the back of the head. At last he found the sum was correct and put the money into a big black purse. But now when he was about to say to the traveller: 'They're a married couple, don't you think?' the train stopped. The noise of the journey ceased, guards shouted the name of a place, and Raban said nothing.

The train started again so slowly that one could picture the re-volutions of the wheels, but a moment later it was racing down a slope, and all unexpectedly the tall railings of a bridge, outside the windows, were torn apart and pressed together, as it seemed.

Raban was now pleased that the train was going so fast, for he would not have wanted to stay in the last place. 'When it is dark there, when one knows no one there, when it is such a long way home. But then it must be terrible there by day. And is it different at the next station or at the previous ones or at the later ones or at the village I am going to?'

The traveller was suddenly talking more loudly. 'It's a long way yet,' Raban thought. 'Sir, you know just as well as I do, these manufacturers send their travellers round the most god-forsaken little villages, they go crawling to the seediest of little shopkeepers, and do you think they offer them prices different from those they offer us big business men? Sir, take it from me; exactly the same prices, only yesterday I saw it black on white. I call it villainy. They're squeezing us out of existence, under current conditions it's simply impossible for us to do business.'

Again he looked at Raban; he was not ashamed of the tears in his eyes; he pressed the knuckles of his left hand to his mouth because his lips were quivering. Raban leaned back and tugged faintly at his moustache with his left hand.

The shop-woman opposite woke up and smilingly passed her hands over her forehead. The traveller talked more quietly. Once again the woman shifted as though settling down to sleep, half-lying on her bundle, and sighed. The skirt was drawn tight over her right hip.

Behind her sat a gentleman with a travelling-cap on his head, reading a large newspaper. The girl opposite him, who was probably a relative of his, urged him – at the same time inclining her head towards her right shoulder – to open the window, because it was so very hot. He said, without looking up, he would do it in a moment, only he must first finish reading an article in the newspaper, and he showed her which article he meant.

The shop-woman could not go to sleep again, she sat upright and looked out of the window, then for a long time she looked at the oil-lamp and the flame burning yellow near the ceiling of the carriage. Raban shut his eyes for a little while.

When he glanced up, the shop-woman was just biting into a piece of cake that was spread with brown jam. The bundle next her was open. The traveller was smoking a cigar in silence and kept on fidgeting as though he were tapping the ash off the end of it. The other was poking about in the works of a pocket-watch with the tip of a knife, so that one could hear the scraping of it.

With his eyes almost shut Raban still had time to see, in a blurred way, the gentleman in the travelling-cap pulling at the window-strap. There came a gust of cool air, and a straw hat fell from a hook. Raban thought he was waking up and that was why his cheeks were so refreshed, or someone was opening the door and drawing him into the room, or he was in some way mistaken about things, and, breathing deeply, he quickly fell asleep.

II

The steps of the coach were still shaking a little when Raban climbed down them. Into his face, coming out of the air of the carriage, the rain beat, and he shut his eyes. It was raining noisily on to the corrugated iron roof of the station building, but out in the open country the rain fell only in such a way that it sounded like the uninterrupted blowing of the wind. A bare-foot boy came running up – Raban did not see from where – and breathlessly asked Raban to let him carry the suit-case, for it was raining, but Raban said: Yes, it was raining, and he would therefore go by omnibus. He did not need him, he said. Thereupon the boy pulled a face as though he thought it grander to walk in the rain and have one's suit-case carried than to go by bus, and instantly turned round and ran away. When Raban wanted to call him it was already too late.

There were two lighted lamps to be seen, and a station official came out of a door. Without hesitation he walked through the rain to the engine, stood there motionless, with his arms folded, and waited until the engine-driver leaned over his rail and talked to him. A porter was called, came, and was sent back again. At many of the windows in the train there were passengers standing, and since what they had to look at was an ordinary railway-station their gaze was probably dim, the eyelids close together, as while the train was in motion. A girl who came hurrying along from the road to the platform under a parasol with a flowered pattern on it, set the open parasol on the ground and sat down, pushing her legs apart so that her skirt should dry better, and ran her fingertips over the tight-stretched skirt. There were only two lamps alight, her face was indistinguishable. The porter, who came past, complained that puddles were forming under the parasol, held his arms in a semi-circle before him in order to demonstrate the size of these puddles, and then moved his hands through the air, one after the other, like fishes sinking into deeper water, in order to make it clear that traffic was also being impeded by this parasol.

The train started, disappeared like a long sliding-door, and behind the poplars on the far side of the railway-track there was the landscape, so massive that it took away one's breath. Was it a dark view through a gap or was it woods, was it a pool or a house, in which the people were already asleep, was it a church steeple or a ravine between the hills? Nobody must dare to go there, but who could restrain himself?

And when Raban caught sight of the official – he was already at the step up to his office – he ran in front of him and stopped him: 'Excuse me, please, is it far to the village? That's where I want to go.'

'No, a quarter of an hour, but by bus – as it's raining – you'll be there in five minutes.'

'It's raining. It's not a very fine spring,' Raban said.

The official had put his right hand on his hip, and through the triangle formed by the arm and the body Raban saw the girl, who had now shut the parasol, on the seat where she sat.

'If one is going to one's summer holidays now and is going to stay there, one can't but regret it. Actually I thought I should be met.' He glanced round to make it seem plausible.

'You will miss the bus, I'm afraid. It doesn't wait so long. Nothing to thank me for. That's the road, between the hedges.'

The road outside the railway station was not lighted; only from three ground-floor windows in the building there came a misty glimmer, but it did not extend far. Raban walked on tiptoe through the mud and shouted 'Driver!' and 'Hello there!' and 'Omnibus!' and 'Here I am!' many times. But when he landed among scarcely interrupted puddles on the dark side of the road, he had to tramp onwards with his heels down, until suddenly a horse's moist muzzle touched his forehead.

There was the omnibus, he quickly climbed into the empty compartment, sat down by the window-pane behind the driver's box and hunched his back into the corner, for he had done all that was necessary. For if the driver is asleep, he will wake up towards morning, if he is dead, then a new driver will come, or the innkeeper, and should that not happen either, then passengers will come by the early morning train, people in a hurry, making a noise. In any case one can be quiet, one may even draw the curtains over the windows and wait for the jerk with which the vehicle must start.

'Yes, after all I have already accomplished it is certain that tomorrow I shall get to Betty and to Mamma, nobody can prevent that. Yet it is true, and was indeed to be foreseen, my letter will arrive only tomorrow, so that I might very well have remained in town and spent an agreeable night at Elvy's, without having to be afraid of the next day's work, the sort of thing that otherwise ruins every pleasure for me. But look, I've got my feet wet.'

He lit a stub of candle that he had taken out of his waistcoat pocket and set it on the seat opposite. It was bright enough, the darkness outside made it appear as though the omnibus had black distempered walls and no glass in the windows. There was no need to think that there were wheels under the floor and in front the horse between the shafts. Raban rubbed his feet thoroughly on the seat, pulled on clean socks and sat up straight. Then he heard some-one from the station shouting: 'Hi!', if there was anyone in the bus he might say so. 'Yes, yes, and he would like to start now, too,' Raban answered, leaning out of the door, which he had opened, holding on to the doorpost with his right hand, the left hand held open, close to his mouth.

The rain gushed down the back of his neck, inside his collar.

Wrapped in the canvas of two sacks that had been cut up, the driver came over, the reflection of his stable-lantern jumping through the puddles at his feet. Irritably he began an explanation: Listen here, he said, he had been playing cards with Lebeda and they had just been getting on fine when the train came. It would really have been impossible for him to take a look outside then, still, he did not mean to abuse anyone who did not understand that. Apart from that, this place here was a filthy dump, and no half-measures, and it was hard to see what business a gentleman like this could have here, and he would be getting there soon enough anyway, so that he need not go and complain anywhere. Only just now Herr Pirkershofer — if you please, that's the junior assistant clerk — had come in and had said he thought a small fair man had been wanting to go by the omnibus. Well, so he had at once come and asked, or hadn't he at once come and asked?

The lantern was attached to the end of the shaft, the horse, having been shouted at in a muffled voice, began to pull, and the water on top of the bus, now set stirring, dripped slowly through a crack into the carriage.

The road was perhaps hilly, there was surely mud flying up into the spokes, fans of puddle-water formed, with a rushing sound, behind the turning wheels, it was for the most part with loose reins that the driver guided the dripping horse. – Could not all this be used as reproaches against Raban? Many puddles were unexpectedly lit up by the lantern trembling on the shaft, and split up, in ripples, under the wheel. This happened solely because Raban was travelling to his fiancée, to Betty, an oldish pretty girl. And who, if one were going to speak of it at all, would appreciate what merits Raban here had, even if it was only that he bore those reproaches, which admittedly nobody could make openly. Of course, he was doing it gladly, Betty was his fiancée, he was fond of her, it would be disgusting if she were to thank him for that as well, but all the same.

Without meaning to he often bumped his head against the panel he was leaning against, then for a while he would look up at the ceiling. Once his right hand slipped down from his thigh, where he had been resting it. But his elbow remained in the angle between belly and leg.

The omnibus was now travelling between houses, here and there the inside of the coach had a share of the light from a room, there were some steps – to see the first of them Raban would have had to stand up – built up to a church, outside a park gate there was a lamp with a large flame burning in it, but a statue of a saint stood out in black relief only because of the light from a draper's shop, and Raban saw his candle, which had burnt down, the trickle of wax hanging motionless from the seat.

When the bus stopped outside the inn, and the rain could be heard loudly and – probably there was a window open – so could the voices of the guests, Raban wondered which would be better, to get out at once or to wait until the innkeeper came to the coach. What the custom was in this township he did not know, but it was pretty certain that Betty would have spoken of her fiancé, and according to whether his arrival here was magnificent or feeble, so the esteem in which she was held here would increase or diminish, and with that, again, his own too. But, of course, he knew neither what people felt about her nor what she had told them about him, and so everything was all the more disagreeable and difficult. Oh beautiful city and beautiful the way home! If it rains there one goes home by tram over wet cobbles, here one goes in a cart through mud to an inn. – 'The city is far from here, and if I were now in danger of dying of homesickness, nobody could get me back there today. – Well, anyway, I shouldn't die – but there I get the meal expected for that evening set on the table, on the right behind my plate the newspaper, on the left the lamp, here I shall be given some dreadfully greasy dish – they don't know that I have a weak stomach, and even if they did know – an unfamiliar newspaper – Many people, whom I can already hear, will be there, and one lamp will be lit for all. What sort of light can it provide? Enough to play cards by – but for reading a newspaper?

'The innkeeper isn't coming, he's not interested in guests, he is probably an unfriendly man. Or does he know that I am Betty's fiancé, and does that give him a reason for not coming to fetch me in? It would be in accord with that that the driver kept me waiting so long at the station. Betty has often told me, after all, how much she has been bothered by lecherous men and how she has had to rebuff their insistence, perhaps it is that here too . . .' [*Text breaks off.*]

[Second Manuscript (B)]

When Eduard Raban, coming along the passage, walked into the open doorway, he could now see how it was raining. It was not raining much.

On the pavement straight in front of him, not higher, not lower, there were, in spite of the rain, many passers-by. Every now and again one would step forward and cross the road.

A little girl was carrying a grey dog on her outstretched arms. Two gentlemen were exchanging information on some subject, at times turning the whole front of their bodies to each other, and then slowly turning aside themselves again; it was like doors ajar in the wind. The one held his hands palm-upward, raising and lowering them in regular motion, as though he were balancing a load, testing the weight of it. Then one caught sight of a slim lady whose face twitched slightly, like the flickering light of the stars, and whose flat hat was loaded high and to the brim with unrecognizable objects; she appeared to be a stranger to all the passers-by, without intending it, as though by some law. And hurrying past was a young man with a thin walking-stick, his left hand, as though paralysed, lying flat on his chest. Many were out on business; in spite of the fact that they walked fast one saw them longer than others, now on the pavement, now below, their coats fitted them badly, they did not care how they carried themselves, they let themselves be pushed by the people and they pushed too. Three gentlemen — two holding light-weight overcoats on their crooked fore-arms — walked from the front of the building to the edge of the pavement, in order to see what was going on on the carriage-way and on the farther pavement.

Through the gaps between the passers-by, now fleetingly, then comfortably, one saw the regularly laid cobbles of the carriage-way, on which carriages, swaying on their wheels, were swiftly drawn by horses with craning necks. The people who sat at ease on the upholstered seats gazed in silence at the pedestrians, the shops, the balconies, and the sky. If it happened that one carriage overtook another, then the horses would press against each other, and the harness-straps hung dangling. The animals tugged at the shafts, the carriage bowled along, swaying as it gathered speed, until the swerve round the carriage ahead was completed and the horses moved apart again, still with their narrow heads inclined towards each other.

An elderly gentleman came quickly towards the front entrance, stopped on the dry mosaic paving, turned round. And he then gazed into the rain, which, wedged in by the narrow street, fell confusedly.

Raban put down the suit-case with the black cloth cover, bending his right knee a little in doing so. The rain-water was already running along the edge of the carriage-way in streaks that almost extended to the lower-lying gutters.

The elderly gentleman stood upright near Raban, who was supporting himself slightly against the wooden doorpost, and from time to time glanced towards Raban, even though to do so he had to twist his neck sharply. Yet he did this only out of the natural desire, now that he happened to be unoccupied, to observe everything exactly, at least in his vicinity. The result of this aimless glancing hither and thither was that there was a great deal he did not notice. So, for instance, it escaped him that Raban's lips were very pale, not much less so than the very faded red of his tie, which had a once striking Moorish pattern. Now, had he noticed this, he would certainly have made a fuss about it, at least inwardly, which, again, would not have been the right thing, for Raban was always pale, even if, it was a fact, various things might have been making him especially tired just recently.

'What weather!' the gentleman said in a low voice, shaking his head, consciously, it was true, but still in a slightly senile way.

'Yes, indeed, and when one's supposed to be starting on a journey, too,' Raban said, quickly straightening up.

'And it isn't the kind of weather that will improve,' the gentleman said and, in order to make sure of it once more for the last time, bent forward to glance in scrutiny up the street, then down, and then at the sky, 'it may last for days, even for weeks. So far as I recall, nothing better is forecast for June and the beginning of July, either. Well, it's no pleasure to anyone, I for instance shall have to do without my walks, which are extremely important to my health.'

Hereupon he yawned and seemed to become exhausted, since he had now heard Raban's voice and, occupied with this conversation, no longer took any interest in anything, not even in the conversation.

This made quite an impression on Raban, since after all the gentleman had addressed him first, and he therefore tried to show off a little, although it might not even be noticed. 'True,' he said, 'in town one can very easily manage to go without what isn't good for one. If one does not do without it, then one has only oneself to blame for the bad consequences. One will be sorry and in this way come to see for the first time really clearly how to manage the next time. And even if in matters of detail ... [*two pages missing*] ... 'I don't mean anything by it. I don't mean anything at all,' Raban hastened to say, prepared to excuse the gentleman's absent-mindedness in any way possible, since after all he wanted to show off a little more. 'It's all just out of the book previously mentioned, which I, like other people, happen to have been reading in the evening recently. I have been mostly alone. Owing to family circumstances, you see. But apart from anything else, a good book is what I like best after supper. Always has been. Just recently I read in a prospectus a quotation from some writer or other: "A good book is the best friend there is," and that's really true, it is so, a good book is the best friend there is.'

'Yes, when one is young —' the gentleman said, meaning nothing in particular by this, merely wanting to indicate how it was raining, that the rain was heavier again, and that now it was not going to stop at all, but to Raban it sounded as though at sixty the gentleman still thought of himself as young and energetic and considered Raban's thirty years nothing in comparison, and as though he meant to say besides, in so far as it was permissible, that at the age of thirty he had of course been more sensible than Raban. And that he believed even if one had nothing else to do, like himself, for instance, an old man, yet it was really wasting one's time to stand about here in this hall, looking at the rain, but if one spent the time, besides, in chatter, one was wasting it doubly.

Now Raban believed that for some time nothing other people said about his capabilities or opinions had been able to affect him, on the contrary, that he had positively abandoned the position where he had listened, all submissively, to everything that was said, so that people were now simply wasting their breath whether they happened to be against him or for him. And so he said: 'We are talking about different things, since you did not wait to hear what I was going to say.'

'Please go on, please go on,' the gentleman said.

'Well, it isn't so important,' Raban said, 'I was only going to say books are useful in every sense and quite especially in respects in which one would not expect it. For when one is about to embark on some enterprise, it is precisely the books whose contents have nothing at all in common with the enterprise that are the most useful. For the reader, who does after all intend to embark on that enterprise, that is to say, who has somehow become enthusiastic (and even if, as it were, the effect of the book can penetrate only as far as that enthusiasm), will be stimulated by the book to all kinds of thoughts concerning his enterprise. Now, however, since the contents of the book are precisely something of entire indifference, the reader is not at all impeded in those thoughts, and he passes through the midst of the book with them, as once the Jews passed through the Red Sea, that's how I should like to put it.'

For Raban the whole person of the old gentleman now assumed

an unpleasant expression. It seemed to him as though he had drawn particularly close to him — but it was merely trifling ... [*two pages missing*] ... 'The newspaper too. — But I was about to say, I am only going into the country, that's all, only for a fortnight, I am taking a holiday, for the first time for quite a long period, and it's necessary for other reasons too, and yet for instance a book that I was, as I have mentioned, reading recently taught me more about my little journey than you could imagine.'

'I am listening,' the gentleman said.

Raban was silent and, standing there so straight, put his hands into his overcoat pockets, which were rather too high. Only after a while did the old gentleman say: 'This journey seems to be of some special importance to you.'

'Well, you see, you see,' Raban said, once more supporting himself against the doorpost. Only now did he see how the passage had filled up with people. They were standing even round the foot of the staircase, and an official, who had rented a room in the apartment of the same woman as Raban had, when he came down the stairs had to ask the people to make way for him. To Raban, who only pointed at the rain, he called out over several heads, which now all turned to Raban, 'Have a good journey,' and reiterated a promise, obviously given earlier, definitely to visit Raban the next Sunday.

[*Two pages missing*] ... has a pleasant job, with which he is indeed satisfied and which has always been kept open for him. He has such powers of endurance and is inwardly so gay that he does not need anyone to keep him entertained, but everyone needs him. He has always been healthy. Oh, don't try to tell me.'

'I am not going to argue,' the gentleman said.

'You won't argue, but you won't admit your mistake either. Why do you stick to it so? And however sharply you may recollect now, you would, I dare wager, forget everything if you were to talk to him. You would reproach me for not having refuted you more effectively now. If he so much as talks about a book. He's instantly ecstatic about everything beautiful ...'

Translated by Ernst Kaiser and Eithne Wilkins

Letter to His Father[1]

Dearest Father,

You asked me recently why I maintain I am afraid of you. As usual, I was unable to think of my answer to your question, partly for the very reason that I am afraid of you, and partly because an explanation of the grounds for this fear would mean going into far more details than I could even approximately keep in mind while talking. And if I now try to give you an answer in writing, it will still be very incomplete, because even in writing this fear and its consequences hamper me in relation to you and because [anyway] the magnitude of the subject goes far beyond the scope of my memory and power of reasoning.

To you the matter always seemed very simple, at least in as far as you talked about it in front of me, and without discrimination in front of many other people. It looked to you more or less as follows: you have worked hard all your life, have sacrificed everything for your children, above all for me, consequently I have lived 'like a fighting-cock', have been completely at liberty to learn whatever I wanted, and have had no cause for material worries, which means worries of any kind at all. You have not expected any gratitude for this, knowing what 'children's gratitude' is like, but have expected at least some sort of obligingness, some sign of sympathy. Instead I have always dodged you and hidden from you, in my room, among my books, with crazy friends, or with extravagant ideas. I have never talked to you frankly, I have never come to you when you were in the synagogue, never visited you at Franzensbad, nor indeed ever shown any family feeling, I have never taken any interest in the business or your other concerns, I left the factory on your hands and left you in the lurch, I encouraged Ottla[2] in her obstinacy, and never lifted a finger for you (never even got you a theatre-ticket), while I do everything for my friends. If you sum up your judgement of me, the result you get is that although you don't charge me with anything downright improper or wicked (with the exception perhaps of my latest marriage-plan), you do charge me with coldness, estrangement, and ingratitude. And, what is more, you charge me with it in such a way as to make it seem it were my fault, as though I might have been able, with something like a touch on the steering-wheel, to make everything quite different, while you aren't in the slightest to blame, unless it were for having been too good to me.

This, your usual way of representing it, I regard as accurate only in as far as I too believe you are entirely blameless in the matter of our estrangement. But I also am entirely blameless. If I could get you to acknowledge this, then what would be possible is – not, I think, a new life, we are both much too old for that – but still, a kind of peace; no cessation, but still, a diminution of your unceasing reproaches.

Oddly enough you have some sort of notion of what I mean. For instance, a short time ago you said to me: 'I have always been fond of you, even though outwardly I didn't act towards you as other fathers do, and this precisely because I can't pretend as other people can.' Now, Father, on the whole I have never doubted your goodness towards me, but this remark is one I consider wrong. You can't pretend, that's a fact, but merely for that reason to maintain that other fathers pretend is either mere opinionatedness, and as such beyond discussion, or on the other hand – and this in my view is what it really is – a veiled expression of the fact that something is wrong in our relationship and that you have played your part in causing it to be so, but without its being your fault. If you really mean that, then we are in agreement.

I'm not going to say, of course, that I have become what I am only as a result of your influence. That would be very much exaggerated (and I am indeed inclined to this exaggeration). It is indeed quite possible that even if I had grown up entirely free from your influence I still could not have become a person after your own heart. I should probably have still become a weakly, timid, hesitant, restless person, neither Robert Kafka nor Karl Hermann, but yet quite different from what I really am, and we might have got on with each other excellently. I should have been happy to have you as a friend, as a chief, an uncle, a grandfather, even indeed (though this rather more hesitantly) as a father-in-law. Only as what you are, a father, you have been too strong for me, particularly since my brothers died when they were small and my sisters only came along much later, so that I had to bear the whole brunt of it all alone, something I was too weak for.

Compare the two of us: I, to put it in a very much abbreviated form, a Löwy[3] with a certain basis of Kafka, which however is not set in motion by the Kafka will to life, business, and conquest, but by a Löwyish spur that urges more secretly, more diffidently, and in another direction, and which often fails to work entirely. You, on the other hand, a true Kafka in strength, health, appetite, loudness of voice, eloquence, self-satisfaction, worldly dominance, endurance, presence of mind, knowledge of human nature, a certain way of doing things on a grand scale, of course also with all the defects and weaknesses that go with all these advantages and into which your temperament and sometimes your hot temper drive you. You are perhaps not wholly a Kafka in your general outlook, in so far as I can compare you with Uncle Philipp, Ludwig, and Heinrich. That is odd, and here I don't see quite clearly either. After all, they were all more cheerful, fresher, more informal, more easy-going, less severe than you. (In this, by the way, I have inherited a great deal from you and taken much too good care of my inheritance, without, admittedly, having the necessary counter-weights in my own nature, as you have.) Yet you too, on the other hand, have in this respect gone through various phases. You were perhaps more cheerful before your children, in particular I, disappointed you and depressed you at home (when other people came in, you were quite different) and perhaps have become more cheerful again since then, now that your grandchildren and your son-in-law again give you something of that warmth which your children, except perhaps Valli, could not give you. However it was, we were so different and in our difference so dangerous to each other that, if anyone had tried to calculate in advance how I, the slowly developing child, and you, the full-grown man, would stand to each other, he could have assumed that you would simply trample me underfoot so that nothing was left of me. Well, that didn't happen. Nothing alive can be calculated. But perhaps something worse happened. And in saying this I would all the time beg of you not to forget that I never, and not even for a single moment, believe any guilt to be on your side. The effect you had on me was the effect you could not help having. But you should stop considering it some particular malice on my part that I succumbed to that effect.

I was a timid child. For all that, I am sure I was also obstinate, as children are. I am sure that Mother spoilt me too, but I cannot believe I was particularly difficult to manage, I cannot believe that a kindly word, a quiet taking of me by the hand, a friendly look, could not have got me to do anything that was wanted of me. Now you are after all at bottom a kindly and soft-hearted person (what follows will not be in contradiction to this, I am speaking only of the impression you made on the child), but not every child has the endurance and fearlessness to go on searching until it comes to the kindliness that lies beneath the surface. You can only treat a child in the way you yourself are constituted, with vigour, noise, and hot temper, and in this case this seemed to you, into the bargain, extremely suitable, because you wanted to bring me up to be a strong brave boy.

Your educational methods in the very early years I can't of course directly describe today, but I can more or less imagine them by drawing retrospective conclusions from the later years and from your treatment of Felix.[4] What must be considered as heightening the effect is that you were then younger and hence more energetic, wilder, more untrammelled and still more reckless than you are today and that you were, besides, completely tied to the business, scarcely able to be with me even once a day, and therefore made all the more profound an impression on me, never really levelling out into the flatness of habit.

There is only one episode in the early years of which I have a direct memory. You may remember it too. Once in the night I kept on whimpering for water, not, I am certain, because I was thirsty, but probably partly to be annoying, partly to amuse myself. After several vigorous threats had failed to have any effect, you took me out of bed, carried me out on to the *pavlatche*[5] and left me there alone for a while in my nightshirt, outside the shut door. I am not going to say that this was wrong – perhaps at that time there was really no other way of getting peace and quiet that night

— but I mention it as typical of your methods of bringing up a child and their effect on me. I dare say I was quite obedient afterwards at that period, but it did me inner harm. What was for me a matter of course, that senseless asking for water, and the extraordinary terror of being carried outside were two things that I, my nature being what it was, could never properly connect with each other. Even years afterwards I suffered from the tormenting fancy that the huge man, my father, the ultimate authority, would come almost for no reason at all and take me out of bed in the night and carry me out on to the *pavlatche*, and that therefore I was such a mere nothing for him.

That then was only a small beginning, but this sense of nothingness that often dominates me (a feeling that is in another respect, admittedly, also a noble and fruitful one) comes largely from your influence. What I would have needed was a little encouragement, a little friendliness, a little keeping open of my road, instead of which you blocked it for me, though, of course, with the good intention of making me go another road. But I was not fit for that. You encouraged me for instance when I saluted and marched smartly, but I was no future soldier, or you encouraged me when I was able to eat heartily or even drink beer with my meals, or when I was able to repeat songs, singing what I had not understood, or prattle to you using your own favourite expressions, imitating you, but nothing of this had anything to do with my future. And it is characteristic that even today you really only encourage me in anything when you yourself are involved in it, when what is at stake is your own sense of self-importance, which I damage (for instance by my intention of marrying) or which is damaged in me (for instance when Pepa[6] is abusive to me). Then I receive encouragement, I am reminded of my worth, the matches I would be entitled to make are pointed out to me, and Pepa is condemned utterly. But apart from the fact that at the age I have now reached I am almost quite unsusceptible to encouragement, what help could it be to me anyway, when it only comes where it isn't primarily a matter of myself at all?

At that time, and at that time everywhere, I would have needed encouragement. I was, after all, depressed even by your mere physical presence. I remember for instance how we often undressed together in the same bathing-hut. There was I, skinny, weakly, slight, you strong, tall, broad. Even inside the hut I felt myself a miserable specimen, and what's more not only in your eyes, but in the eyes of the whole world, for you were for me the measure of all things. But then when we went out of the bathing-hut before the people, I with you holding my hand, a little skeleton, unsteady, barefoot on the boards, frightened of the water, incapable of copying your swimming-strokes, which you, with the best of intentions, but actually to my profound humiliation, always kept on showing me, then I was frantic with desperation and all my bad experiences in all spheres at such moments fitted magnificently together. What made me feel best was when you sometimes undressed first and I was able to stay behind in the hut alone and put off the disgrace of showing myself in public until at length you came to see what I was doing and drove me out of the hut. I was grateful to you for not seeming to notice my extremity, and besides, I was proud of my father's body. For the rest, this difference between us remains much the same to this very day.

In keeping with that, furthermore, was your intellectual domination. You had worked your way up so far alone, by your own energies, and as a result you had unbounded confidence in your opinion. For me as a child that was not yet as dazzling as later for the boy growing up. From your armchair you ruled the world. Your opinion was correct, every other was mad, wild, *meschugge*, not normal. With all this your self-confidence was so great that you had no need to be consistent at all and yet never ceased to be in the right. It did sometimes happen that you had no opinion whatsoever about a matter and as a result all opinions that were at all possible with respect to the matter were necessarily wrong, without exception. You were capable, for instance, of running down the Czechs, and then the Germans, and then the Jews, and what is more not only selectively but in every respect, and finally nobody was left except yourself. For me you took on the enigmatic quality that all tyrants have whose rights are based on their person and not on reason. At least so it seemed to me.

Now where I was concerned you were in fact astonishingly often in the right, which was a matter of course in talk, for there was hardly ever any talk between us, but also in reality. Yet this too was nothing particularly incomprehensible: in all my thinking I was, after all, under the heavy pressure of your personality, even in that part of it – and particularly in that – which was not in accord with yours. All these thoughts, seemingly independent of you, were from the beginning loaded with the burden of your harsh and dogmatic judgements; it was almost impossible to endure this and yet to work out one's thoughts with any measure of completeness and permanence. I am not here speaking of any sublime thoughts, but of every little enterprise in childhood. It was only necessary to be happy about something or other, to be filled with the thought of it, to come home and speak of it, and the answer was an ironical sigh, a shaking of the head, a tapping of the table with one finger: 'Is that all you're so worked up about?' or 'I wish I had your worries!' or 'The things some people have time to think about!' or 'What can you buy yourself with that?' or 'What a song-and-dance about nothing!' Of course you couldn't be expected to be enthusiastic about every childish triviality, toiling and moiling as you used to. But that wasn't the point. The point was, rather, that you could not help always and on principle causing the child such disappointments, by virtue of your antagonistic nature, and further that this antagonism was ceaselessly intensified through accumulation of its material, that it finally became a matter of established habit even when for once you were of the same opinion as myself, and that finally these disappointments of the child's were not disappointments in ordinary life but, since what it concerned was your person, which was the measure of all things, struck to the very core. Courage, resolution, confidence, delight in this and that, did not endure to the end when you were against whatever it was or even if your opposition was merely to be assumed; and it was to be assumed in almost everything I did.

This applied to thoughts as well as to people. It was enough that I should take a little interest in a person – which in any case did not happen often, as a result of my nature – for you, without any consideration for my feelings or respect for my judgement, to butt in with abuse, defamation, and denigration. Innocent, childlike people such as for instance the Yiddish actor Löwy had to pay for that. Without knowing him you compared him, in a dreadful way that I have now forgotten, to vermin and as was so often the case with people I was fond of you were automatically ready with the proverb of the dog and its fleas.[7] I here particularly recall the actor because at that time I made a note of your pronouncements about him, with the comment: 'This is how my father speaks of my friend (whom he does not even know), simply because he is my friend. I shall always be able to bring this up against him whenever he reproaches me with a lack of a child's affection and gratitude.' What was always incomprehensible to me was your total lack of feeling for the suffering and shame you could inflict on me with your words and judgements. It was as though you had no notion of your power. I too, I am sure, often hurt you with what I said, but then I always knew, and it pained me, but I could not control myself, could not keep the words back, I was sorry even while I was saying it. But you struck out with your words without more ado, you weren't sorry for anyone, either during or afterwards, one was utterly defenceless against you.

But that was what your whole method of upbringing was like. You have, I think, a gift for bringing up children; you could, I am sure, have been of use to a human being of your own kind with your methods; such a person would have seen the reasonableness of what you told him, would not have troubled about anything else, and would quietly have done things the way he was told. But for me as a child everything you shouted at me was positively a heavenly commandment, I never forgot it, it remained for me the most important means of forming a judgement of the world, above all of forming a judgement of you yourself, and there you failed entirely. Since as a child I was together with you chiefly at meals, your teaching was to a large extent teaching about proper behaviour at table. What was brought to the table had to be eaten up, there could be no discussion of the goodness of the food – but you yourself often found the food uneatable, called it 'this swill', said 'that brute' (the cook) had ruined it. Because in accordance with your strong appetite and your particular habit you ate everything fast, hot and in big mouthfuls, the child had to hurry, there was a sombre silence at table, interrupted by admonitions: 'Eat first, talk afterwards,' or 'Faster, faster, faster,' or 'There you are, you see, I finished ages ago.' Bones musn't be cracked with the teeth, but you could. Vinegar must not be sipped noisily, but you could. The main thing was that the bread should be cut straight. But it didn't matter that you did it with a knife dripping with gravy. One had to take care that no scraps fell on the floor. In the end it was under your chair that there were most scraps. At table one wasn't allowed to do anything but eat, but you cleaned and cut your fingernails, sharpened pencils, cleaned your ears with the toothpick. Please, Father, understand me rightly, these would in themselves have been utterly insignificant details, they only became depressing for me because you, the man who was so tremendously the measure of all things for me, yourself did not keep the commandments you imposed on me. Hence the world was for me divided into three parts: one in which I, the slave, lived under laws that had been invented only for me and which I could, I did not know why, never completely comply with; then a second world, which was infinitely remote from mine, in which you lived, concerned with government, with the issuing of orders and with annoyance about their not being obeyed; and finally a third world where everybody else lived happily and free from orders and from having to obey. I was continually in disgrace, either I obeyed your orders, and that was a disgrace, for they applied, after all, only to me, or I was defiant, and that was a disgrace too, for how could I presume to defy you, or I could not obey because for instance I had not your strength, your appetite, your skill, in spite of which you expected it of me as a matter of course; this was the greatest disgrace of all. What moved in this way was not the child's reflections, but his feelings.

My situation at that time becomes clearer, perhaps, if I compare it with that of Felix.* You do, of course, treat him in a similar way, even indeed employing a particularly terrible method against him in his upbringing: whenever at meals he does anything that is in your opinion uncleanly you are not content to say to him, as you used to say to me at that time: 'What a swine you are,' but add: 'a thorough Hermann' or 'just like your father'. Now this may perhaps – one can't say more than 'perhaps' – not really harm Felix in any essential way, for where he is concerned you are actually no more than a grandfather, an especially important one, of course, but still, not everything, as you were for me; and besides, Felix is of a quiet, even at this stage to a certain extent manly character, one who may perhaps be disconcerted by a great voice thundering at him, but not conditioned permanently by it, but above all he is, of course, only comparatively seldom together with you, and apart from that he is also under other influences, you are for him more something of an endearing curiosity from which he can pick and choose whatever he likes. For me you were nothing in the least like a curiosity, I couldn't pick and choose, I had to take everything.

And this, besides, without being able to produce any arguments against any of it, for it is fundamentally impossible for you to talk calmly about a subject you don't approve of or which simply is not suggested by you; your hectoring temperament doesn't allow of that. In recent years you have been explaining this as due to your nervous heart-condition. I don't know that you were ever essentially different. At the most the nervous heart-condition is a means by which you exercise your domination more severely, since the thought of it necessarily chokes off the last opposition from others. This is of course not a reproach, only a statement of fact. Rather as in Ottla's case, what you say is: 'One simply can't talk to her at all, she flies straight in your face,' but in reality she does not begin by flying out at all. You mistake the person for the thing. The thing under discussion is what flies in your face and you immediately make up your mind about it without listening to the person; whatever is brought forward afterwards merely serves to irritate you further, never to convince you. Then all one gets from you is: 'Do whatever you like. So far as I'm concerned you have a free hand. You're of age, I've no advice to give you,' and all this with that frightful hoarse undertone of anger and utter condemnation that only makes me tremble less today than in my childhood because the child's exclusive sense of guilt has been partly replaced by insight into our helplessness, yours and mine.

The impossibility of getting on calmly together had one more result, actually a very natural one: I lost the capacity to talk. I dare say I should never have been a very eloquent person in any case, but I should after all have had the usual fluency of human language at my command. But at a very early stage you forbade me to talk. Your threat: 'Not a word of contradiction!' and the raised hand that accompanied it have gone with me ever since. What I got from you – and you are, as soon as it is a matter of your own affairs, an excellent talker – was a hesitant, stammering mode of speech, and even that was still too much for you, and finally I kept silence, at first perhaps from defiance, and then because I couldn't either think or speak in your presence. And because you were the person who really brought me up, this has had its repercussions throughout my life. It is altogether a remarkable mistake for you to believe I never fell in with your wishes. 'Always agin you' was really not my basic principle where you were concerned, as you believe and as you reproach me. On the contrary: if I had obeyed you less, I am sure you would have been much better pleased with me. As it is, all your educational measures hit the mark exactly. There was no hold I tried to escape. As I now am, I am (apart, of course, from the fundamentals and the influence of life itself) the result of your upbringing and of my obedience. That this result is nevertheless distressing to you, indeed that you unconsciously refuse to acknowledge it as the result of your methods of upbringing, is due to the fact that your hand and the material I offered were so alien to each other. You would say: 'Not a word of contradiction!' thinking that that was a way of silencing the oppositional forces in me that were disagreeable to you, but the effect of it was too strong for me, I was too docile, I became completely dumb, cringed away from you, hid from you, and only dared to stir when I was so far away from you that your power could no longer reach me, at any rate directly. But you were faced with all that, and it all seemed to you to be 'agin', whereas it was only the inevitable consequence of your strength and my weakness.

Your extremely effective rhetorical methods in bringing me up, which never failed to work with me anyway, were: abuse, threats, irony, spiteful laughter and – oddly enough – self-pity.

I can't recall your ever having abused me directly and in downright abusive terms. Nor was that necessary, you had so many other methods, and besides, in talk at home and particularly at business the words of abuse went flying around me in such swarms, as they were flung at other people's heads, that as a little boy I was sometimes almost stunned and had no reason not to apply them to myself too, for the people you were abusing were certainly no worse than I was and you were certainly not more displeased with them than with me. And here again, too, was your enigmatic innocence and inviolability, you cursed and swore without the slightest scruple about it, indeed you condemned cursing and swearing in other people and would not have it.

You reinforced abusiveness with threats, and this applied to me too. How terrible for me was, for instance, that 'I'll tear you apart like a fish,' in spite of knowing, of course, that there was nothing worse to follow (admittedly, as a little child I didn't know that), but it was almost exactly in accord with my notions of your power and I saw you as being capable of doing this too. What was also terrible was when you ran round the table, shouting, to grab one, obviously not really trying to grab, but still pretending to, and Mother (in the end) had to rescue one, as it seemed. Once again one had, so it seemed to the child, remained alive through your mercy and bore one's life henceforth as an undeserved gift from you. This too is the place to mention the threats about the consequences of disobedience. When I began to do something you did not like and you threatened me with the prospect of failure, my veneration for your opinion was so great that the failure then became inevitable, even though perhaps it happened only at some later time. I lost confidence in my own actions. I was wavering, doubtful. The older I became the more material there was for you to bring forward against me as evidence of my worthlessness; gradually you began really to be right in a certain respect. Once again I am careful not to assert that I became like this solely through you; you only intensified what was already there, but you did greatly intensify it, simply because where I was concerned you were very powerful and you employed all your power to that end.

You put special trust in bringing children up by means of irony, and this was most in keeping with your superiority over me. An admonition from you generally took this form: 'Can't you do it in such-and-such a way? That's too hard for you, I suppose. You haven't the time, of course?' and so on. And each such question would be accompanied by malicious laughter and a malicious face. One was so to speak already punished before one even knew that one had done something bad. What was also maddening were those rebukes when one was treated as a third person, in other words accounted not worthy even to be spoken to angrily: that is to say, when you would speak in form to Mother, but in fact to me, sitting there at the same time. For instance: 'Of course that's too much to expect of our worthy son' and the like. (This then produced a corollary in that, for instance, I did not dare to ask, and later from habit did not even really much think of asking, you anything directly when Mother was there. It was much less dangerous for the child to put questions to Mother, sitting there beside you, and to ask Mother: 'How is Father?' so guarding oneself against surprises.) There were of course also cases when one was entirely in agreement with even the worst irony, namely when it referred to someone else, for instance Elli, with whom I was on bad terms for years. There was an orgy of malice and spiteful delight for me when such things were said of her, as they were at almost every meal: 'She has to sit six feet away from the table, the great fat lump' and when you, morosely sitting on your chair without the slightest trace of pleasantness or humour, a bitter enemy, would exaggeratedly imitate the way she sat, which you found utterly loathsome. How often such things happened, over and over again, and how little you really achieved as a result of them! I think the reason was that the expenditure of anger and malice seemed to be in no proper relation to the subject itself, one did not have the feeling that the anger was caused by this trifle of sitting some way back from the table, but that the whole bulk of it was already there to begin with and only by chance happened to settle on this matter as a pretext for breaking out. Since one was convinced that a pretext would be found anyway, one did not bother particularly, and anyway one's feelings became dulled by these continual threats. One had gradually become pretty sure of not getting a beating, anyway. One became a glum, inattentive, disobedient child, always trying to escape from something and in the main to escape within oneself. So you suffered, and so we suffered. From your own point of view you were quite right when, clenching your teeth and with that gurgling laughter that gave the child its first notions of hell, you used bitterly to say (as you did only just recently in connection with a letter from Constantinople): 'A *nice* crowd that is!'

What seemed to be quite incompatible with this attitude to your children was, and it happened very often, that you complained in public. I confess that as a child (though doubtless this was rather later) I was completely callous about this and could not understand how you could possibly expect to get any sympathy from anyone. You were so huge, a giant in every respect. What could you care for our pity or even our help? Our help, indeed, you could not but despise, as you so often despised us ourselves. Hence I did not take these complaints at their face-value and looked for some hidden motive behind them. Only later did I come to understand that you really suffered a great deal because of your children, but at that time, when these complaints might in other circumstances still have met with a childish candid sympathy that would not have counted the cost but would have been ready to offer any help it could, to me they could only seem to be overemphatic means of drilling me and humiliating me, as such not in themselves very intense, but with the harmful accompanying effect that the child became used to not taking very seriously the very things it should have taken seriously.

Fortunately there were, I admit, exceptions to all these things, mostly when you suffered in silence, and affection and kindliness by their own strength overcame all obstacles, and moved me immediately. Admittedly this was rare, but it was wonderful. For instance, when in earlier times, in hot summers, when you were tired after lunch, I saw you having a nap at the office, your elbow on the desk; or when you joined us in the country, in the summer holidays, on Sundays, worn out from work at the office; or the time when Mother was gravely ill and you stood holding on to the bookcase, shaking with sobs; or when, during my last illness, you came tiptoeing to Ottla's room to see me, stopping in the doorway, craning your neck to see me, and out of consideration for me only waved your hand to me. At such times one would lie back and weep for happiness, and one weeps again now, writing it down.

You have a particularly beautiful, very rare way of quietly, contentedly, approving smilingly, a way of smiling that can make the person for whom it is meant entirely happy. I can't recall its ever having expressly been my lot in my childhood, but I dare say it may have happened, for why should you have refused it to me at that time when I still seemed blameless to you and was your great hope? For the rest, such friendly impressions in the long run brought about nothing but an increase in my sense of guilt, making the world still more incomprehensible to me.

I would rather keep to the practical and permanent. In order to assert myself a very little in relation to you, and partly, too, from a kind of vengefulness, I soon began to observe little ridiculous things about you, collecting them and exaggerating them. For instance, there was the way you so easily let yourself be dazzled by people who were for the most part only seemingly your social superiors; you would keep on talking about them, as of some Imperial Councillor or other and the like (on the other hand such things pained me too, to see you, my father, believing you had any need of such trifling confirmations of your own value, and boasting about them). Or I would observe your taste for indecent expressions, which you would produce in the loudest possible voice, laughing about them as though you had said something particularly good, while in point of fact it was only a banal little obscenity (at the same time this again was for me a humiliating manifestation of your vitality). There were of course plenty of such observations. I was happy about them, they were for me an occasion for whispering and joking, you sometimes noticed it and were angry about it, taking it to be malice and lack of respect for you, but believe me it was for me nothing other than a means – moreover, a useless one – of attempted self-preservation, they were jokes of the kind that is made everywhere about gods and kings, jokes that are not only compatible with the profoundest respect but which are indeed part and parcel of it.

Incidentally, you too, in keeping with your similar position where I was concerned, tried a similar form of self-defence. You were in the habit of pointing out how exaggeratedly well off I was and how well I had in fact been treated. That is correct, but I don't believe it was of any real use to me in the circumstances that actually prevailed.

It was true that Mother was illimitably good to me, but all that was for me in relation to you, that is to say, in no good relation. Mother unconsciously played the part of a beater during a hunt. Even if your method of upbringing might in some unlikely case have set me on my own feet by means of producing defiance, dislike, or even hate in me, Mother cancelled that out again by kindness, by talking sensibly (in the maze and chaos of my childhood she was the very pattern of good sense and reasonableness), by pleading for me, and I was again driven back into your orbit, which I might perhaps otherwise have broken out of, to your advantage and to my own. Or it was so that no real reconciliation ever came about, that Mother merely shielded me from you in secret, secretly gave me something, or allowed me to do something, and then where you were concerned I was again the furtive creature, the cheat, the guilty one, who in his worthlessness could only pursue backstairs methods even to get things he regarded as his right. Of course I then became used to taking such courses also in quest of things to which, even in my own view, I had no right. This again meant an increase in the sense of guilt.

It is also true that you hardly ever really gave me a whipping. But the shouting, the way your face got red, the hasty undoing of the braces and the laying of them ready over the back of the chair, all that was almost worse for me. It is like when someone is going to be hanged. If he is really hanged, then he's dead and it's all over. But if he has to go through all the preliminaries to being hanged and only when the noose is dangling before his face is told of his reprieve, then he may suffer from it all his life long. Besides, from so many occasions when I had, as you clearly showed you thought, deserved to be beaten, when you were, however, gracious enough to let me off at the last moment, here again what accumulated was only a huge sense of guilt. On every side I was to blame, I was in debt to you.

You have always reproached me (and what is more either alone or in front of others, you having no feeling for the humiliation of this latter, your children's affairs always being public affairs) for living in peace and quiet, warmth, and abundance, lacking for nothing, thanks to your hard work. I think here of remarks that must positively have worn grooves in my brain, like: 'When I was only seven I had to push the barrow from village to village.' 'We all had to sleep in one room.' 'We were glad when we got potatoes.' 'For years I had open sores on my legs from not having enough clothes to wear in winter.' 'I was only a little boy when I was sent away to Pisek to go into business.' 'I got nothing from home, not even when I was in the army, even then I was sending money

home.' 'But for all that, for all that – Father was always Father
to me. Ah, nobody knows what that means these days! What do
these children know of things? Nobody's been through that! Is
there any child that understands such things today?' Under other
conditions such stories might have been very educational, they
might have been a way of encouraging one and strengthening one
to endure similar torments and deprivations to those one's father
had undergone. But that wasn't what you wanted at all, the situation had, after all, become quite different as a result of all your
efforts, and there was no opportunity to distinguish oneself in the
world as you had done. Such an opportunity would first of all have
had to be created by violence and revolution, it would have meant
breaking away from home (assuming one had had the resolution
and strength to do so and that Mother wouldn't have worked
against it, for her part, with other means). But all that was not
what you wanted at all, that you termed ingratitude, extravagance,
disobedience, treachery, madness. And so while on the one hand
you tempted me to it by means of example, story, and humiliation,
on the other hand you forbade it with the utmost severity. Otherwise you ought for instance really to have been delighted, apart
from the accompanying circumstances, with Ottla's Zürau escapade.[8] She wanted to get back to the country, from which you had
come, she wanted work and hardship such as you had had, she did
not want to batten on the results of your work, just as you yourself were independent of your father. Were those such dreadful
intentions? Was that so remote from your example and your pre-
cept? Well, Ottla's intentions came to nothing finally in practice,
were indeed perhaps carried out in a somewhat ridiculous way,
with too much fuss, and she did not have enough consideration for
her parents. But was that exclusively her fault and not also the
fault of the circumstances and above all of the fact that you were
so estranged from her? Was she any less estranged from you (as
you later tried to convince yourself) in the business than afterwards
at Zürau? And would you not quite certainly have had the power
(assuming you could have brought yourself to do so) to turn that
escapade into something very good by means of encouragement,
advice, and supervision, perhaps even merely by means of tolera-
tion?

In connection with such experiences you were in the habit of saying, in bitter jest, that we were too well off. But this joke is in a certain sense no joke at all. What you had to fight for we received from your hand, but the fight for external life, a fight that was instantly open to you and which we were naturally not spared either, we have to fight for only late in life, in our majority but with only childish strength. I do not say that our situation is therefore inevitably less favourable than yours was, on the contrary, it is probably no better and no worse (although this is said without reference to our different natures), only we have the disadvantage of not being able to boast of our wretchedness and not being able to humiliate anyone with it as you have done with your wretchedness. Nor do I deny that it would have been possible for me really to enjoy the fruits of your great and successful work, that I could have turned them to account and continued to work with them, so giving you joy, but what stood in the way of this was, here again, our estrangement. I could enjoy what you gave, but only in humiliation, weariness, weakness, and with a sense of guilt. That was why I could be grateful to you for everything only as a beggar is, and never show it by doing the right things.

The next external result of this whole method of upbringing was that I fled from everything that even remotely reminded me of you. First there was the business. In itself, particularly in my childhood, so long as it was a shop, I ought to have liked it very much, it was so animated, the lights lit at evening, so much to see and hear, being able to help now and then and to distinguish oneself, but above all to admire you for your magnificent commercial talents, the way you sold things, managed people, made jokes, were untiring, knew the right decision to make at once in doubtful cases, and so forth; even the way you wrapped up a parcel or opened a crate was a spectacle worth watching, and all this was certainly not the worst school for a child. But since you gradually began to terrify me on all sides and the business and you became one for me, the business too made me feel uneasy. Things that had at first been a matter of course for me there now began to torment and shame me, particularly the way you treated the staff. I don't know, perhaps it was like that in most business (in the *Assicurazioni Generali*, for instance, in my time it was really similar, and the explanation I gave the director for my resignation was, though not strictly in accordance with the truth, still not entirely a lie, my not being able to bear the cursing and swearing, which incidentally had not actually been directed at me; it was a matter about which I was too painfully sensitive from home), but in my childhood other businesses did not concern me. But you I heard and saw shouting, cursing, and raging in the shop, in a way that in my opinion at that time had not its equal anywhere in the world. And not only cursing, but other sorts of tyrannizing. For instance, the way you would push goods you did not want to have mixed up with others, knocking them off the counter – only the thoughtlessness of your rage was some slight excuse – and the assistant had to pick them up. Or your constant mode of referring to an assistant with T.B. lungs: 'Sooner he dies the better, the mangey dog.' You called the employees 'paid enemies', and that was what they were too, but even before they became such you seemed to me to be their 'paying enemy'. There too I learnt the great lesson that you could be unjust; in my own case I would not have noticed it so soon, for here was too much accumulated sense of guilt, ready to admit that you were right; but there, in my childish view, later of course a little but not overmuch corrected, were strangers, who were after all working for us and because of that had to live in constant dread of you. Of course there I exaggerated, and this because I simply assumed you had as terrible an effect on these people as on me. If it had been so, they could not have lived at all; since however they were grown-up people, most of them with excellent nerves, they shook off this abuse without any trouble and in the end it did you much more harm than it did them. But it made the business insufferable to me, reminding me far too much of my relations with you: quite apart from your proprietary interest and apart from your mania for domination even as a business man, you were so greatly superior to all those who ever came to learn the business from you that nothing they ever did could satisfy you, and you must, as I assumed, in the same way be for ever dissatisfied with me too. That was why I could not but side with the staff, incidentally also because, from sheer nervousness, I could not understand how anyone could be so abusive to a stranger, and hence from sheer nervousness tried somehow to reconcile the staff, which in my opinion must be in a terrible state of indignation, with you, with our family, if for no other reason than that of my own security. To this end it was not sufficient to behave in an ordinary decent way to the staff, not even modestly, on the contrary I had to be humble, not only to be first in saying 'good morning' or 'good evening' but if it was at all possible also to prevent any return of the greeting. And even if I, insignificant creature that I was, had licked their feet down below, it would still have been no compensation for the way that you, the master, were lashing out at them up above. This relationship that I came to have towards my fellow men extended beyond the limits of the business and on into the future (something similar, but not as dangerous and deep-going as in my case is for instance Ottla's taste for associating with poor people, sitting together with the maids, which annoys you so much, and the like). In the end I was almost afraid of the business, and in any case it had long ceased to be any concern of mine even before I went to the *Gymnasium* and hence was taken even farther away from it. Besides, it seemed to be entirely beyond my resources and capacities, since, as you said, it exhausted even yours. You then tried (to me this today seems touching and shaming) to extract, nevertheless, some little sweetness for yourself from my dislike of the business, of your handiwork – a dislike that was after all very distressing to you – by asserting that I had no business sense, I had loftier ideas in my head, and the like. Mother was of course delighted with this explanation that you wrung from yourself, and I too, in my vanity and wretchedness, let myself be influenced by it. But if it had really been only or mainly 'loftier ideas' that turned me against the business (which I now, but only now, have come really and honestly to hate), they would have had to express themselves differently, instead of letting me float quickly and timidly through my schooling and my law studies until finally I landed up at a clerk's desk.

If I was to flee from you, I had to flee from the family as well, even from Mother. True, one could always get protection from her, but only in relation to you. She loved you too much and was too devoted and loyal to you to have been able to constitute an independent spiritual force, in the long run, in the child's struggle. It was, incidentally, a true instinct the child had, for with the passing of the years Mother became ever more closely allied to you; while, where she herself was concerned, she always kept her independence, within the narrowest limits, delicately and beautifully, and without ever essentially hurting you, still, with the passing of the years she did more and more completely, emotionally rather than intellectually, blindly adopt your judgements and your condemnations with regard to the children, particularly in the case – certainly a grave one – of Ottla. Of course it must always be borne in mind how tormenting and utterly wearing Mother's position in the family was. She toiled in the business and in the house, and suffered doubly in watching all the family illnesses, but the culmination of all this was what she suffered in her position midway between us and you. You were always affectionate and considerate to her, but in this respect you spared her exactly as little as we spared her. We all hammered ruthlessly away at her, you from your side, we from ours. It was a diversion, nobody meant any harm, thinking of the battle that you were waging with us and that we were waging with you, and it was Mother on whom we relieved our wild feelings. Nor was it at all a good contribution to the children's upbringing the way you – of course without being in the slightest to blame for it yourself – tormented her on our account. It even seemed to justify our otherwise unjustifiable behaviour towards her. How much she suffered from us on your account and from you on our account, quite without counting those cases where you were in the right because she was spoiling us, even though this 'spoiling' may sometimes have been only a quiet, unconscious counter-demonstration against your system. Of course Mother could not have borne all this if she had not drawn the strength to bear it from her love for us all and her happiness in that love.

My sisters were only partly on my side. The one who was happiest in her relation to you was Valli. Being closest to Mother, she fell in with your wishes in a similar way, without much effort and without suffering much harm. But, just because she reminded you of Mother, you did accept her in a more friendly spirit, although there was little Kafka material in her. But perhaps precisely that was what you wanted; where there was nothing of the Kafka, even you could not demand anything of the sort; nor had you the feeling, as with the rest of us, that here something was getting lost which had to be saved by force. For the rest, it may be that you were never particularly fond of the Kafka element as it manifested itself in women. Valli's relationship to you would perhaps even have become still more friendly if the rest of us had not slightly interfered with it.

Elli is the only example of the almost complete success of a breaking out from our orbit. When she was a child she was the last person I should have expected it of. For she was such a clumsy, tired, timid, bad-tempered, guilt-ridden, over-meek, malicious, lazy, greedy, miserly child, I could hardly bring myself to look at her, far from speaking to her, so much did she remind me of myself, in so very much the same way was she under the same spell of our up-bringing. Her miserliness in particular was abhorrent to me, since I had it to an, if possible, even greater extent. Miserliness is, after all, one of the most reliable signs of profound unhappiness; I was so unsure of everything that in fact I possessed only what I actually had in my hands or in my mouth or what was at least on the way there, and this was precisely what she, being in a similar situation, most enjoyed taking away from me. But all this changed when, at an early age – this is the most important thing – she left home, married, had children, and became cheerful, carefree, brave, generous, unselfish, and hopeful. It is almost incredible how you actually did not notice this change at all, or at any rate did not give it its due, blinded as you were by the grudge you have always borne Elli and at bottom still bear her to this day, only this grudge matters much less now, since Elli no longer lives with us and, besides, your love for Felix and affection for Karl[9] have made it less important. It is only Gerti who sometimes has to suffer for it still.

Of Ottla I scarcely dare [to] write; I know by doing so I risk ruin-ing the whole effect I hope for from this letter. In ordinary cir-cumstances, that is, so long as she is not in particular need or danger, all you feel for her is hatred; you have yourself confessed to me that in your opinion she is always intentionally causing you suffering and annoyance, and while you are suffering on her account she is satisfied and pleased. In other words, a sort of fiend. What an immense estrangement, greater still than that between you and me, must have come about between you and her, for such an immense misunderstanding to be possible. She is so remote from you that you scarcely see her any more, but set a spectre in the place where you suppose her to be. I grant you that you have had a particularly difficult time with her. I don't of course quite see to the bottom of this very complicated case, but at any rate here was something like a kind of Löwy, equipped with the best Kafka weapons. Between us there was no real struggle; I was soon finished off; what remained was flight, embitterment, melancholy, and inner struggle. But you two were always in fighting-position, always fresh, always energetic. A sight as magnificent as it was desperate. At the very beginning you were, I am sure, very close to each other, for even today Ottla is, of the four of us, perhaps the purest representation of the marriage between you and Mother and of the forces there combined. I don't know what it was that deprived you both of the happiness of the harmony between father and child, but I can't help believing that the development in this case was similar to that in mine. On your side there was the tyranny of your own nature, on her side the Löwy defiance, touchiness, sense of justice, restlessness, and all that, backed up by the consciousness of Kafka vigour. Doubtless I too influenced her, but scarcely of my own doing, simply through the fact of my existence. Besides, as the last to arrive she found herself in a situation where the balance of power was already established, and was able to form her own judgement from the large amount of material at her disposal. I can even imagine that she may, in her inmost being, have wavered for some time as to whether she should fling herself into your arms or into those of the enemies, and it is obvious that at that time there was something you failed to do and that you rebuffed her, but if it had been possible, the two of you would have become a magnificently harmonious pair. In that way of course I should have lost an ally, but the sight of the two of you would have richly compensated me, and besides, as a result of the unforeseeable happiness of finding complete contentment at least in one child you would have altered greatly to my advantage. All this, however, is today only a dream. Ottla has no contact with her father and has to seek her way alone, like me, and the degree of confidence, self-confidence, health, and ruthlessness by which she surpasses me makes her in your eyes more wicked and treacherous than I seem to you. I understand that. From your point of view she can't be different. Indeed she is herself capable of regarding herself with your eyes, of feeling what you suffer and of being – not desperate, despair is my business – but very sad. You do see us together often enough, in apparent contradiction to this, whispering and laughing, and now and then you hear us talking of you. The impression you get is that of impudent conspirators – strange conspirators. You are, admittedly, a chief subject of conversation between us, as of our thoughts ever since we can remember, but truly it is not in order to plot something against you that we sit together, but in order to discuss – with all our might and main, jokingly and seriously, in affection, defiance, anger, revulsion, submission, consciousness of guilt, with all the resources of our head and heart – this terrible trial that is pending between us and you, to discuss it in all its details, from all sides, on all occasions, from far and near – a trial in which you keep on claiming to be the judge, whereas, at least in the main (here I leave a margin for all the mistakes I may naturally make), you are a party too, just as weak and deluded as we are.

An example of the effect of your methods of upbringing, one that is very instructive in the context of the whole situation, is the case of Irma. On the one hand she was after all a stranger, already grown up when she entered your business, and had to do with you mainly as her employer, so that she was only partially exposed to your influence and this at an age when she had already developed powers of resistance; yet on the other hand she was also a blood-relation, venerating you as her father's brother, and the power you had over her was far greater than that of a mere employer. And for all this she, who, with her frail body, was so efficient, intelligent, hard-working, modest, trustworthy, unselfish, and loyal, who loved you as her uncle and admired you as her employer, she who stood the test in previous and in subsequent situations, was not a very good clerk to you. The fact was that, under pressure from us too of course, she came near to being in the relation, to you, of one of your own children, and the power of your personality to bend others was, even in her case, so great that what developed in her (admittedly only in relation to you and, it is to be hoped, without the deeper suffering a child experiences) was forgetfulness, carelessness, a grim sardonic sort of humour, and perhaps even a shade of defiance, in so far as she was capable of that at all, and in all this

I am not taking any account whatsoever of the fact that she was inclined to be ailing, and not very happy in other respects either, and that she was burdened by the bleakness of her life at home. What was so illuminating to me in your relation to her, you yourself summed up in a remark that became classical for us, one that was almost blasphemous, but at the same time extraordinary evidence of the *naïvety* of your way of treating people: 'The late lamented in the Lord has left me a damned mess to clear up.'

I might go on to describe further orbits of your influence and of struggle against it, but there I would be entering uncertain ground, and would have to construct things, and apart from that, the farther you are at a remove from your business and your family the pleasanter you have always become, easier to get on with, better-mannered, more considerate, and more sympathetic (I mean outwardly too), in exactly the same way as for instance an autocrat, when he happens to be outside the frontiers of his own country, has no reason to go on being tyrannical and is able to associate good-humouredly even with the lowest of the low. In point of fact, in the group photographs taken at Franzensbad, for instance, you always looked as big and jolly, among those sulky little people, as a king upon his travels. This was something, I grant you, from which your children might have benefited too, only they would have had to be capable of recognizing this even as little children, which was impossible, and I, for instance, would have had not to live constantly in, as it were, the inmost, strictest, strangling ring of your influence, as I did of course in reality.

In this way, did I lose my family feeling, as you say? On the contrary, I tended, rather, to preserve my feeling for the family, although mainly in a negative sense, in the sense of breaking away (which of course could never be completed) from you. Relations to people outside the family, however, suffered if possible still more as a result of your influence. You are entirely mistaken if you believe I do everything for other people, out of affection and loyalty, and for you and the family nothing, out of coldness and treachery. I repeat for the tenth time: even in other circumstances I should probably have become a shy and nervous person, but it is a long dark road from there to where I have really come to. (Up to this point there is in this letter relatively little I have intentionally passed over in silence, but now and later I shall have to be silent on certain matters that it is still too hard for me to confess – to you and to myself. I say this in order that, if the picture as a whole should be somewhat blurred here and there, you should not believe that what is to blame is any lack of evidence; on the contrary, there is evidence that might well make the picture unbearably stark. It is not easy to strike a medium position.) Here, it is enough to remind you of early days. I had lost my self-confidence where you were concerned, and in its place had developed a boundless sense of guilt. (In recollection of this boundlessness I once wrote of someone, accurately: 'He is afraid the shame will outlive him, even.') I could not suddenly undergo a transformation when I came into the company of other people; on the contrary, with them I came to feel an even deeper sense of guilt, for, as I have already said, in their case I had to make good the wrongs done them by you in the business, wrongs in which I too had my share of responsibility. Besides, you always, of course, had some objection to make, frankly or covertly, to everyone I associated with, and for this too I had to beg his pardon. The mistrust that you tried to instil into me, at business and at home, towards most people (tell me of any single person who was of importance to me in my childhood whom you didn't at least once tear to shreds with your criticism), this mistrust, which oddly enough was no particular burden to you (the fact was that you were strong enough to bear it, and besides, it was in reality perhaps only a token of the autocrat), this mistrust, which for me as a little boy was nowhere confirmed in my own eyes, since I everywhere saw only people excellent beyond all hope of emulation, in me turned into mistrust of myself and into perpetual anxiety in relation to everything else. There, then, I was in general certain of not being able to escape from you. The fact that you were mistaken on this point was perhaps due to your actually never learning anything about my association with other people, and to your mistrustful and jealous (I don't deny, do I? that you are fond of me) assumption that I had to get compensation elsewhere for what was missing in life at home, since it was after all impossible that outside my home I should live in the same way. Incidentally, it was precisely in my childhood that I found a certain comfort, in this respect, in my very mistrust of my own judgement. I would say to myself: 'Oh, you're exaggerating, you tend too much to feel trivialities as great exceptions, the way young people always do.' But this comfort was one that I later lost almost entirely, with an increasing perspective of the world.

I found equally little means of escape from you in Judaism. Here some escape would, in principle, have been thinkable, but more than that, it would have been thinkable that we might both have found each other in Judaism or even that we might have begun from there in harmony. But what sort of Judaism was it I got from you?! In the course of the years I have taken roughly three different attitudes to it.

As a child I reproached myself, in accord with you, for not going to the synagogue enough, for not fasting, and so on. I thought that in this way I was doing a wrong not to myself but to you, and I was penetrated by a sense of guilt, which was of course always ready to hand.

Later, as a boy, I could not understand how, with the insignificant scrap of Judaism you yourself possessed, you could reproach me for not (if for no more than the sake of piety, as you put it) making an effort to cling to a similar insignificant scrap. It was indeed really, so far as I could see, a mere scrap, a joke, not even a joke. On four days in the year you went to the synagogue, where you were, to say the least of it, closer to the indifferent than to those who took it seriously, patiently went through the prayers by way of formality, sometimes amazed me by being able to show me in the prayer-book the passage that was being said at the moment, and for the rest, so long (and this was the main thing) as I was there in the synagogue I was allowed to hang about wherever I liked. And so I yawned and dozed through the many hours (I don't think I was ever again so bored, except later at dancing lessons) and did my best to enjoy the few little bits of variety there were, as for instance when the Ark of the Covenant was opened, which always reminded me of the shooting-stands where a cupboard door would open in the same way whenever one got a bull's-eye, only with the difference that there something interesting always came out and here it was always just the same old dolls with no heads. Incidentally, it was also very frightening for me there, not only, as goes without saying, because of all the people one came into close contact with, but also because you once mentioned, by the way, that I too might be called up to read the Torah. That was something I went in dread of for years. But otherwise I was not fundamentally disturbed in my state of boredom, unless it was by the Barmizwah, but that meant no more than some ridiculous learning by heart, in other words, led to nothing but something like the ridiculous passing of an examination, and then, so far as you were concerned, by little, not very significant incidents, as when you were called up to read the Torah and came well out of the affair, which to my way of feeling was purely social, or when you stayed on in the synagogue for the prayers for the dead, and I was sent away, which for a long time, obviously because of being sent away and lacking, as I did, any deeper interest, aroused in me the more or less unconscious feeling that what was about to take place was something indecent. – That was how it was in the synagogue, and at home it was if possible even more poverty-stricken, being confined to the first evening of Passover, which more and more developed into a farce, with fits of hysterical laughter, admittedly under the influence of the growing children. (Why did you have to give way to that influence? Because you brought it about in the first place.) And so there was the religious material that was handed on to me, to which may be added at most the outstretched hand pointing to 'the sons of the millionaire Fuchs', who were in the synagogue with their father at great festivals. How one could do anything better with this material than get rid of it as fast as possible was something I could not understand; precisely getting rid of it seemed to me the most effective act of 'piety' one could perform.

But later on still I did see it again differently and came to realize why it was possible for you to think that in this respect too I was showing ill will and betraying you. You had really brought some traces of Judaism with you from that ghetto-like little village community; it was not much and it dwindled a little more in town and while you were doing your military service, but still, the impression and memories of your youth did just about suffice to make some sort of Jewish life, especially since you did not, after all, need much of that kind of help, coming as you did of a vigorous stock and being personally scarcely capable of being shaken by religious scruples, if they were not very much mixed up with social scruples.

At bottom the faith that ruled your life consisted in your believing in the unconditional rightness of the opinions prevailing in a particular class of Jewish society, and hence actually, since these opinions were part and parcel of your own nature, in believing in yourself. Even in this there was still Judaism enough, but it was too little to be handed on to the child; it all trickled away while you were passing it on. In part it was youthful memories of your own, of a kind that could not be conveyed to others; in part it was your dreaded personality. It was also impossible to make a child, over-acutely observant from sheer nervousness, understand that the few flimsy gestures you performed in the name of Judaism, and with an indifference in keeping with their flimsiness, could have any higher meaning. For you they had their meaning as little souvenirs of earlier times, and that was why you wanted to pass them on to me, but this, since after all even for you they no longer had any value in themselves, was something you could do only by means of persuasion or threats; this could, on the one hand, not be successful and could not, on the other hand, but make you, since you utterly failed to recognize your weak position here, very angry with mè on account of my apparent obstinacy.

The whole thing is of course not an isolated phenomenon. It was much the same with a large section of this transitional generation of Jews, which had migrated from the still comparatively devout countryside to the towns. The situation arose automatically; only it did, as it happened, bring one more source of acrimony, and a fairly painful one, into our relationship, which was already far from lacking in sources of acrimony. On the other hand, although you ought, on this point too, just like myself, to believe in your own blamelessness, you ought, however, to explain this blamelessness by your personality and the conditions of the time, but not merely by external circumstances, that is, not by saying, for instance, that you had too much other work and too many other worries to be able to give your mind to such things as well. This is the manner in which you are in the habit of twisting your undoubted innocence into an unjust reproach to others. That can be very easily refuted everywhere and here too. It was not a matter of any sort of instruction you ought to have given your children, but of an exemplary life. Had your Judaism been stronger, then your example would have been compelling too; this goes without saying and is, again, by no means a reproach, but only a refutation of your reproaches. You have recently been reading Franklin's memoirs of his youth. I did in fact give you this book to read on purpose, but not, as you ironically commented, because of a little passage on vegetarianism, but because of the relationship between the author and his father, as it is there described, and of the relationship between the author and his son, as it is spontaneously revealed in these memoirs written for that son. I do not wish to dwell here on matters of detail.

I have received a certain retrospective confirmation of this view of your Judaism from your attitude in recent years, when it seemed to you that I was taking more interest in Jewish things. As you have a dislike in advance of every one of my activities and particularly of the nature of my interest, so you have had it here too. But in spite of this general attitude, one would really have expected that here you would make a little exception. It was, after all, Judaism of your Judaism that was here stirring, and thus with it the possibility too of the start of new relations between us. I do not deny that if you had shown interest in them these things might, for that very reason, have become suspect in my eyes. For I do not dream of asserting that I am in this respect in any way better than you. But it never came to putting it to the test. Through my mediation Judaism became abhorrent to you and Jewish writings unreadable; they 'nauseated' you. – This may have meant that you were insisting that only that Judaism which you had shown me in my childhood was the right one, and beyond that there was nothing. But that you should insist on that was, after all, scarcely thinkable. But then the 'nausea' (apart from the fact that it was directed primarily not against Judaism but against me personally) could only mean that unconsciously you did acknowledge the weakness of your Judaism and of my Jewish upbringing, did not wish to be reminded of it in any way, and reacted to all reminders with frank hatred. Incidentally, your negative high esteem of my new Judaism was much exaggerated; first of all it bore your curse within it, and secondly, in its development the fundamental relationship to one's fellow men was decisive, in my case that is to say fatal.

You struck nearer home with your dislike of my writing and all that, unknown to you, was connected with it. Here I had in fact got some distance away from you, by my own efforts, even if it was slightly reminiscent of the worm that, as a foot tramples on the tail end of it, breaks loose with its top end and drags itself aside. To a certain extent I was in safety; there was a chance to breathe freely. The dislike that you naturally and immediately had of my writing too was, by way of exception, welcome to me. My vanity and my ambition did suffer, it is true, under your soon proverbial way of hailing the arrival of my books: 'Put it on my bedside table!' (as it happened, you were usually playing cards when a book came), but fundamentally I was thoroughly glad of it, not only out of rebellious malice, not only out of delight at a new confirmation of my view of our relationship, but quite spontaneously, because to me that formula sounded something like: 'Now you are free!' Of course it was a delusion; I was not, or, to put it most optimistically, was not *yet*, free. My writing was all about you; all I did there, after all, was to bemoan what I could not bemoan upon your breast. It was an intentionally long-drawn-out leave-taking from you, only although it was brought about by force on your part, it did take its course in the direction determined by me. But how little all this amounted to! It is all only worth talking about at all because it has happened in my life; otherwise it would not be worthy of remark at all; and then too for the reason that in my childhood it ruled my life as a premonition, later as a hope, and still later often as despair, dictating – it may be said, yet again in your shape – my few little decisions to me.

For instance, the choice of a career. True, here you gave me complete freedom, in your magnanimous and, in this regard, even indulgent manner. Admittedly, here too you were conforming with the general method of treating sons in the Jewish middle class, which was the measure of things for you, or at least with the values of that class. Finally, what also played a part in this was one of your misunderstandings with respect to my person. The fact is, for reasons of paternal pride, ignorance of my real life, and conclusions drawn from my feebleness, you have always regarded me as a particularly keen worker. As a child, in your view I was always at my lessons, and later always at my writing. Now this does not even remotely correspond to the facts. It would be correct, and much less exaggerated, to say that I paid little attention to my lessons and learnt nothing; the fact that something did stick in my mind after those many years, seeing that I had a moderately good memory and a capacity for learning that was not of the most inferior kind, is after all not very remarkable, but, be that as it may, the total sum of knowledge and particularly of a solid basis for knowledge is extremely pitiable in comparison with the expenditure of time and money in the course of an outwardly untroubled, quiet life, particularly too in comparison with almost all the people I knew. It is pitiable, but to me understandable. As far as I can think I have had such anxieties, of the very deepest kind, about asserting my spiritual existence that everything else was a matter of indifference to me. Jewish schoolboys in our country often tend to be odd; among them one finds the most unlikely things; but something like my cold indifference, scarcely disguised, indestructible, childishly helpless, approaching the ridiculous, and brutishly complacent, the indifference of a self-sufficient but coldly imaginative child, I have never found anywhere else, but admittedly here it was the sole defence against destruction of the child's nerves by fear and a sense of guilt. All that occupied my mind was worry about myself, and this in various ways. There was for instance the worry about my health; it began imperceptibly enough, with now and then a little anxiety about digestion, hair falling out, a spinal curvature, and so on, this intensifying in innumerable gradations, finally ending with a real illness. But since there was nothing at all I was certain of, since I needed to be provided at every instant with a new confirmation of my existence, since nothing was in my very own, undoubted, sole possession, determined unequivocally only by me – in sober truth a disinherited son – naturally even the thing nearest at hand, my own body, became insecure; I shot up, tall and lanky, without knowing what to do with my lankiness, the burden being too heavy, the back becoming bent; I scarcely dared to move or least of all to do gymnastics, and so I remained weakly: I was amazed by everything (that did not trouble me) as by a miracle, for instance my good digestion; that sufficed to make me lose it, and so now the way was open to every sort of hypochondria, until finally under the strain of the superhuman effort of wanting to marry (of this I shall speak later) blood came from the lung, something in which, of course, the apartment in the Schönbornpalais – which, however, I needed only because I believed I needed it for my writing, so that even that comes under the same heading – may have quite a fair share. Well, so all this did not originate in excessive work, as you always imagine. There were years in which, being in perfectly good health, I lazed away more time on the sofa than you in all your life, including all your illnesses. When I rushed away from you, frightfully busy, it was generally in order to lie down in my room. My total achievement in work done, both at the office (where admittedly, laziness is nothing particularly striking, and mine, furthermore, was kept in bounds by my timidity) and at home as well, is minute; if you had any real idea of it, you would be aghast. Probably I am constitutionally not lazy at all, but there was nothing for me to do. In the place where I lived I was spurned, condemned, fought to a standstill, and although I did make the utmost endeavours to escape to some other place, that was not work, for there it was a matter of something impossible, something that was, apart from small exceptions, unattainable for one of my resources.

This then was the state in which I was given the liberty to choose my career. But was I still at all capable of really making use of such liberty? Had I still any confidence in my own capacity to achieve a real career? My valuation of myself was much more dependent on you than on anything else, say for instance some external success. *That* was strengthening for a moment, nothing more, but on the other side your weight always dragged me down much more strongly. Never, I thought, should I pass out of the first class at elementary school, but I succeeded, I even got a prize; but I should certainly not pass the entrance exam for the *Gymnasium*, yet I succeeded in that; but now I should certainly fail in the first class at the *Gymnasium*, no, I did not fail, and I went on and on succeeding. What this produced, however, was not confidence, on the contrary, I was always convinced – and I positively had the proof of it in your forbidding expression – that the more things I was successful in, the worse the final outcome would inevitably be. Often in my mind's eye I saw the terrible assembly of the masters (the *Gymnasium* is only the most integral example, but it was the same all around me), as they would meet, when I had passed out of

the first class, and then in the second class, when I had passed out
of that, and then in the third, and so on, meeting in order to
examine this unique, outrageous case, to discover how I, the most
incapable and in any case the most ignorant of all, had succeeded
in creeping up as far as this class, which now, when everybody's
attention had at last been focused on me, would of course instantly
spew me out, to the high delight of all the righteous, now liberated
from this nightmare. Living with such fantasies is not easy for a
child. In these circumstances, what could I care about my lessons?
Who was capable of striking a spark of real interest out of me?
Lessons, and not only lessons but everything round about me, at
that decisive age, interested me pretty much as a defaulting bank-
clerk, still holding his job and trembling at the thought of discovery, is interested in the small current business of the bank,
which he still has to deal with as a clerk. That was how small and
far-away everything was in comparison to the main thing. So it
went on up to matriculation, which I passed really, this time, partly
only by means of cheating, and then everything stagnated, for now
I was free. If I had been concerned only with myself up to now, in
spite of the discipline of the *Gymnasium*, how much more now that
I was free. So there was actually no such thing for me as liberty
to choose my career, for I knew: compared to the main thing
everything would be exactly as much a matter of indifference to me
as all the subjects taught at school, and so it was a matter of finding a profession that would be most likely to allow me to indulge
this indifference without overmuch injuring my vanity. So the law
was the obvious choice. Little contrary attempts on the part of
vanity, of senseless hope, such as a fortnight's study of chemistry, or
six months' German studies, only reinforced that fundamental conviction. So I studied law. This meant that in the few months before
the exams, and in a way that told severely on my nerves, I was
positively living, in an intellectual sense, on sawdust, which had,
moreover, already been chewed for me in thousands of other
people's mouths. But in a certain sense this very thing was to my
taste, as in a certain sense too the *Gymnasium* had previously been
and later my job as a clerk was, for all this was utterly appropriate
to my situation. At any rate I here showed astonishing foresight;
even as a small child I had had fairly clear premonitions with regard

to my studies and career. This was something from which I expected no rescue; here I had long ago given up.

But I showed no foresight at all with regard to the significance and possibility of a marriage for me; this up to now greatest terror of my life has come upon me almost completely unexpectedly. The child had developed so slowly, these things were outwardly all too remote from him; now and then the necessity of thinking of them did arise; but that here a permanent, decisive and indeed the most grimly bitter ordeal was imminent was something that could not be recognized. In reality, however, the plans to marry became the most large-scale and hopeful attempt at escape, and then the failure was on a correspondingly large scale, too.

I am afraid that, because in this sphere everything I try is a failure, I shall also fail to make these attempts to marry comprehensible to you. And yet on this depends the success of this whole letter, for in these attempts there was, on the one hand, concentrated everything I had at my disposal in the way of positive forces, and on the other hand here there also accumulated, and with downright fury, all the negative forces that I have described as being the result in part of your method of upbringing, that is to say, the weakness, the lack of self-confidence, the sense of guilt, and they positively drew a cordon between myself and marriage. The explanation will be hard for me also because I have spent so many days and nights thinking and burrowing through the whole thing over and over again that now even I myself am bewildered by the mere sight of it. The only thing that makes the explanation easier for me is your – in my opinion – complete misunderstanding of the matter; slightly to correct so complete a misunderstanding does not seem excessively difficult.

First of all you rank the failures of the marriages with the rest of my failures; I should have nothing against this, provided you accepted my previous explanation of my failure as a whole. It does in fact form part of the same series, only you underrate the importance of the matter, underrating it to such an extent that whenever we talk of it we are actually talking about quite different things. I venture to say that nothing has happened to you in your whole life that had such importance for you as the attempts at marriage have had for me. By this I do not mean that you have not experienced anything in itself as important; on the contrary, your life was much richer and more care-laden and more concentrated than mine, but for this very reason nothing of this sort has happened to you. It is as when one person has to climb five low steps and another person only one step, but one that is, at least for him, as high as all the other five put together; the first person will not only manage the five, but hundreds and thousands more as well, he will have led a great and very strenuous life, but none of the steps he has climbed will have been of such importance to him as for the second person that one, first, high step, that step which it is impossible for him to climb even by exerting all his strength, that step which he cannot get up and which he naturally cannot get past either.

Marrying, founding a family, accepting all the children that come, supporting them in this insecure world and even guiding them a little as well, is, I am convinced, the utmost a human being can succeed in doing at all. That seemingly so many succeed in this is no evidence to the contrary, for, first, there are not many who do in fact succeed, and secondly these not-many usually don't 'do' it, it merely 'happens' to them; although this is not that Utmost, yet it is still very great and very honourable (particularly since 'doing' and 'happening' cannot be kept clearly distinct). And finally it is not a matter of this Utmost at all, anyway, but only of some distant but decent approximation; it is after all not necessary to fly right into the middle of the sun, but it is necessary to crawl to a clean little spot on the earth where the sun sometimes shines and one can warm oneself a little.

How, then, was I prepared for this? As badly as possible. This is apparent even from what has been said hitherto. But in so far as there is a direct preparing of the individual and a direct creating of the general basic conditions, you did not intervene much outwardly. Nor is it otherwise possible; what is decisive here is the general sexual morality of class, nation, and time. All the same, you did intervene here too – not much, for the precondition for such intervention can only be great mutual trust, and both of us had been lacking in this even long before the decisive time came – and not very happily, because our needs were after all quite different; what grips me need hardly touch you at all, and vice versa, what is innocence in you may be guilt in me, and vice versa, what has no consequences for you may be the last nail in my coffin.

I remember going for a walk one evening with you and Mother; it was on the Josefsplatz near where the *Länderbank* is today; and I began talking about these interesting things, in a stupidly boastful, superior, proud, cool (that was spurious), cold (that was genuine), and stammering manner, as indeed I usually talked to you, reproaching the two of you for my having been left uninstructed, for the fact that it was my school-mates who first had to take me in hand, that I had been in the proximity of great dangers (here I was brazenly lying, as was my way, in order to show myself brave, for as a consequence of my timidity I had, except for the usual sexual misdemeanours of city children, no very exact notion of these 'great dangers'), but finally hinted that now, fortunately, I knew everything, no longer needed any advice, and that everything was all right. I had begun talking about this in any case mainly because it gave me pleasure at least to talk about it, and then too out of curiosity, and finally too in order somehow to avenge myself on the two of you for something or other. In keeping with your nature you took it quite simply, only saying something to the effect that you could give me some advice about how I could go in for these things without danger. Perhaps it was just such an answer that I had wanted to lure out of you, for it was in keeping with the pruriency of a child over-fed with meat and all good things, physically inactive, everlastingly occupied with himself, but still, my outward sense of shame was so hurt by this, or I believed it must be so hurt, that against my will I could not go on talking to you about this and with arrogant impudence cut the conversation short.

It is not easy to judge the answer you gave me then; on the one hand there was, after all, something staggeringly frank, in a manner of speaking primeval, about it, on the other hand, however, as regards the instruction itself, it was uninhibited in a very modern way. I don't know how old I was at the time, certainly not much over sixteen. It was nevertheless a very remarkable answer for such a boy to be given, and the distance between the two of us is also shown in the fact that this was actually the first direct instruction bearing on real life that I ever received from you. But its real meaning, which sank into my mind even then, but only much later came partly to the surface of my consciousness, was this: what you were advising me to do was, after all, in your opinion and, still far more, in my opinion at that time, the filthiest thing possible. The fact that you were prepared to see to it that physically speaking I should not bring any of the filth home with me was incidental, for in that way you were only protecting yourself, your own household. The main thing was, rather, that you remained outside your own advice, a married man, a pure man, exalted above these things; this was intensified for me at the time probably even more through the fact that marriage too seemed to me to be shameless and hence it was impossible for me to refer the general information I had picked up about marriage to my parents. In this way you became still more pure, rose still higher. The thought that you might perhaps have given yourself similar advice too before marriage was to me utterly unthinkable. So there was almost no smudge of earthly filth on you at all. And precisely you were pushing me, just as though I were predestined to it, down into this filth, with a few frank words. And so if the world consisted only of me and you, a notion I was much inclined to have, then this purity of the world came to an end with you and, by virtue of your advice, the filth began with me. In itself it was, of course, incomprehensible that you should thus condemn me; only old guilt and profoundest contempt on your side could explain it to me. And so this again was something that struck home to my innermost being, and very hard too.

Here is perhaps where it becomes most clear how we were both not to blame. A gives B a piece of advice that is frank, in keeping with his attitude to life, not very lovely but still even today perfectly usual in town, a piece of advice that might prevent damage to health. This piece of advice is for B morally not very invigorating – but why should he not be able to work his way out of this, and repair the damage, in the course of the years? – besides, he does not even have to take the advice at all, and in any case in the advice itself there is no occasion for B's whole future world, say, to come tumbling down upon him. And yet something of this kind does happen, but only for the very reason that A is you and B is myself.

The extent to which we are both not to blame is something I

can get a particularly good general view of because a similar clash between us took place in quite different circumstances some twenty years later, as a fact horrible, though in itself much less damaging – for where was there anything in me, the thirty-six-year-old, that could still be damaged? I am referring to a little discussion on one of the few agitated days after I had informed you of my last marriage-project. What you said to me was more or less as follows: 'She probably put on some specially chosen blouse, the thing these Prague Jewesses are good at, and straightaway, of course, you made up your mind to marry her. And, what's more, as fast as possible, in a week, tomorrow, today. I can't make you out, after all, you're a grown man, here you are in town, and you can't think of any way of managing but going straight off and marrying the next best girl. Isn't there anything else you can do? If you're frightened, I'll go along with you myself.' You put it in more detail and more plainly, but I can no longer recall the particular points, perhaps too things became a little misty before my eyes, I was almost more interested in Mother, as she, though perfectly in agreement with you, nevertheless took something from the table and left the room with it.

You have, I suppose, scarcely ever humiliated me more deeply with words and have never more clearly shown me your contempt. When you spoke to me in a similar way twenty years earlier, looking at it through your eyes one might even have seen in it some respect for the precocious city boy, who in your opinion could already be initiated into life without more ado. Today this consideration could only intensify the contempt, for the boy who was about to take his first leap into life got stuck half-way and seems to you today to be richer by no experience but only more pitiable by twenty years. My deciding on a girl meant nothing at all to you. You had (unconsciously) always kept down my power of decision and now believed (unconsciously) that you knew what it was worth. Of my attempts at escape in other directions you knew nothing, thus you could not know anything, either, of the thought-processes that had led me to this attempt to marry, and had to try to guess at them, and your guess was in keeping with your total judgement of me, a guess at the most abominable, crude, and ridiculous thing possible. And you did not for a moment hesitate to say this to me in just such a manner. The shame you inflicted on me with this was nothing to you in comparison to the shame that I would, in your opinion, inflict on your name by this marriage.

Now, as it happens, with regard to my attempts at marriage there is much you can say in reply, and you have indeed done so: you could not have much respect for my decision since I had twice broken the engagement to F. and twice renewed it again, since I had dragged you and Mother to Berlin to celebrate the engagement, and all for nothing, and the like. All this is true – but how did it come about?

The fundamental idea of both attempts at marriage was quite a right and proper one: to set up house, to become independent. It is an idea that does after all appeal to you, only then in reality it always turns out like the children's game where one holds and even presses the other's hand, calling out: 'Oh, go away, go away, why don't you go?' Which in our case, of course, is complicated by the fact that you have always honestly meant this 'go away!' since you have always, without knowing it, held me, or, rather, held me down, only by virtue of your personality.

Both girls were chosen by chance, it is true, but extraordinarily well. Here again is a sign of your complete misunderstanding, in that you can believe that I, the timid, hesitant, suspicious person, can make up my mind to marry all of a sudden, with a jerk, say out of delight over a blouse. Both marriages would, on the contrary, have been marriages of common sense, in as far as that means that day and night, the first time for years, the second time for months, all my power of thought was concentrated on the plan.

Neither of the girls disappointed me, only I disappointed both of them. My judgement on them is today exactly the same as at that time when I wanted to marry them.

Neither is it the case that in my second attempt at marriage I disregarded the experience gained from the first attempt, that is to say, was rash and careless. The cases were, as it happens, quite different from each other; it was precisely the early experiences that were able to give me hope in the second case, which was altogether much more promising. I don't want to go into details here.

Why then did I not marry? There were individual obstacles, as there are everywhere, but, after all, life consists in taking such obstacles in one's stride. The essential obstacle, however, which was unfortunately independent of the individual case, was that I am obviously intellectually incapable of marrying. This manifests itself in the fact that from the moment when I make up my mind to marry I can no longer sleep, my head burns day and night, life can no longer be called life, I stagger about in despair. It is not actually worries that bring this about; true, in keeping with my sluggishness and pedantry there are countless worries that are involved in all this, but they are not the decisive thing; true, they are like worms completing the work on the corpse, but the decisive blow comes from elsewhere. It is the general pressure of anxiety, of weakness, of self-contempt.

I will try to explain it in more detail. Here, in the attempt to marry, two seemingly antagonistic elements in my relations with you unite more intensely than anywhere else. Marriage is certainly the pledge of the most acute form of self-liberation and independence. I should have a family, the highest thing that one can achieve, in my opinion, and so, too, the highest thing you have achieved, I should be your equal, all old and everlastingly new shame and tyranny would now be mere history. That would, admittedly, be like a fairy-tale, but precisely there does the questionable element lie. It is too much; so much cannot be achieved. It is as if a person were a prisoner and he had not only the intention of escaping, which would perhaps be attainable, but also, and indeed simultaneously, the intention of rebuilding the prison as a pleasure-seat for himself. But if he escapes, he cannot do any rebuilding, and if he rebuilds, he cannot escape. If I want to become independent in the particular unhappy relationship in which I stand to you, I must do something that will have, if possible, no relation to you at all; marrying is, it is true, the greatest thing of all and provides the most honourable independence, but it is also at the same time in the closest relation to you. To try to get out at this point therefore has a touch of madness about it, and every attempt is almost punished with it.

Precisely this close relation does indeed partly lure me towards marrying. I picture this equality that would then arise between us, and which you would be able to understand better than any other form of equality, as so beautiful precisely because I could then be a free, grateful, guiltless, upright son, and you could be an untroubled, untyrannical, sympathetic, contented father. But to this end it would be necessary to make all that has happened be as though it had never happened, which means, we ourselves should have to be cancelled out.

But we being what we are, marrying is barred to me through the fact that it is precisely and peculiarly your most intimate domain. Sometimes I imagine the map of the world spread out flat and you stretched out diagonally across it. And what I feel then is that only those territories come into question for my life that either are not covered by you or are not within your reach. And, in keeping with the conception that I have of your magnitude, these are not many and not very comforting territories, and above all marriage is not among them.

This very comparison proves that I am far from wishing to say that you, by your example, drove me out of marriage as you did, for instance, out of the business. On the contrary, in spite of all the remote similarity. In your and Mother's marriage I had before me an in many ways model marriage, a model as regards constancy, mutual help, number of children, and even when the children grew up and increasingly disturbed the peace, the marriage as such remained untouched by this. It was perhaps precisely from this example that I formed my high idea of marriage; the desire for marriage was powerless simply for other reasons. These lay in your relation to your children, which is, after all, what this whole letter is about.

There is a view according to which fear of marriage sometimes has its source in a fear that one's children would some time pay one out for the sins one has oneself committed against one's own parents. This, I believe, in my case has no very great significance, for my sense of guilt actually originates, of course, in you, and goes so much with the deep conviction of its uniqueness, indeed this feeling of uniqueness is an essential part of its tormenting nature, that a repetition is unthinkable. All the same I must say that I should find such a mute, glum, dry, doomed son unbearable; I dare say, if there were no other possibility, I should flee from him, emigrate, as you at first meant to do on account of my marriage. And so there may be some influence of this too in my incapacity to marry.

What is, however, much more important in all this is the anxiety about myself. This is to be understood as follows: I have already indicated that in writing and in what is connected with it I have made some attempts at independence, attempts at escape, with the very smallest of success; they will scarcely lead any farther; much confirms this for me. Nevertheless it is my duty to watch over them, or, rather, my life consists in this, letting no danger that I can avert, indeed no possibility of such a danger, approach them. Marriage is the possibility of such a danger, admittedly also the possibility of the greatest advancement, for me, however, it is enough that it is the possibility of a danger. What should I do if it turned out to be a danger after all! How could I go on living in matrimony in the perhaps undemonstrable, but nevertheless irrefutable sense of this danger! Faced with this I can, indeed, waver, but the final outcome is certain, I must renounce. The simile of the bird in the hand and the two in the bush has only a very remote application here. In my hand I have nothing, in the bush there is everything, and yet — so it is decided by the conditions of battle and the exigency of life — I must choose the nothing. I had, after all, to make a similar choice in choosing my profession too.

The most important obstacle to marriage, however, is the no longer eradicable conviction that what is essential to supporting a family and, more, to guiding it is what I have recognized in you, and indeed everything rolled into one, good and bad, as it is organically combined in you, that is to say, strength, and scorn of the other, health and a certain immoderation, eloquence and inadequacy, self-confidence and dissatisfaction with everyone else, a superior attitude to the world and tyranny, knowledge of human nature and mistrust of most people, then also good qualities without any drawback, such as industry, endurance, presence of mind, and fearlessness. Of all this I had by comparison almost nothing or only very little, and was it with this I wanted to risk marrying, while I could see for myself that even you had to fight hard in your marriage and where the children were concerned even failed? This question I did not of course put to myself in so many words and did not answer in so many words, otherwise everyday thinking would after all have taken the matter over and shown me other men who are different from you (to name one, near at hand, who is very different from you: Uncle Richard) and yet have married and at least have not collapsed under the strain, which is in itself a great deal and would have been quite enough for me. But there it is, I did not ask this question, but experienced it from childhood on. I tested myself after all not only then when I was faced with marriage, but in the face of every little thing; in the face of every little thing you by your example and your method of upbringing convinced me, as I have tried to describe, of my incapacity, and what turned out to be right in the case of every little thing, proving you to be in the right, naturally could not but turn out to be tremendously right when it came to the greatest thing of all, that is to say, when it came to marriage. Up to the time of the attempts at marriage I grew up more or less like a business man who lives from day to day, it is true with worries and forebodings, but still without keeping any proper books. He makes a few small profits, which as a consequence of their rarity he keeps on pampering and exaggerating in his imagination, and for the rest only daily losses. Everything is entered, but never balanced. Now comes the necessity of drawing a balance, that is, the attempt at marriage. And with the large sums that have to be taken into account here, it is as though there had never been even the smallest profit, everything one single great liability. And now marry without going mad!

That is what my life with you has been like up to now, and these are the prospects inherent in it for the future.

Surveying my reasoned account of the fear I have of you, you might answer: 'You maintain I make things easy for myself by explaining my relation to you simply as being your fault, but I believe that in spite of outward effort you make things at least no more difficult for yourself, only much more profitable. First you too repudiate all guilt and responsibility; in this, then, our method is the same. But whereas I then attribute the sole guilt to you as frankly as I mean it, you are at the same time trying to be "too clever" and "too affectionate" and to acquit me too of all blame. Of course in this latter you only apparently succeed (and you do not want more, either), and what appears between the lines, in spite of all the "turns of phrase" about character and nature and antagonism and helplessness, is that actually I have been the aggressor, while everything you were up to was only self-defence. And so for the time being, by means of your insincerity, you would have

achieved enough, for you have proved three things, first that you
are blameless, secondly that I am to blame, and thirdly that out
of sheer magnanimity you are prepared not only to forgive me but,
what is both more and less, also to prove, into the bargain, and to
try to believe it yourself, that I, contrary to the truth, am also
blameless. One would think that would be enough for you now, but
it is still not enough. What you are in fact set upon is living entirely
on me. I admit that we fight with each other, but there are two
kinds of fighting. There is chivalrous fighting, in which the forces
of independent opponents are measured against each other, each one
remaining alone, losing alone, winning alone. And there is the
fighting of vermin, which not only sting but, at the same time,
suck the blood, too, to sustain their own life. That is after all what
the professional soldier really is, and that is what you are. You
are unfit for life; but in order to be able to settle down in it comfortably, without worries and without self-reproaches, you prove
that I have deprived you of all your fitness for life and put it into
my pockets. What does it matter to you now if you are unfit for
life, now it is my responsibility, but you calmly lie down and let
yourself be hauled along through life, physically and mentally, by
me. For example: when you recently wanted to marry, you wanted
– and this you do after all admit in this letter – at the same time
not to marry, but in order not to have to exert yourself you wanted
me to help you with this not-marrying, through my forbidding you
to make this marriage on account of the "disgrace" that this union
would bring upon my name. Now as it happened I did not dream
of doing this. First of all, here as elsewhere, I never wanted "to be
an obstacle to your happiness", and secondly I never want to have
to hear such a reproach from my own child. But was my having
overcome my own feelings, and so leaving your way open to this
marriage, any help to me? Not in the slightest. My dislike of the
marriage would not have prevented it; on the contrary, it would in
itself have been for you an added stimulus to marry the girl, for the
"attempt at escape", as you put it, would thus of course have become complete. And my consent to the marriage did not prevent
your reproaching me, for you do prove that I am in any case to
blame for your not marrying. At bottom, however, here and in everything else you have to my way of thinking proved nothing but that

all my reproaches were justified and that among them there was indeed one especially justified reproach missing, namely the charge of insincerity, obsequiousness, and parasitism. If I am not very much mistaken, you are preying upon me even now with this letter as such.'

To this I answer that first of all this whole rejoinder, which can also be partly turned against you, does not originate in you but, in fact, in me. Not even your mistrust of yourself, after all, is as great as my self-mistrust which you inculcated in me. A certain justification for the rejoinder, which in itself also contributes new material to the characterization of our relationship, I do not deny. Naturally things cannot in reality fit together in the way the evidence does in my letter; life is more than a Chinese puzzle. But with the correction that results from this rejoinder – a correction that I neither can nor will elaborate in detail – in my opinion something has yet been achieved that is so closely approximate to the truth that it may be able to reassure us both a little and make our living and our dying easier.

Franz.

Translated by Ernst Kaiser and Eithne Wilkins

Notes

By Max Brod

1. This 'letter' was written by Franz Kafka in November 1919, in Schelesen near Liboch, Bohemia. Since it was never delivered to the person to whom it was addressed, and hence never fulfilled the function of a letter, although it was undoubtedly intended to have that function (the details of this matter can be found in the first chapter of my *Life of Kafka*), I have included this work not in the volumes containing Kafka's correspondence, but among

his literary works, in which it represents the most comprehensive attempt at an autobiography that he ever made. The original is typewritten by Kafka himself and corrected by him by hand. It covers forty-four and a quarter large sheets of typing paper, with an average of thirty-four lines. The forty-fifth page is for the most part blank. The manuscript breaks off in the middle of a sentence, at the words 'You are unfit for life; but in order ...' (*Lebensuntüchtig bist Du; um es Dir aber ...*). Nevertheless the two and a half final pages are attached on smaller paper and written by hand, so that there is no lacuna in the text.

2. The youngest of Franz Kafka's three sisters. The two elder sisters, who are also mentioned in this letter, were called Elli and Valli. Since all three sisters were murdered by the Nazis (together with many other members of the family), I no longer have the qualms that in 1937 (when I published my *Life of Kafka*) compelled me to quote only extracts from the letter. The letter as now published is reproduced without any abbreviation or change whatsoever. Only the punctuation has been slightly supplemented in places.

3. Kafka's mother was a member of the Löwy family, a family whose peculiar spiritual and almost eccentric character is described in my *Life of Kafka*.

4. Franz Kafka's nephew. He too was murdered.

5. This word, Czech in origin, signifies a long balcony of the kind that ran round the inner courtyard of many of the more ancient houses in Prague. It was generally shared by several apartments.

6. A relative of Franz Kafka's.

7. *Wer sich mit Hunden niederlegt, steht mit Flöhen auf*: He who lies down with dogs gets up with fleas.

8. Kafka's sister took on the management of a farm in the little German–Bohemian town of Zürau. The writer stayed with her there for some time in his illness (1917–18).

9. In explanation of the relationships in the family it should be noted that Karl was Elli's husband and Felix and Gerti were their children.

Two Dialogues

From a work later destroyed:
DESCRIPTION OF A STRUGGLE

1. Conversation with the Suppliant

There was a time when I went every day into a church, since a girl I was in love with knelt there in prayer for half an hour in the evening and I was able to look at her in peace.

Once when she had not come and I was reluctantly eyeing the other supplicants, I noticed a young fellow who had thrown his whole lean length along the floor. Every now and then he clutched his head as hard as he could and sighing loudly beat it in his upturned palms on the stone flags.

Only a few old women were in the church, and they kept turning their shawled heads sideways to watch the young man at his devotions. Their awareness of him seemed to please him, for before each of his pious outbursts he cast his eyes around to see whether many of them were looking. This I found unseemly, and I made up my mind to accost him as he left the church and to ask him why he prayed in such a manner. Yes, I felt irritable because my girl had not come.

But an hour elapsed before he stood up, crossed himself punctiliously, and strode jerkily towards the basin of holy water. I set myself in a direct line between the basin and the door, knowing that I was not going to let him pass without an explanation. I screwed up my mouth as I always do when I want to speak decisively. I advanced my right leg and rested all my weight upon it, balancing my left leg carelessly on the points of my toes; that, too, gives me a sense of firmness.

Now it is possible that the young man had already caught sight of me when he was sprinkling himself with the holy water, or he might even have remarked me sooner with some dismay, for he made a sudden unexpected dash out through the doorway. The glass door banged shut. And when I came out immediately behind him I could not see him anywhere, for there were several narrow streets and plenty of traffic.

He stayed away for the next few days, but my girl was there. She was wearing her black dress with the transparent lace top over the shoulders, the crescent of her petticoat showed under it – from the lower edge of which the silk hung in a beautifully cut ruffle. And since she had come I forgot the young man and did not even concern myself with him when he continued to appear regularly to do his devotions in the usual manner. Yet, whenever he passed me he always seemed in a great hurry and turned his face away. Perhaps it was only that I could not think of him except in motion and so even when he was standing still he seemed to me to be slithering past.

One evening I stayed too long in my room. All the same, I went along to the church. My girl was not in it, and I thought of going home again. But there was the young fellow lying on the floor. I was reminded of my first encounter with him and my curiosity revived.

I went on tip-toe to the doorway, gave a coin to the blind beggar who sat there, and squeezed in beside him behind the open half of the door; and for a whole hour there I sat, perhaps with a crafty look on my face. I liked being there and made up my mind to come again often. In the second hour I began to think it foolish to sit there because of a man at his prayers. Yet for a third hour in growing irritation I let the spiders creep over my clothes while the last of the people came, drawing deep breaths, out of the darkness of the church.

And then he too came. He was walking cautiously, trying the ground lightly with his feet before setting them down.

I rose up, took a large stride forward, and seized him.

'Good evening,' I said, and with my hand on his collar pushed him down the steps into the lighted square.

When we were down on the level he said in a fluttering voice: 'Good evening, my dear, dear sir, don't be angry with me, your most devoted servant.'

'Well,' said I, 'I want to ask you some questions, sir; you slipped through my fingers the other time but you'll hardly do that to-night.'

'Sir, you are a compassionate man and you'll let me go home. I'm a poor creature, that's the truth.'

'No,' I cried, against the noise of a passing tram, 'I won't let you go. This is the kind of encounter I like. You're a lucky catch for me. I congratulate myself.'

Then he said: 'Oh God, your heart is alive but your head is a block of wood. You call me a lucky catch, what good luck you must be sure of! For my bad luck is like a see-saw teetering on a very fine point, and it will fall on anyone's head who lays a questioning finger on it. Good night, sir.'

'Right,' said I, and held his right hand fast, 'if you don't give me an answer I'll begin to yell here in the street. And all the shop-girls that are coming out now and all their sweethearts waiting for them so happily will come running up, for they'll think a carriage-horse has fallen down or some accident has happened. And then I'll point you out to the people.'

At that he tearfully kissed my hands, one after the other. 'I'll tell you what you want to know, but please let us rather go into the side-street over there.' I nodded, and we crossed to it.

But it was not enough for him to be in the dusk of the little street where only a few yellow lamps hung at wide intervals, he drew me into the low hall-way of an old house underneath a tiny lamp that hung dripping before a wooden stair. There he took out his handkerchief gravely and spread it on a step, saying: 'Do sit down, my dear sir, and you will be better able to ask questions, while I stand here, for so I'll be better able to answer them. Only don't torment me.'

So I sat down and said, looking up at him with narrowed eyes: 'You're an utter lunatic, that's what you are! Look at the way you carry on in the church! How irritating it is and how unpleasant for onlookers! How can anyone compose himself to worship if he has to look at you?'

He kept his body pressed against the wall, only his head could move freely to and fro. 'Don't be angry – why should you be angry about things that don't concern you? I get angry when I behave badly; but if someone else does the wrong thing I am delighted. So don't be angry if I tell you that it is the aim of my life to get people to look at me.'

'What a thing to say,' I cried, much too loudly for the low-roofed hall-way, but I was afraid to let my voice die away again, 'truly, what a thing to say. Of course I can guess, of course I guessed the first time I saw you, what kind of state you are in. I've had some experience, and I don't mean it as a joke when I tell you it's like being seasick on dry land. It's a condition in which you can't remember the real names of things and so in a great hurry you fling temporary names at them. You do it as fast as you can. But you've hardly turned your back on them before you've forgotten what you called them. A poplar in the fields which you called "the tower of Babel", since you either didn't or wouldn't know that it was a poplar, stands wavering anonymously again, and so you have to call it "Noah in his cups".'

I was somewhat disconcerted when he said: 'I'm thankful to say that I don't understand what you've been talking about.'

With annoyance I answered quickly: 'Your saying that you're thankful shows that you do know what I was talking about.'

'Of course it shows that, my dear sir, but what you said was rather peculiar too.'

I laid my hands on a step above me, leaned right back and in this almost untacklable position, which is the last resource of a wrestler, asked him: 'Haven't you a comic way of wriggling out of things, projecting your own state of mind like that on other people?'

That made him pluck up courage. He clasped his hands together to give his body unity and put up some resistance, saying: 'No, I don't do that with anyone, not even with you for instance, because I can't. But I should be glad if I could, for then I wouldn't need to make people look at me in church. Do you know why I need to?'

This question rather dished me. Of course I didn't know, and I believe I didn't want to know. I never wanted to come here, I said to myself, but the creature forced me to give him a hearing. So all I had to do was to shake my head, to convey that I didn't know, yet I found myself unable to move my head at all.

The young man standing opposite me smiled. Then he dropped on his knees and with a dreamy look on his face told me: 'There has never been a time in which I have been convinced from within myself that I am alive. You see, I have only such a fugitive awareness of things around me that I always feel they were once real and are now fleeting away. I have a constant longing, my dear sir, to catch a glimpse of things as they may have been before they show themselves to me. I feel that then they were calm and beautiful. It must be so, for I often hear people talking about them as though they were.'

Since I made no answer and only through involuntary twitchings in my face betrayed my uneasiness, he asked: 'Don't you believe that people talk like that?'

I knew I ought to nod assent but could not do it.

'You don't really believe it? Why, listen; once when I was a child and just waking up from a short afternoon nap, still half asleep, I heard my mother calling down from the balcony in the most natural voice: "What are you doing, my dear? It's so hot." And a woman answered from the garden: "I'm revelling in the grass." She said it quite simply and without insistence, as if it were to be taken for granted.'

I thought an answer was expected from me, so I felt in my hip trouser pocket as if I were looking for something. But I wasn't looking for anything, I only wanted to shift my position to show that I was paying attention. And then I said that the incident was remarkable enough and quite beyond my comprehension. I added also that I didn't believe it was true and that it must have been invented for some special purpose which I could not fathom. Then I shut my eyes for they were hurting me. 'Oh, how glad I am that you agree with me, and it was most unselfish of you to stop me in order to let me know it. Why indeed should I feel ashamed – or why should we feel ashamed – because I don't walk upright and ponderously, striking my walking-stick on the pavement and brushing the clothes of the people who pass by so loudly. Shouldn't I rather venture to complain with justified resentment at having to flit along the house walls like a shadow with hunched shoulders, many a time disappearing from sight in the plate-glass of the shop windows.

'What dreadful days I have to live through! Why are all our buildings so badly put together that tall houses sometimes collapse without any discernible external cause? I go clambering over the ruins asking everyone I meet: "Now how could such a thing happen! In our town – a brand new house – that's the fifth one today – just think of it." And nobody can give me an answer.

'And people often fall down in the street and lie there dead. Then all the tradesmen open their doors that are hung with a litter of goods, come trotting out, carry the dead man into a house, and then appear again, with smiling eyes and lips, saying: "Good morning – the sky is overcast – I'm selling a lot of head-clothes – yes, the war." I go slinking into the house and after timidly raising my hand several times with the fingers ready crooked knock at last on the porter's little glass window. "My dear fellow," I say to him in a friendly way, "a dead man was just brought in here. Do let me see him, please." And when he shakes his head as if undecided, I say positively: "My dear chap. I'm from the secret police. Show me that dead man at once." "A dead man?" he asks, almost in an injured voice. "No, there's no dead man here. This is a respectable house." And I take my leave and go.

'And then if I have to cross a large open space I forget everything. The difficulty of this enterprise confuses me, and I can't help thinking: "If people must build such large squares out of pure wantonness why don't they add a stone balustrade to help one across? There's a gale from the south-west today. The air in the square is swirling about. The tip of the Town Hall is teetering in small circles. All this agitation should be controlled. Every window-pane is rattling and the lamp-posts are bending like bamboos. The very robe of the Virgin Mary on her column is fluttering and the stormy wind is snatching at it. Is no one aware of this? The ladies and gentlemen who should be walking on the paving-stones are driven along. When the wind slackens they come to a stop, exchange a few words, and bow to each other, but when the wind blows again they can't help themselves, all their feet leave the ground at the same moment. They have to hold on to their hats, of course, but their eyes twinkle merrily as if there were only a gentle breeze. No one's afraid but me." '

Smarting as I was, I said: 'The story you told me about your mother and the woman in the garden seems to me not in the least remarkable. Not only have I heard many like it and experienced them, but I've even played a part in some of them. It was quite a natural incident. Do you think that if I had been on the balcony I couldn't have said the same thing and got the same answer from the garden? Such a simple affair.'

When I said that, he seemed very delighted. He remarked that I was well dressed and he particularly liked my tie. And what fine skin I had. And admissions became most clear and unequivocal when one withdrew them.

2. Conversation with the Drunken Man

I took a small step out of the front door and at once the sky, with moon and stars in its great vault, and the spacious square with the Town Hall, the Virgin Mary on her column, and the church, overwhelmed me.

I passed calmly from shadow to moonlight, unbuttoned my overcoat and warmed myself; then I raised my hands to still the roaring of the night and began to meditate.

'Now what does it mean, your behaving like this as if you were real? Can you be trying to make me believe that I am unreal, a comic figure standing on the greenish pavement? And yet it's a long time since you were real, you heavens, and as for you, Old Town Square, you have never been real.

'True, you still have the advantage of me, but only so long as I leave you alone.

'God be thanked, Moon, you have ceased being Moon, but perhaps it's careless of me to go on calling you Moon simply because that has been your name. Why are you so much less supercilious when I call you "Forgotten Paper Lantern of a queer colour"? And why do you almost vanish from sight when I call you "Mary Column", and you, Mary Column, seem much less threatening when I call you "Moon casting a yellow light"?

'It really looks as if you take harm from being thought about; your courage and your well-being dwindle.

'God, how salutary it must be for a thinking man to learn from a drunken one!

'Why has everything grown so still? I believe the wind has stopped. And the little houses that often reel across the square as if on tiny wheels are standing quite firm – still – still – no, there's no sign of the thin black line that usually separates them from the ground.'

And I began to run. I ran three times round the great square without let or hindrance, and since I met no drunken man I ran without slackening speed and without perceptible effort in the direction of Charles Street. My shadow ran beside me on the wall, often smaller than myself, as if it were in a ditch between the house walls and the street.

As I passed the Fire Station I heard a noise from the Small Square, and swerving into it I saw a drunken man standing at the trellis-work of the fountain, his arms stretched bolt upright and his feet, that were thrust into wooden clogs, stamping on the ground.

I stopped for a moment to control my breathing and then I went up to him, swept off my top-hat, and introduced myself:

'Good evening, gentle nobleman, I am twenty-three years old but I have as yet no name. But you, I am sure, have come with a re-markable, yes, with a ringing name from the great city of Paris. The quite artificial odour of the wanton Court of France surrounds you.

'Undoubtedly with those farded eyes of yours you have seen the great ladies who stand on a high light terrace, turning ironically on slender waists, while the ends of their embroidered trains, wide-spread over the steps, still trail over the sand of the garden. It's true, isn't it, that lackeys in dashing grey livery-coats and white breeches are climbing up long poles disposed at intervals, each with his legs curled round a pole but his body sometimes bent backwards and sideways, since they have to haul up by ropes from the ground enormous grey canvas covers and stretch them on high because the great lady desires a cloudy morning?' He belched and I said almost in alarm: 'Is it really true, sir, that you have come from our Paris, from Paris the tempestuous, from the hail-storm of enthusiasm?' When he belched again I said diffidently: 'I know that I am being greatly honoured.'

And with quick fingers I buttoned up my overcoat, then I said to him with shy insistence:

'I know that you don't think me worthy of an answer, but I should have led a miserable life had I not questioned you today.

'Pray, my fine gentleman, are the tales true that I have heard? Does one find in Paris people who are nothing but gaily bedecked, clothes and houses that have only entrance portals, and is it true that on summer days the sky is a fleeting blue with little white clouds pasted over it as a decoration, all in the shape of hearts? And isn't there a thronged panopticon with nothing but trees in it on which little placards have been hung bearing the names of the most famous heroes, criminals and lovers?

'And then to hear such news from Paris! Such obviously lying news!

'The streets of Paris have suddenly begun to ramify, isn't that it? They have grown restless, isn't that all? Things can't always be kept in order, how could they be? Some accident is bound to happen, people come flocking, pouring out of the side-streets with the mincing city gait that hardly touches the pavement; they are all filled with curiosity, of course, but also afraid of being disappointed; they breathe quickly and poke their little heads forward. But when they brush against each other they bow low and beg each other's pardon: "I am so sorry – it was quite unintentional – there is such a crowd, excuse me, please – it was very clumsy of me – my fault entirely. My name is – my name is Jerome Faroche, I am a spice merchant in the Rue du Cabotin – permit me to invite you to luncheon tomorrow – my wife will be delighted." That's how they speak, even while the street is filled with clamour and the smoke of the chimneys falls between the houses. That's how it must be. And it would be possible suddenly to see on a crowded boulevard in some fashionable quarter a couple of carriages come to a stop. Lackeys gravely open the carriage doors. Eight noble Siberian wolf-hounds prance out and with great bounds course along the roadway, baying. And someone says that they are young Persian dandies in disguise.'

He had shut his eyes tight. As I stopped talking he thrust both hands into his mouth and wrenched at his lower jaw. His clothes were all befouled. Perhaps he had been thrown out of a tavern and still did not know how he stood.

It was about the moment when there is a small, hushed pause between day and night, when one's head unexpectedly hangs heavy and without one's being aware of it everything holds its breath because no one is looking, and then slips out of sight. Meanwhile one stands there drooping and then looks up and finds that one can see nothing, that one no longer feels the very air moving, but clings inwardly to the remembrance of houses standing a certain distance off, with roofs and blessedly sharp-cornered chimneys through which the darkness seeps into the houses, right through the garrets into the different rooms. And it is a blessing that tomorrow will be another day, in which, incredible as it may seem, one will be able to see everything.

Then the drunken man raised his eyebrows so high that a sheen was visible between them and his eyes, and announced in spasms: 'It's like this, you see – I'm sleepy, you see, so I'm going to bed. I have a brother-in-law in Wenceslas Square, you see – that's where I'm going, for that's where I'm staying, for that's where I have a bed. I'm going there now. Only I don't know what his name is and where he lives – seems I've forgotten that – but it doesn't matter, for I'm not even sure that I have a brother-in-law at all. Well, I'm going. Do you think I'll ever find him?'

I answered him unthinkingly: 'Of course you will. But you are a stranger here and somehow you have mislaid your retinue. Allow me to escort you.'

He made no answer. So I offered him my arm and he took it.

Translated by Willa and Edwin Muir

Meditation

Children on a Country Road

I heard the waggons rumbling past the garden fence, sometimes I even saw them through gently swaying gaps in the foliage. How the wood of their spokes and shafts creaked in the summer heat! Labourers were coming from the fields and laughing so that it was a scandal.

I was sitting on our little swing, just resting among the trees in my parents' garden.

On the other side of the fence the traffic never stopped. Children's running feet were past in a moment; harvest waggons with men and women perched on and around the sheaves darkened the flower-beds; towards evening I saw a gentleman slowly promenading with a walking-stick and a couple of girls who met him arm-in-arm stepped aside into the grass as they greeted him.

Then birds flew up as if in showers, I followed them with my eyes and saw how high they soared in one breath, till I felt not that they were rising but that I was falling, and holding fast to the ropes began to swing a little out of sheer weakness. Soon I was swinging more strongly as the air blew colder and instead of soaring birds trembling stars appeared.

I was given my supper by candle-light. Often both my arms were on the wooden board and I was already weary as I bit into my bread and butter. The much-pierced window-curtains bellied in the warm wind and many a time some passer-by outside would stay them with his hands as if he wanted to see me better and speak to me. Usually the candle soon went out and in the sooty candle-smoke the assembled midges went on circling for a while. If anyone asked me a question from the window I would gaze at him as if at a distant mountain or into vacancy, nor did he particularly care whether he got an answer or not. But if one jumped over the windowsill and announced that the others were already waiting, then I did get to my feet with a sigh.

'What are you sighing for? What's wrong? Has something dreadful happened that can never be made good? Shan't we ever recover from it? Is everything lost?'

Nothing was lost. We ran to the front of the house. 'Thank God, here you are at last!' 'You're always late!' 'Why just me?' 'Especially you, why don't you stay at home if you don't want to come?' 'No quarter!' 'No quarter? What kind of way is that to talk?'

We ran our heads full tilt into the evening. There was no daytime and no night-time. Now our waistcoat buttons would be clacking together like teeth, again we would be keeping a steady distance from each other as we ran, breathing fire like wild beasts in the tropics. Like cuirassiers in old wars, stamping and springing high, we drove each other down the short alley and with this impetus in our legs a farther stretch along the main road. Stray figures went into the ditch, hardly had they vanished down the dusky escarpment when they were standing like newcomers on the field-path above and looking down.

'Come on down!' 'Come on up first!' 'So's you can push us down, no thanks, we're not such fools!' 'You're afraid, you mean. Come on up, you cowards!' 'Afraid? Of the likes of you? You're going to push us down, are you? That's a good one.'

We made the attempt and were pushed head over heels into the grass of the roadside ditch, tumbling of our own free will. Everything was equally warm to us, we felt neither warmth nor chill in the grass, only one got tired.

Turning on one's right side, with a hand under the ear, one could easily have fallen asleep there. But one wanted to get up again with chin uplifted, only to roll into a deeper ditch. Then with an arm thrust out cross-wise and legs threshing to the side one thought to launch into the air again only to fall for certain into a still deeper ditch. And of this one never wanted to make an end.

How one might stretch oneself out properly to sleep in the extremity of the last ditch of all, especially on one's knees, was something scarcely thought of, and one simply lay on one's back, like an invalid, inclined to weep a little. One blinked as now and then a youngster with elbows pressed to his sides sprang over one's head with dark-looming soles, in a leap from the escarpment to the roadway.

The moon was already some way up in the sky, in its light a mail-coach drove past. A small wind began to blow everywhere, even in the ditch one could feel it, and near by the forest began to rustle. Then one was no longer so anxious to be alone.

'Where are you?' 'Come here!' 'All together!' 'What are you hiding for, drop your nonsense!' 'Don't you know the mail's gone past already?' 'Not already?' 'Of course, it went past while you were sleeping.' 'I wasn't sleeping. What an idea!' 'Oh shut up, you're still half asleep.' 'But I wasn't.' 'Come on!'

We ran bunched more closely together, many of us linked hands, one's head could not be held high enough, for now the way was downhill. Someone whooped an Indian war-cry, our legs galloped us as never before, the wind lifted our hips as we sprang. Nothing could have checked us; we were in such full stride that even in overtaking others we could fold our arms and look quietly around us.

At the bridge over the brook we came to a stop; those who had overrun it came back. The water below lapped against stones and roots as if it were not already late evening. There was no reason why one of us should not jump on to the parapet of the bridge.

From behind clumps of trees in the distance a railway train came past, all the carriages were lit up, the window-panes were certainly let down. One of us began to sing a popular catch, but we felt like singing. We sang much faster than the train was going, we waved our arms because our voices were not enough, our voices rushed together in an avalanche of sound that did us good. When one joins in song with others it is like being drawn on by a fishhook.

So we sang, the forest behind us, for the ears of the distant travellers. The grown-ups were still awake in the village, the mothers were making down the beds for the night.

Our time was up. I kissed the one next me, reached hands to the three nearest, and began to run home, none called me back. At the first cross-roads where they could no longer see me I turned off and ran by the field-paths into the forest again. I was making for that city in the south of which it was said in our village:

'There you'll find queer folk! Just think, they never sleep!'

'And why not?'

'Because they never get tired.'

'And why not?'

'Because they're fools.'

'Don't fools get tired?'

'How could fools get tired!'

Unmasking a Confidence Trickster

At last, about ten o'clock at night, I came to the doorway of the fine house where I was invited to spend the evening, after the man beside me, whom I was barely acquainted with, and who had once again thrust himself unasked upon me, had marched me for two long hours around the streets.

'Well!' I said, and clapped my hands to show that I really had to bid him good-bye. I had already made several less explicit attempts to get rid of him. I was tired out.

'Are you going straight in?' he asked. I heard a sound in his mouth that was like the snapping of teeth.

'Yes.'

I had been invited out, I told him when I met him. But it was to enter a house where I longed to be that I had been invited, not to stand here at the street door looking past the ears of the man before me. Nor to fall silent with him, as if we were doomed to stay for a long time on this spot. And yet the houses around us at once took a share in our silence, and the darkness over them, all the way up to the stars. And the steps of invisible passers-by, which one could not take the trouble to elucidate, and the wind persistently buffeting the other side of the street, and a gramophone singing behind the closed windows of some room – they all announced themselves in this silence, as if it were their own possession for the time past and to come.

And my companion subscribed to it in his own name and – with a smile – in mine too, stretched his right arm up along the wall and leaned his cheek upon it, shutting his eyes.

But I did not wait to see the end of that smile, for shame suddenly caught hold of me. It had needed that smile to let me know that the man was a confidence trickster, nothing else. And yet I had been months in the town and thought I knew all about confidence tricksters, how they came slinking out of side-streets by night to meet us with outstretched hands like tavern-keepers, how they haunted the advertisement pillars we stood beside, sliding round them as if playing hide-and-seek and spying on us with at least one eye, how they suddenly appeared on the kerb of the pavement at cross-streets when we were hesitating! I understood them so well, they were the first acquaintances I had made in the town's small taverns, and to them I owed my first inkling of a ruthless hardness which I was now so conscious of, everywhere on earth, that I was even beginning to feel it in myself. How persistently they blocked our way, even when we had long shaken ourselves free, even when, that is, they had nothing more to hope for! How they refused to give up, to admit defeat, but kept shooting glances at us that even from a distance were still compelling! And the means they employed were always the same: they planted themselves before us, looking as large as possible, tried to hinder us from going where we purposed, offered us instead a habitation in their own bosoms, and when at last all our balked feelings rose in revolt they welcomed that like an embrace into which they threw themselves face foremost.

And it had taken me such a long time in this man's company to recognize the same old game. I rubbed my finger-tips together to wipe away the disgrace.

My companion was still leaning there as before, still believing himself a successful trickster, and his self-complacency glowed pink on his free cheek.

'Caught in the act!' said I, tapping him lightly on the shoulder. Then I ran up the steps, and the disinterested devotion on the servants' faces in the hall delighted me like an unexpected treat. I looked at them all, one after another, while they took my great-coat off and wiped my shoes clean.

With a deep breath of relief and straightening myself to my full height I then entered the drawing-room.

The Sudden Walk

When it looks as if you had made up your mind finally to stay at home for the evening, when you have put on your house-jacket and sat down after supper with a light on the table to the piece of work or the game that usually precedes your going to bed, when the weather outside is unpleasant so that staying indoors seems natural, and when you have already been sitting quietly at the table for so long that your departure must occasion surprise to everyone, when, besides, the stairs are in darkness and the front door locked, and in spite of all that you have started up in a sudden fit of restlessness, changed your jacket, abruptly dressed yourself for the street, explained that you must go out and with a few curt words of leave-taking actually gone out, banging the flat door more or less hastily according to the degree of displeasure you think you have left behind you, and when you find yourself once more in the street with limbs swinging extra freely in answer to the unexpected liberty you have procured for them, when as a result of this decisive action you feel concentrated within yourself all the potentialities of decisive action, when you recognize with more than usual significance that your strength is greater than your need to accomplish effortlessly the swiftest of changes and to cope with it, when in this frame of mind you go striding down the long streets – then for that evening you have completely got away from your family, which fades into insubstantiality, while you yourself, a firm, boldly-drawn black figure, slapping yourself on the thigh, grow to your true stature.

All this is still heightened if at such a late hour in the evening you look up a friend to see how he is getting on.

Resolutions

To lift yourself out of a miserable mood, even if you have to do it by strength of will, should be easy. I force myself out of my chair, stride round the table, exercise my head and neck, make my eyes sparkle, tighten the muscles round them. Defy my own feelings, welcome A. enthusiastically supposing he comes to see me, amiably tolerate B. in my room, swallow all that C. says, whatever pain and trouble it may cost me, in long draughts.

Yet even if I manage that, one single slip, and a slip cannot be avoided, will stop the whole process, easy and painful alike, and I will have to shrink back into my own circle again.

So perhaps the best resource is to meet everything passively, to make yourself an inert mass, and, if you feel that you are being carried away, not to let yourself be lured into taking a single unnecessary step, to stare at others with the eyes of an animal, to feel no compunction, in short, with your own hand to throttle down whatever ghostly life remains in you, that is, to enlarge the final peace of the graveyard and let nothing survive save that.

A characteristic movement in such a condition is to run your little finger along your eyebrows.

Excursion into the Mountains

'I don't know,' I cried without being heard, 'I do not know. If nobody comes, then nobody comes. I've done nobody any harm, nobody's done me any harm, but nobody will help me. A pack of nobodies. Yet that isn't all true. Only, that nobody helps me – a pack of nobodies would l e rather fine, on the other hand. I'd love to go on an excursion – why not? – with a pack of nobodies. Into the mountains, of course, where else? How these nobodies jostle each other, all these lifted arms linked together, these numberless feet treading so close! Of course they are all in dress suits. We go so gaily, the wind blows through us and the gaps in our company. Our throats swell and are free in the mountains! It's a wonder that we don't burst into song.'

Bachelor's Ill Luck

It seems so dreadful to stay a bachelor, to become an old man struggling to keep one's dignity while begging for an invitation whenever one wants to spend an evening in company, to lie ill gazing for weeks into an empty room from the corner where one's bed is, always having to say good night at the front door, never to run up a stairway beside one's wife, to have only side-doors in one's room leading into other people's living-rooms, having to carry one's supper home in one's hand, having to admire other people's children and not even being allowed to go on saying: 'I have none myself,' modelling oneself in appearance and behaviour on one or two bachelors remembered from one's youth.

That's how it will be, except that in reality, both today and later, one will stand there with a palpable body and a real head, a real forehead, that is, for smiting on with one's hand.

The Tradesman

It is possible that some people are sorry for me, but I am not aware of it. My small business fills me with worries that make my forehead and temples ache inside yet without giving any prospect of relief, for my business is a small business.

I have to spend hours beforehand making things ready, jogging the caretaker's memory, warning him about mistakes he is likely to commit, and puzzling out in one season of the year what the next season's fashions are to be, not such as are followed by the people I know but those that will appeal to inaccessible peasants in the depths of the country.

My money is in the hands of strangers; the state of their affairs must be a mystery to me; the ill luck that might overwhelm them I cannot foresee; how could I possibly avert it! Perhaps they are running into extravagance and giving a banquet in some inn-garden, some of them may be attending the banquet as a brief respite before their flight to America.

When at the close of a working day I turn the key on my business and suddenly see before me hours in which I shall be able to do nothing to satisfy its never-ending demands, then the excitement which I drove far away from me in the morning comes back like a returning tide, but cannot be contained in me and sweeps me aimlessly away with it.

And yet I can make no use of this impulse, I can only go home, for my face and hands are dirty and sweaty, my clothes are stained and dusty, my working cap is on my head, and my shoes are scratched with the nails of crates. I go home as if lifted on a wave, snapping the fingers of both hands, and caress the hair of any children I meet.

But the way is short. Soon I reach my house, open the door of the lift, and step in.

I see that now, of a sudden, I am alone. Others who have to climb stairways tire a little as they climb, have to wait with quick panting breath till someone opens the door of the flat, which gives them an excuse for being irritable and impatient, have to traverse the hall-way where hats are hung up, and not until they go down a lobby past several glass doors and come into their own room are they alone.

But I am alone in the lift, immediately, and on my knees gaze into the narrow looking-glass. As the lift begins to rise, I say: 'Quiet now, back with you, is it the shadow of the trees you want to make for, or behind the window-curtains, or into the garden arbour?'

I say that behind my teeth, and the staircase flows down past the opaque glass panes like running water.

'Fly then; let your wings, which I have never seen, carry you into the village hollow or as far as Paris, if that's where you want to go.

'But enjoy yourselves there looking out of the window, see the processions converging out of three streets at once, not giving way to each other but marching through each other and leaving the open space free again as their last ranks draw off. Wave your handkerchiefs, be indignant, be moved, acclaim the beautiful lady who drives past.

'Cross over the stream on the wooden bridge, nod to the children bathing and gape at the Hurrah! rising from the thousand sailors on the distant battleship.

'Follow the trail of the inconspicuous little man, and when you have pushed him into a doorway, rob him, and then watch him, each with your hands in your pockets, as he sadly goes his way along the left-hand street.

'The police dispersed on galloping horses rein in their mounts and thrust you back. Let them, the empty streets will dishearten them, I know. What did I tell you, they are riding away already in couples, slowly round the corners, at full speed across the squares.'

Then I have to leave the lift, send it down again and ring the bell, and the maid opens the door while I say 'Good evening.'

Absent-minded Window-gazing

What are we to do with these spring days that are now fast coming on? Early this morning the sky was grey, but if you go to the window now you are surprised and lean your cheek against the latch of the casement.

The sun is already setting, but down below you see it lighting up the face of the little girl who strolls along looking about her, and at the same time you see her eclipsed by the shadow of the man behind overtaking her.

And then the man has passed by and the little girl's face is quite bright.

The Way Home

See what a persuasive force the air has after a thunderstorm! My merits become evident and overpower me, though I don't put up any resistance, I grant you.

I stride along and my tempo is the tempo of all my side of the street, of the whole street, of the whole quarter. Mine is the responsibility, and rightly so, for all the raps on doors or on the flat of a table, for all toasts drunk, for lovers in their beds, in the scaffolding of new buildings, pressed to each other against the house walls in dark alleys, or on the divans of a brothel.

I weigh my past against my future, but find both of them admirable, cannot give either the preference, and find nothing to grumble at save the injustice of Providence that has so clearly favoured me.

Only as I come into my room I feel a little meditative, without having met anything on the stairs worth meditating about. It doesn't help me much to open the window wide and hear music still playing in a garden.

Passers-by

When you go walking by night up a street, and a man, visible a long way off — for the street mounts uphill and there is a full moon — comes running towards you, well, you don't catch hold of him, not even if he is a feeble and ragged creature, not even if someone chases yelling at his heels, but you let him run on.

For it is night, and you can't help it if the street goes uphill before you in the moonlight, and besides, these two have maybe started that chase to amuse themselves, or perhaps they are both chasing a third, perhaps the first is an innocent man and the second wants to murder him and you would become an accessory, perhaps they don't know anything about each other and are merely running separately home to bed, perhaps they are night-birds, perhaps the first man is armed.

And anyhow, haven't you a right to be tired, haven't you been drinking a lot of wine? You're thankful that the second man is now long out of sight.

On the Tram

I stand on the end platform of the tram and am completely unsure of my footing in this world, in this town, in my family. Not even casually could I indicate any claims that I might rightly advance in any direction. I have not even any defence to offer for standing on this platform, holding on to this strap, letting myself be carried along by this tram, nor for the people who give way to the tram or walk quietly along or stand gazing into shop-windows. Nobody asks me to put up a defence, indeed, but that is irrelevant.

The tram approaches a stopping-place and a girl takes up her position near the step, ready to alight. She is as distinct to me as if I had run my hands over her. She is dressed in black, the pleats of her skirt hang almost still, her blouse is tight and has a collar of white fine-meshed lace, her left hand is braced flat against the side of the tram, the umbrella in her right hand rests on the second top step. Her face is brown, her nose, slightly pinched at the sides, has a broad round tip. She has a lot of brown hair and stray little tendrils on the right temple. Her small ear is close-set, but since I am near her I can see the whole ridge of the whorl of her right ear and the shadow at the root of it.

At that point I asked myself: How is it that she is not amazed at herself, that she keeps her lips closed and makes no such remark?

Clothes

Often when I see clothes with manifold pleats, frills, and append-ages which fit so smoothly on to lovely bodies I think they won't keep that smoothness long, but will get creases that can't be ironed out, dust lying so thick in the embroidery that it can't be brushed away, and that no one would want to be so unhappy and so foolish as to wear the same valuable gown every day from early morning till night.

And yet I see girls who are lovely enough and display attractive muscles and small bones and smooth skin and masses of delicate hair, and none the less appear day in, day out, in this same natural fancy dress, always propping the same face on the same palms and letting it be reflected from the looking-glass.

Only sometimes at night, on coming home late from a party, it seems in the looking-glass to be worn-out, puffy, dusty, already seen by too many people and hardly wearable any longer.

Rejection

When I meet a pretty girl and beg her: 'Be so good as to come with me,' and she walks past without a word, this is what she means to say:

'You are no Duke with a famous name, no broad American with a Red Indian figure, level, brooding eyes and a skin tempered by the air of the prairies and the rivers that flow through them, you have never journeyed to the seven seas and voyaged on them wherever they may be, I don't know where. So why, pray, should a pretty girl like myself go with you?'

'You forget that no automobile swings you through the street in long thrusts; I see no gentlemen escorting you in a close half-circle, pressing on your skirts from behind and murmuring blessings on your head; your breasts are well laced into your bodice, but your thighs and hips make up for that restraint; you are wearing a taffeta dress with a pleated skirt such as delighted all of us last autumn, and yet you smile – inviting mortal danger – from time to time.'

'Yes, we're both in the right, and to keep us from being irrevocably aware of it, hadn't we better go our separate ways home?'

Reflections for Gentlemen Jockeys

When you think it over, winning a race is nothing to sigh for. The fame of being hailed as the best rider in the country is too intoxicating a pleasure when the applause tunes up not to bring a reaction the morning after.

The envy of your opponents, cunning and fairly influential men, must trouble you in the narrow enclosure you now traverse after the flat race-course, which soon lay empty before you save for some laggards of the previous round, small figures charging the horizon.

Many of your friends are rushing to gather their winnings and only cry 'Hurrah!' to you over their shoulders from distant pay-boxes; your best friends laid no bet on your horse, since they feared that they would have to be angry with you if you lost, and now that your horse has come in first and they have won nothing, they turn away as you pass and prefer to look along the stands.

Your rivals behind you, firmly in the saddle, are trying to ignore the bad luck that has befallen them and the injustice they have somehow suffered; they are putting a brave new face on things, as if a different race were due to start, and this time a serious one after such child's play.

For many ladies the victor cuts a ridiculous figure because he is swelling with importance and yet cannot cope with the never-ending hand-shaking, saluting, bowing and waving, while the defeated keep their mouths shut and casually pat the necks of their whinnying horses.

And finally from the now overcast sky rain actually begins to fall.

The Street Window

Whoever leads a solitary life and yet now and then wants to attach himself somewhere, whoever, according to changes in the time of day, the weather, the state of his business and the like, suddenly wishes to see any arm at all to which he might cling – he will not be able to manage for long without a window looking on to the street. And if he is in the mood of not desiring anything and only goes to his window-sill a tired man, with eyes turning from his public to heaven and back again, not wanting to look out and having thrown his head up a little, even then the horses below will draw him down into their train of waggons and tumult, and so at last into the human harmony.

The Wish to be a Red Indian

If one were only an Indian, instantly alert, and on a racing horse, leaning against the wind, kept on quivering jerkily over the quivering ground, until one shed one's spurs, for there needed no spurs, threw away the reins, for there needed no reins, and hardly saw that the land before one was smoothly-shorn heath when horse's neck and head would be already gone.

The Trees

For we are like tree-trunks in the snow. In appearance they lie sleekly and a light push should be enough to set them rolling. No, it can't be done, for they are firmly wedded to the ground. But see, even that is only appearance.

Unhappiness

When it was becoming unbearable – once towards evening in November – and I ran along the narrow strip of carpet in my room as on a race-track, shrank from the sight of the lit-up street, then turning to the interior of the room found a new goal in the depths of the looking-glass and screamed aloud, to hear only my own scream which met no answer nor anything that could draw its force away, so that it rose up without check and could not stop even when it ceased being audible, the door in the wall opened towards me, how swiftly, because swiftness was needed and even the cart-horses down below on the paving-stones were rising in the air like horses driven wild in a battle, their throats bare to the enemy.

Like a small ghost a child blew in from the pitch-dark corridor, where the lamp was not yet lit, and stood a-tip-toe on a floorboard that quivered imperceptibly. At once dazzled by the twilight in my room she made to cover her face quickly with her hands, but contented herself unexpectedly with a glance at the window, where the mounting vapour of the street-lighting had at last settled under its cover of darkness behind the cross-bars. With her right elbow she supported herself against the wall in the open doorway and let the draught from outside play along her ankles, her throat, and her temples.

I gave her a brief glance, then said 'Good day', and took my jacket from the hood of the stove, since I didn't want to stand there half undressed. For a little while I let my mouth hang open, so that my agitation could find a way out. I had a bad taste in my mouth, my eyelashes were fluttering on my cheeks, in short this visit, though I had expected it, was the one thing needful.

The child was still standing by the wall on the same spot, she had pressed her right hand against the plaster and was quite taken up with finding, her cheeks all pink, that the white-washed walls had a rough surface and chafed her fingertips. I said: 'Are you really looking for me? Isn't there some mistake? Nothing easier than to make a mistake in this big building. I'm called So-and-so and I live on the third floor. Am I the person you want to find?'

'Hush, hush,' said the child over her shoulder, 'it's all right.'

'Then come farther into the room, I'd like to shut the door.'

'I've shut it this very minute. Don't bother. Just be easy in your mind.'

'It's no bother. But there's a lot of people living on this corridor, and I know them all, of course; most of them are coming back from work now; if they hear someone talking in a room, they simply think they have a right to open the door and see what's happening. They're just like that. They've turned their backs on their daily work and on their provisionally free evenings they're not going to be dictated to by anyone. Besides, you know that as well as I do. Let me shut the door.'

'Why, what's the matter with you? I don't mind if the whole house comes in. Anyhow, as I told you, I've already shut the door, do you think you're the only person who can shut doors? I've even turned the key in the lock.'

'That's all right then. I couldn't ask for more. You didn't need to turn the key, either. And now that you are here, make yourself comfortable. You are my guest. You can trust me entirely. Just make yourself at home and don't be afraid. I won't compel you either to stay or to go away. Do I have to tell you that? Do you know me so little?'

'No. You really didn't need to tell me that. What's more, you shouldn't have told me. I'm just a child; why stand on so much ceremony with me?'

'It's not so bad as that. A child, of course. But not so very small. You're quite big. If you were a young lady, you wouldn't dare to lock yourself so simply in a room with me.'

'We needn't worry about that. I just want to say: my knowing you so well isn't much protection to me, it only relieves you from the effort of keeping up pretences before me. And yet you're paying me a compliment. Stop it, I beg you, do stop it. Anyhow, I don't know you everywhere and all the time, least of all in this darkness. It would be much better if you were to light up. No, perhaps not. At any rate I'll keep it in mind that you have been threatening me.'

'What? Am I supposed to have threatened you? But, look here. I'm so pleased that you've come at last. I say "at last" because it's already rather late. I can't understand why you've come so late. But it's possible that in the joy of seeing you I have been speaking at random and you took up my words in the wrong sense. I'll admit ten times over that I said something of the kind, I've made all kinds of threats, anything you like – only no quarrelling, for Heaven's sake! But how could you think of such a thing? How could you hurt me so? Why do you insist on spoiling this brief moment of your presence here? A stranger would be more on-coming than you are.'

'That I can well believe; that's no great discovery. No stranger could come any nearer to you than I am already by nature. You know that, too, so why all this pathos? If you're only wanting to stage a comedy I'll go away immediately.'

'What? You have the impudence to tell me that. You make a little too bold. After all, it's my room you're in. It's my wall you're rubbing your fingers on like mad. My room, my wall! And besides, what you are saying is ridiculous as well as impudent. You say your nature forces you to speak to me like that. Is that so? Your nature forces you? That's kind of your nature. Your nature is mine, and if I feel friendly to you by nature, then you mustn't be anything else.'

'Is that friendly?'

'I'm speaking of earlier on.'

'Do you know how I'll be later on?'

'I don't know anything.'

And I went to the bed-table and lit the candle on it. At that time I had neither gas nor electric light in my room. Then I sat for a while at the table till I got tired of it, put on my great-coat, took my hat from the sofa, and blew out the candle. As I went out I tripped over the leg of a chair.

On the stairs I met one of the tenants from my floor.

'Going out again already, you rascal?' he asked, pausing with his legs firmly straddled over two steps.

'What can I do?' I said. 'I've just had a ghost in my room.'

'You say that exactly as if you had just found a hair in your soup.'

'You're making a joke of it. But let me tell you, a ghost is a ghost.'

'How true. But what if one doesn't believe in ghosts at all?'

'Well, do you think I believe in ghosts? But how can my not believing help me?'

'Quite simply. You don't need to feel afraid if a ghost actually turns up.'

'Oh, that's only a secondary fear. The real fear is a fear of what caused the apparition. And that fear doesn't go away. I have it fairly powerfully inside me now.' Out of sheer nervousness I began to hunt through all my pockets.

'But since you weren't afraid of the ghost itself, you could easily have asked it how it came to be there.'

'Obviously you've never spoken to a ghost. One never gets straight information from them. It's just a hither and thither. These ghosts seem to be more dubious about their existence than we are, and no wonder, considering how frail they are.'

'But I've heard that one can feed them up.'

'How well-informed you are. It's quite true. But is anyone likely to do it?'

'Why not? If it were a feminine ghost, for instance,' said he, swinging on to the top step.

'Aha,' said I, 'but even then it's too much to expect.'

I thought of something else. My neighbour was already so far up that in order to see me he had to bend over the well of the staircase. 'All the same,' I called up, 'if you steal my ghost from me all is over between us, for ever.'

'Oh, I was only joking,' he said and drew his head back.

'That's all right,' said I, and now I really could have gone quietly for a walk. But because I felt so forlorn I preferred to go upstairs again and so went to bed.

Translated by Willa and Edwin Muir

The Judgement

A Story for F.

It was a Sunday morning in the very height of spring. George Bendemann, a young merchant, was sitting in his own room on the first floor of one of a long row of small ramshackle houses stretching beside the river which were scarcely distinguishable from each other except in height and colouring. He had just finished a letter to an old friend of his who was now living abroad, had put it into its envelope in a slow and dreamy fashion, and with his elbows propped on the writing-table was gazing out of the window at the river, the bridge and the hills on the farther bank with their tender green.

He was thinking about his friend, who had actually run away to Russia some years before, being dissatisfied with his prospects at home. Now he was carrying on a business in St Petersburg, which had flourished to begin with but had long been going downhill, as he always complained on his increasingly rare visits. So he was wearing himself out to no purpose in a foreign country, the unfamiliar full beard he wore did not quite conceal the face George had known so well since childhood, and his skin was growing so yellow as to indicate some latent disease. By his own account he had no regular connection with the colony of his fellow-countrymen out there and almost no social intercourse with Russian families, so that he was resigning himself to becoming a permanent bachelor.

What could one write to such a man, who had obviously run off the rails, a man one could be sorry for but could not help. Should one advise him to come home, to transplant himself and take up his old friends again – there was nothing to hinder him – and in general to rely on the help of his friends? But that was as good as telling him, and the more kindly the more offensively, that all his efforts hitherto had miscarried, that he should finally give up, come back home, and be gaped at by everyone as a returned prodigal, that only his friends knew what was what and that he himself was just a big child who should do what his successful and home-keeping friends prescribed. And was it certain, besides, that all the pain one would have to inflict on him would achieve its object? Perhaps it would not even be possible to get him to come home at all – he said himself that he was now out of touch with commerce in his native country – and then he would still be left an alien in a foreign land embittered by his friends' advice and more than ever estranged from them. But if he did follow their advice and then didn't fit in at home – not out of malice, of course, but through force of circumstances – couldn't get on with his friends or without them, felt humiliated, couldn't be said to have either friends or a country of his own any longer, wouldn't it have been better for him to stay abroad just as he was? Taking all this into account, how could one be sure that he would make a success of life at home?

For such reasons, supposing one wanted to keep up correspondence with him, one could not send him any real news such as could frankly be told to the most distant acquaintance. It was more than three years since his last visit, and for this he offered the lame excuse that the political situation in Russia was too uncertain, which apparently would not permit even the briefest absence of a small business-man while it allowed hundreds of thousands of Russians to travel peacefully abroad. But during these three years George's own position in life had changed a lot. Two years ago his mother had died, since when he and his father had shared the household together, and his friend had of course been informed of that and had expressed his sympathy in a letter phrased so dryly that the grief caused by such an event, one had to conclude, could not be realized in a distant country. Since that time, however, George had applied himself with greater determination to the business as well as to everything else.

Perhaps during his mother's lifetime his father's insistence on having everything his own way in the business had hindered him from developing any real activity of his own, perhaps since her death his father had become less aggressive, although he was still active in the business, perhaps it was mostly due to an accidental run of good fortune – which was very probable indeed – but at any rate during those two years the business had developed in a most unexpected way, the staff had had to be doubled, the turnover was five times as great, no doubt about it, further progress lay just ahead.

But George's friend had no inkling of this improvement. In earlier years, perhaps for the last time in that letter of condolence, he had tried to persuade George to emigrate to Russia and had enlarged upon the prospects of success for precisely George's branch of trade. The figures quoted were microscopic by comparison with the range of George's present operations. Yet he shrank from letting his friend know about his business success, and if he were to do it now retrospectively that certainly would look peculiar.

So George confined himself to giving his friend unimportant items of gossip such as rise at random in the memory when one is idly thinking things over on a quiet Sunday. All he desired was to leave undisturbed the idea of the home-town which his friend must have built up to his own content during the long interval. And so it happened to George that three times in three fairly widely separated letters he had told his friend about the engagement of an unimportant man to an equally unimportant girl, until indeed, quite contrary to his intentions, his friend began to show some interest in this notable event.

Yet George preferred to write about things like these rather than to confess that he himself had got engaged a month ago to a Fräulein Frieda Brandenfeld, a girl from a well-to-do family. He often discussed this friend of his with his fiancée and the peculiar relationship that had developed between them in their correspondence. 'So he won't be coming to our wedding,' said she, 'and yet I have a right to get to know all your friends.' 'I don't want to trouble him,' answered George, 'don't misunderstand me, he would probably come, at least I think so, but he would feel that his hand had been forced and he would be hurt, perhaps he would envy me and certainly he'd be discontented and without being able to do anything about his discontent he'd have to go away again alone. Alone – do you know what that means?' 'Yes, but may he not hear about our wedding in some other fashion?' 'I can't prevent that, of course, but it's unlikely, considering the way he lives.' 'Since your friends are like that, George, you shouldn't ever have got engaged at all.'

'Well, we're both to blame for that; but I wouldn't have it any other way now.' And when, breathing quickly under his kisses, she still brought out: 'All the same, I do feel upset,' he thought it could not really involve him in trouble were he to send the news to his friend. 'That's the kind of man I am and he'll have to take me as I am,' he said to himself. 'I can't cut myself to another pattern that might make a more suitable friend for him.'

And in fact he did inform his friend, in the long letter he had been writing that Sunday morning, about his success in love, with these words: 'I have saved my best news to the end. I have got engaged to a Fräulein Frieda Brandenfeld, a girl from a well-to-do family, who only came to live here a long time after you went away, so that you're hardly likely to know her. There will be time to tell you more about her later, for today let me just say that I am very happy and as between you and me the only difference in our relationship is that instead of a quite ordinary kind of friend you will now have in me a happy friend. Besides that, you will acquire in my fiancée, who sends her warm greetings and will soon write you herself, a genuine friend of the opposite sex, which is not without importance to a bachelor. I know that there are many reasons why you can't come to see us, but would not my wedding be precisely the right occasion for giving all obstacles the go-by? Still, however that may be, do just as seems good to you without regarding any interests but your own.'

With this letter in his hand George had been sitting a long time at the writing-table, his face turned towards the window. He had barely acknowledged, with an absent smile, a greeting waved to him from the street by a passing acquaintance.

At last he put the letter in his pocket and went out of his room across a small lobby into his father's room, which he had not entered for months. There was in fact no need for him to enter it, since he saw his father daily at business and they took their midday meal together at an eating-house; in the evening, it was true, each did as he pleased, yet even then, unless George – as mostly happened – went out with friends or, more recently, visited his fiancée, they always sat for a while, each with his newspaper, in their common sitting-room.

It surprised George how dark his father's room was even on this sunny morning. So it was overshadowed so much as that by the high wall on the other side of the narrow courtyard. His father was sitting by the window in a corner hung with various mementoes of George's dead mother, reading a newspaper which he held to one side before his eyes in an attempt to overcome a defect of vision. On the table stood the remains of his breakfast, not much of which seemed to have been eaten.

'Ah, George,' said his father, rising at once to meet him. His heavy dressing-gown swung open as he walked and the skirts of it fluttered round him. 'My father is still a giant of a man,' said George to himself. 'It's unbearably dark here,' he said aloud.

'Yes, it's dark enough,' answered his father.

'And you've shut the window, too?'

'I prefer it like that.'

'Well, it's quite warm outside,' said George, as if continuing his previous remark, and sat down.

His father cleared away the breakfast dishes and set them on a chest.

'I really only wanted to tell you,' went on George, who had been vacantly following the old man's movements, 'that I am now sending the news of my engagement to St Petersburg.' He drew the letter a little way from his pocket and let it drop back again.

'To St Petersburg?' asked his father.

'To my friend there,' said George trying to meet his father's eye. In business hours he's quite different, he was thinking, how solidly he sits here with his arms crossed.

'Oh yes. To your friend,' said his father, with peculiar emphasis.

'Well, you know, Father, that I wanted not to tell him about my engagement at first. Out of consideration for him, that was the only reason. You know yourself he's a difficult man. I said to myself that someone else might tell him about my engagement, although he's such a solitary creature that that was hardly likely – I couldn't prevent that – but I wasn't ever going to tell him myself.'

'And now you've changed your mind?' asked his father, laying his enormous newspaper on the window-sill and on top of it his spectacles, which he covered with one hand.

'Yes, I've been thinking it over. If he's a good friend of mine, I said to myself, my being happily engaged should make him happy too. And so I wouldn't put off telling him any longer. But before I posted the letter I wanted to let you know.'

'George,' said his father, lengthening his toothless mouth, 'listen to me! You've come to me about this business, to talk it over with me. No doubt that does you honour. But it's nothing, it's worse than nothing, if you don't tell me the whole truth. I don't want to stir up matters that shouldn't be mentioned here. Since the death of our dear mother certain things have been done that aren't right. Maybe the time will come for mentioning them, and maybe sooner than we think. There's many a thing in the business I'm not aware of, maybe it's not done behind my back – I'm not going to say that it's done behind my back – I'm not equal to things any longer, my memory's failing, I haven't an eye for so many things any longer. That's the curse of Nature in the first place, and in the second place the death of our dear mother hit me harder than it did you – but since we're talking about it, about this letter, I beg you George, don't deceive me. It's a trivial affair, it's hardly worth mentioning, so don't deceive me. Do you really have this friend in St Petersburg?'

George rose in embarrassment. 'Never mind my friends. A thousand friends wouldn't make up to me for my father. Do you know what I think? You're not taking enough care of yourself. But old age must be taken care of. I can't do without you in the business, you know that very well, but if the business is going to undermine your health, I'm ready to close it down tomorrow for ever. And that won't do. We'll have to make a change in your way of living. But a radical change. You sit here in the dark, and in the sitting-room you would have plenty of light. You just take a bite of breakfast instead of properly keeping up your strength. You sit by a closed window, and the air would be so good for you. No, Father! I'll get the doctor to come, and we'll follow his orders. We'll change your room; you can move into the front room and I'll move in here. You won't notice the change, all your things will be moved with you. But there's time for all that later, I'll put you to bed now for a little, I'm sure you need to rest. Come, I'll help you to take off your things, you'll see I can do it. Or if you would rather go into the front room at once, you can lie down in my bed for the present. That would be the most sensible thing.'

George stood close beside his father, who had let his head with its unkempt white hair sink on his chest.

'George,' said his father in a low voice, without moving.

George knelt down at once beside his father, in the old man's weary face he saw the pupils, over-large, fixedly looking at him from the corners of the eyes.

'You have no friend in St Petersburg. You've always been a leg-puller and you haven't even shrunk from pulling my leg. How could you have a friend out there! I can't believe it.'

'Just think back a bit, Father,' said George, lifting his father from the chair and slipping off his dressing-gown as he stood feebly enough, 'it'll soon be three years since my friend came to see us last. I remember that you used not to like him very much. At least twice I kept you from seeing him, although he was actually sitting with me in my room. I could quite well understand your dislike of him, my friend has his peculiarities. But then, later, you got on with him very well. I was proud because you listened to him and nodded and asked him questions. If you think back you're bound to remember. He used to tell us the most incredible stories of the Russian Revolution. For instance, when he was on a business trip to Kiev and ran into a riot and saw a priest on a balcony who cut a broad cross in blood on the palm of his hand and held the hand up and appealed to the mob. You've told that story yourself once or twice since.'

Meanwhile George had succeeded in lowering his father down again and carefully taking off the woollen drawers he wore over his linen under-pants and his socks. The not particularly clean appearance of this underwear made him reproach himself for having been neglectful. It should have certainly been his duty to see that his father had clean changes of underwear. He had not yet explicitly discussed with his bride-to-be what arrangements should be made for his father in the future, for they had both of them silently taken it for granted that the man would go on living alone in the old house. But now he made a quick, firm decision to take him into his own future establishment. It almost looked, on closer inspection, as if the care he meant to lavish there on his father might come too late.

He carried his father to bed in his arms. It gave him a dreadful feeling to notice that while he took the few steps towards the bed the old man on his breast was playing with his watch-chain. He could not lay him down on the bed for a moment, so firmly did he hang on to the watch-chain.

But as soon as he was lain in bed, all seemed well. He covered himself up and even drew the blankets farther than usual over his shoulders. He looked up at George with a not unfriendly eye.

'You begin to remember my friend, don't you?' asked George, giving him an encouraging nod.

'Am I well covered up now?' asked his father, as if he were not able to see whether his feet were properly tucked in or not.

'So you find it snug in bed already,' said George and tucked the blankets more closely round him.

'Am I well covered up?' asked his father once more, seeming to be strangely intent upon the answer.

'Don't worry, you're well covered up.'

'No!' cried his father, cutting short the answer, threw the blankets off with a strength that sent them all flying in a moment and sprang erect in bed. Only one hand lightly touched the ceiling to steady him.

'You wanted to cover me up, I know, my young sprig, but I'm far from being covered up yet. And even if this is the last strength I have, it's enough for you, too much for you. Of course I know your friend. He would have been a son after my own heart. That's why you've been playing him false all these years. Why else? Do you think I haven't been sorry for him? And that's why you had to lock yourself up in your office – the Chief is busy, mustn't be disturbed – just so that you could write your lying little letters to Russia. But thank goodness a father doesn't need to be taught how to see through his son. And now that you thought you'd got him down, so far down that you could set your bottom on him and sit on him and he wouldn't move, then my fine son makes up his mind to get married!'

George stared at the bogy conjured up by his father. His friend in St Petersburg, whom his father suddenly knew so well, touched his imagination as never before. Lost in the vastness of Russia he saw him. At the door of an empty, plundered warehouse he saw him. Among the wreckage of his show-cases, the slashed remnants of his wares, the falling gas-brackets, he was just standing up. Why did he have to go so far away!

'But attend to me!' cried his father, and George, almost distracted, ran towards the bed to take everything in, yet came to a stop half-way.

'Because she lifted up her skirts,' his father began to flute, 'because she lifted her skirts like this, the nasty creature,' and mimicking her he lifted his shirt so high that one could see the scar on his thigh from his war wound, 'because she lifted her skirts like this and this you made up to her, and in order to make free with her undisturbed you have disgraced your mother's memory, betrayed your friend and stuck your father into bed so that he can't move. But he can move, or can't he?'

And he stood up quite unsupported and kicked his legs out. His insight made him radiant.

George shrank into a corner, as far away from his father as possible. A long time ago he had firmly made up his mind to watch closely every least movement so that he should not be surprised by any indirect attack, a pounce from behind or above. At this moment he recalled this long-forgotten resolve and forgot it again, like a man drawing a short thread through the eye of a needle.

'But your friend hasn't been betrayed after all!' cried his father, emphasizing the point with stabs of his forefinger. 'I've been representing him here on the spot.'

'You comedian!' George could not resist the retort, realized at once the harm done and, his eyes starting in his head, bit his tongue back, only too late, till the pain made his knees give.

'Yes, of course I've been playing a comedy! A comedy! That's a good expression! What other comfort was left to a poor old widower? Tell me – and while you're answering me be you still my living son – what else was left to me, in my back room, plagued by a disloyal staff, old to the marrow of my bones? And my son strutting through the world, finishing off deals that I had prepared for him, bursting with triumphant glee and stalking away from his father with the closed face of a respectable business-man! Do you think I couldn't have loved you, I, whom you turned your back on?'

Now he'll lean forward, thought George; what if he topples and smashes himself! These words went hissing through his mind.

His father leaned forward but did not topple. Since George did not come any nearer, as he had expected, he straightened himself again.

'Stay where you are, I don't need you! You think you have strength enough to come over here and that you're only hanging back of your own accord. Don't be too sure! I am still much the stronger of us two. All by myself I might have had to give way, but your mother has given me so much of her strength that I've established a fine connection with your friend and I have your customers here in my pocket!'

'He has pockets even in his shirt!' said George to himself, and believed that with this remark he could make him an impossible figure for all the world. Only for a moment did he think so, since he kept on forgetting everything.

'Just take your bride on your arm and try getting in my way! I'll sweep her from your very side, you don't know how!'

George made a grimace of disbelief. His father only nodded, confirming the truth of his words, towards George's corner.

'How you amused me today, coming to ask me if you should tell your friend about your engagement. He knows it all already, you stupid boy, he knows it all! I've been writing to him, for you forgot to take my writing things away from me. That's why he hasn't been here for years, he knows everything a hundred times better than you do yourself, in his left hand he crumples your letters unopened while in his right hand he holds up my letters to read through!'

In his enthusiasm he waved his arm over his head.

'He knows everything a thousand times better!' he cried.

'Ten thousand times!' said George, to make fun of his father, but in his very mouth the words turned into deadly earnest.

'For years I've been waiting for you to come with some such question! Do you think I concern myself with anything else? Do you think I read the newspapers? Look!' and he threw George a newspaper sheet which had somehow found its way into his bed. An old newspaper, with a name entirely unknown to George.

'How long a time you've taken to grow up! Your mother had to die, she couldn't see the happy day, your friend is going to pieces in Russia, even three years ago he was yellow enough to be thrown away, and as for me, you see what condition I'm in. You have eyes in your head for that!'

'So you've been lying in wait for me!' cried George.

His father said pityingly, in an off-hand manner: 'I suppose you wanted to say that sooner. But now it doesn't matter.' And in a louder voice: 'So now you know what else there is in the world besides yourself, till now you've known only about yourself! An innocent child, yes, that you were, truly, but still more truly have you been a devilish human being! And therefore take note: I sentence you now to death by drowning!'

George felt himself urged from the room, the crash with which his father fell on the bed behind him was still in his ears as he fled. On the staircase, which he rushed down as if its steps were an inclined plane, he ran into his charwoman on her way up to do the morning cleaning of the room. 'Jesus!' she cried and covered her face with her apron, but he was already gone. Out of the front door he rushed, across the roadway, driven towards the water. Already he was grasping at the railings as a starving man clutches food. He swung himself over, like the distinguished gymnast he had once been in his youth, to his parents' pride. With weakening grip he was still holding on when he spied between the railings a motor-bus coming which would easily cover the noise of his fall, called in a low voice: 'Dear parents, I have always loved you, all the same,' and let himself drop.

At this moment an unending stream of traffic was just going over the bridge.

Translated by Willa and Edwin Muir

A Country Doctor

Short Stories

To My Father

The New Advocate

We have a new advocate, Dr Bucephalus. There is little in his appearance to remind you that he was once Alexander of Macedon's battle-charger. Of course, if you know his story, you are aware of something. But even a simple usher whom I saw the other day on the front steps of the Law Courts, a man with the professional appraisal of the regular small punter on a racecourse, was running an admiring eye over the advocate as he mounted the marble steps with a high action that made them ring beneath his feet.

In general the Bar approves the admission of Bucephalus. With astonishing insight people tell themselves that, modern society being what it is, Bucephalus is in a difficult position, and therefore, considering also his importance ·in the history of the world, he deserves at least a friendly reception. Nowadays – it cannot be denied – there is no Alexander the Great. There are plenty of men who know how to murder people; the skill needed to reach over a banqueting table and pink a friend with a lance is not lacking; and for many Macedonia is too confining, so that they curse Philip, the father – but no one, no one at all, can blaze a trail to India. Even in his day the gates of India were beyond reach, yet the King's sword pointed the way to them. Today the gates have receded to remoter and loftier places; but no one points the way; many carry swords; but only to brandish them, and the eye that tries to follow them is confused.

So perhaps it is really best to do as Bucephalus has done and absorb oneself in law books. In the quiet lamplight, his flanks unhampered by the thighs of a rider, free and far from the clamour of battle, he reads and turns the pages of our ancient tomes.

A Country Doctor

I was in great perplexity; I had to start on an urgent journey; a seriously ill patient was waiting for me in a village ten miles off: a thick blizzard of snow filled all the wide spaces between him and me; I had a gig, a light gig with big wheels, exactly right for our country roads; muffled in furs, my bag of instruments in my hand, I was in the courtyard all ready for the journey; but there was no horse to be had, no horse. My own horse had died in the night, worn out by the fatigues of this icy winter; my servant-girl was now running round the village trying to borrow a horse; but it was hopeless, I knew it, and I stood there forlornly, with the snow gathering more and more thickly upon me, more and more unable to move. In the gateway the girl appeared, alone, and waved the lantern; of course, who would lend a horse at this time for such a journey? I strode through the courtyard once more; I could see no way out; in my confused distress I kicked at the dilapidated door of the year-long-uninhabited pig-sty. It flew open and flapped to and fro on its hinges. A steam and smell as of horses came out from it. A dim stable lantern was swinging inside from a rope. A man, crouching on his hams in that low space, showed an open blue-eyed face. 'Shall I yoke up?' he asked, crawling out on all fours. I did not know what to say and merely stooped down to see what else was in the sty. The servant-girl was standing beside me. 'You never know what you're going to find in your own house,' she said, and we both laughed. 'Hey there, Brother, hey there, Sister!' called the groom, and two horses, enormous creatures with powerful flanks, one after the other, their legs tucked close to their bodies, each well-shaped head lowered like a camel's, by sheer strength of buttocking squeezed out through the door-hole which they filled entirely. But at once they were standing up, their legs long and their bodies steaming thickly. 'Give him a hand,' I said, and the willing girl hurried to help the groom with the harnessing. Yet hardly was she beside him when the groom clipped hold of her and pushed his face against hers. She screamed and fled back to me; on her cheek stood out in red the marks of two rows of teeth. 'You

brute,' I yelled in fury, 'do you want a whipping?' but in the same
moment reflected that the man was a stranger; that I did not know
where he came from, and that of his own free will he was helping
me out when everyone else had failed me. As if he knew my
thoughts he took no offence at my threat but, still busied with the
horses, only turned round once towards me. 'Get in,' he said then,
and indeed, everything was ready. A magnificent pair of horses, I
observed, such as I had never sat behind, and I climbed in happily.
'But I'll drive, you don't know the way,' I said. 'Of course,' said he,
'I'm not coming with you anyway, I'm staying with Rose.' 'No,'
shrieked Rose, fleeing into the house with a justified presentiment
that her fate was inescapable; I heard the door-chain rattle as she
put it up; I heard the key turn in the lock; I could see, moreover,
how she put out the lights in the entrance hall and in further
flight all through the rooms to keep herself from being discovered.
'You're coming with me,' I said to the groom, 'or I won't go, urgent
as my journey is. I'm not thinking of paying for it by handing the
girl over to you.' 'Gee up!' he said; clapped his hands; the gig
whirled off like a log in a freshet; I could just hear the door of my
house splitting and bursting as the groom charged at it and then
I was deafened and blinded by a storming rush that steadily buffeted
all my senses. But this only for a moment, since, as if my patient's
farmyard had opened out just before my courtyard gate, I was
already there; the horses had come quietly to a standstill; the blizzard had stopped; moonlight all around; my patient's parents
hurried out of the house; his sister behind them; I was almost lifted
out of the gig; from their confused ejaculations I gathered not a
word; in the sick-room the air was almost unbreathable; the
neglected stove was smoking; I wanted to push open a window; but
first I had to look at my patient. Gaunt, without any fever, not cold,
not warm, with vacant eyes, without a shirt, the young man heaved
himself up from under the feather bedding, threw his arms round
my neck, and whispered in my ear: 'Doctor, let me die.' I glanced
round the room; no one had heard it; the parents were leaning
forward in silence waiting for my verdict; the sister had set a chair
for my handbag; I opened the bag and hunted among my instruments; the young man kept clutching at me from his bed to remind
me of his entreaty; I picked up a pair of tweezers, examined them

in the candlelight and laid them down again. 'Yes,' I thought
blasphemously, 'in cases like this the Gods are helpful, send the
missing horse, add to it a second because of the urgency, and to
crown everything bestow even a groom —' And only now did I
remember Rose again; what was I to do, how could I rescue her,
how could I pull her away from under that groom at ten miles'
distance, with a team of horses I couldn't control. These horses,
now, they had somehow slipped the reins loose; pushed the windows
open from outside, I did not know how; each of them had stuck
a head in at a window and, quite unmoved by the startled cries
of the family, stood eyeing the patient. 'Better go back at once,'
I thought, as if the horses were summoning me to the return journey, yet I permitted the patient's sister, who fancied that I was
dazed by the heat, to take my fur coat from me. A glass of rum
was poured out for me, the old man clapped me on the shoulder,
a familiarity justified by this offer of his treasure. I shook my head;
in the narrow confines of the old man's thoughts I felt ill; that
was my only reason for refusing the drink. The mother stood by the
bedside and cajoled me towards it; I yielded, and, while one of the
horses whinnied loudly to the ceiling, laid my head to the
young man's breast which shivered under my wet beard. I confirmed what I already knew; the young man was quite sound, something a little wrong with his circulation, saturated with coffee by
his solicitous mother, but sound and best turned out of bed with
one shove. I am no world reformer and so I let him lie. I was the
district doctor and did my duty to the uttermost, to the point where
it became almost too much. I was badly paid and yet generous and
helpful to the poor. I had still to see that Rose was all right, and
then the young man could have his way if he liked and I could die
too. What was I doing there in that endless winter! My horse was
dead, and not a single person in the village would lend me another.
I had to get my team out of the pig-sty; if they hadn't chanced to
be horses I should have had to travel with swine. That was how it
was. And I nodded to the family. They knew nothing about it, and,
had they known, would not have believed it. To write prescriptions
is easy, but to come to an understanding with people is hard. Well,
this should be the end of my visit, I had once more been called
out needlessly, I was used to that, the whole district made my life

a torment with my night-bell, but that I should have to sacrifice Rose this time as well, the pretty girl who had lived in my house for years almost without my noticing her – that sacrifice was too much to ask, and I had somehow to get it reasoned out in my head with the help of what craft I could muster, in order not to let fly at this family, which with the best will in the world could not restore Rose to me. But as I shut my bag and put out an arm for my fur coat, the family meanwhile standing together, the father sniffing at the glass of rum in his hand, the mother, apparently disappointed in me – why, what do people expect? – biting her lips, with tears in her eyes, the sister fluttering a blood-soaked handkerchief, I was somehow ready to admit conditionally that the young man might be ill after all. I went towards him, he welcomed me smiling as if I were bringing him the most nourishing invalid broth – ah, now both horses were whinnying together; the noise, I suppose, was ordained by heaven to assist my examination of the patient – and this time I discovered that the young man was indeed ill. In his right side, near the hip, was an open wound as big as the palm of my hand. Rose-red, in many variations of shade, dark in the grooves, lighter at the edges, softly granulated, with irregular clots of blood, open as a surface-mine to the daylight. That was how it looked from a distance. But on a closer inspection there was another complication. I could not help a low whistle of surprise. Worms, as thick and as long as my little finger, themselves rose-red and blood-spotted as well, were wriggling from their fastness in the interior of the wound towards the light, with small white heads and many little legs. Poor young man, he was past helping. I had discovered his great wound; this blossom in his side was destroying him. The family was pleased; they saw me busying myself; the sister told the mother, the mother the father, the father told several guests who were coming in, through the moonlight at the open door, walking on tip-toe, keeping their balance with outstretched arms. 'Will you save me?' whispered the young man with a sob, quite blinded by the life within his wound. That is what people are like in my district. Always expecting the impossible from the doctor. They have lost their ancient beliefs; the parson sits at home and unravels his vestments, one after another; but the doctor is supposed to be omnipotent with his merciful surgeon's hand. Well, as it pleases them; I have not thrust my services on them; if they misuse me for sacred ends, I let that happen to me too; what better do I want, old country doctor that I am, bereft of my servant-girl! And so they came, the family and the village elders, and stripped my clothes off me; a school choir with the teacher at the head of it stood before the house and sang these words to an utterly simple tune:

> Strip his clothes off, then he'll heal us,
> If he doesn't, kill him dead!
> Only a saw-bones, only a saw-bones.

Then my clothes were off and I looked at the people quietly, my fingers in my beard and my head cocked to one side. I was altogether composed and equal to the situation and remained so, after all there was no help for me, since they now took me by the head and the feet and carried me to the bed. They laid me down in it next to the wall, on the side of the wound. Then they all left the room; the door was shut; the singing stopped; clouds covered the moon; the bedding was warm around me; the horses' heads in the open windows wavered like shadows. 'Do you know,' said a voice in my ear, 'I have very little confidence in you. Why, you were only blown in here, you didn't come on your own feet. Instead of helping me, you're cramping me on my death-bed. What I'd like best is to scratch your eyes out.' 'Right,' I said, 'it is a shame. And yet I am a doctor. What am I to do? Believe me, it is not too easy for me either.' 'Am I supposed to be content with this apology? Oh, I must be, I can't help it. I always have to put up with things. A fine wound is all I brought into the world; that was my sole endowment.' 'My young friend,' said I, 'your mistake is: you have not a wide enough view. I have been in all the sick-rooms, far and wide, and I tell you: your wound is none so bad. Done in a tight corner with two strokes of the axe. Many a one proffers his side and can hardly hear the axe in the forest, far less that it is coming nearer to him.' 'Is that really so, or are you deluding me in my fever?' 'It is really so, take the word of honour of an official doctor.' And he took it and lay still. But now it was time for me to think of escaping. The horses were still standing faithfully in their places. My clothes, my fur coat, my bag were quickly collected; I didn't want to waste time dressing; if the horses raced home as they had come, I should only be springing, as it were, out of this bed into my own. Obediently a horse backed away from the window; I threw my bundle into the gig; the fur coat missed its mark and was caught on a hook only by the sleeve. Good enough. I swung myself on the horse. With the reins loosely trailing, one horse barely fastened to the other, the gig swaying behind, my fur coat last of all in the snow. 'Gee up!' I said, but there was no galloping; slowly, like old men, we crawled through the snowy wastes; a long time echoed behind us the new but faulty song of the children:

> O be joyful, all you patients,
> The doctor's laid in bed beside you!

Never shall I reach home at this rate; my flourishing practice is done for; my successor is robbing me, but in vain, for he cannot take my place; in my house the disgusting groom is raging; Rose is his victim; I do not want to think about it any more. Naked, exposed to the frost of this most unhappy of ages, with an earthly vehicle, unearthly horses, old man that I am, I wander astray. My fur coat is hanging from the back of the gig, but I cannot reach it, and none of my limber pack of patients lifts a finger. Betrayed! Betrayed! A false alarm on the night-bell once answered — it cannot be made good, not ever.

Up in the Gallery

If some frail, consumptive equestrienne in the circus were to be urged round and round on an undulating horse for months on end without respite by a ruthless, whip-flourishing ring-master, before an insatiable public, whizzing along on her horse, throwing kisses, swaying from the waist, and if this performance were likely to continue in the infinite perspective of a drab future to the unceasing roar of the orchestra and hum of the ventilators, accompanied by ebbing and renewed swelling bursts of applause which are really steam-hammers – then, perhaps, a young visitor to the gallery might race down the long stairs through all the circles, rush into the ring, and yell: 'Stop!' against the fanfares of the orchestra still playing the appropriate music.

But since that is not so; a lovely lady, pink and white, floats in between the curtains, which proud lackeys open before her; the ring-master, deferentially catching her eye, comes towards her breathing animal devotion; tenderly lifts her up on the dapple-grey, as if she were his own most precious grand-daughter about to start on a dangerous journey; cannot make up his mind to give the signal with his whip, finally masters himself enough to crack the whip loudly; runs along beside the horse, open-mouthed; follows with a sharp eye the leaps taken by its rider; finds her artistic skill almost beyond belief; calls to her with English shouts of warning; angrily exhorts the grooms who hold the hoops to be most closely attentive; before the great somersault lifts up his arms and implores the orchestra to be silent; finally lifts the little one down from her trembling horse, kisses her on both cheeks and finds that all the ovation she gets from the audience is barely sufficient; while she herself, supported by him, right up on the tips of her toes, in a cloud of dust, with outstretched arms and small head thrown back, invites the whole circus to share her triumph – since that is so, the visitor to the gallery lays his face on the rail before him and, sinking into the closing march as in a heavy dream, weeps without knowing it.

An Old Manuscript

It looks as if much had been neglected in our country's system of defence. We have not concerned ourselves with it until now and have gone about our daily work; but things that have been happening recently begin to trouble us.

I have a cobbler's workshop in the square that lies before the

Emperor's palace. Scarcely have I taken my shutters down, at the first glimmer of dawn, when I see armed soldiers already posted in the mouth of every street opening on the square. But these soldiers are not ours, they are obviously nomads from the North. In some way that is incomprehensible to me they have pushed right into the capital, although it is a long way from the frontier. At any rate, here they are; it seems that every morning there are more of them.

As is their nature, they camp under the open sky, for they abominate dwelling-houses. They busy themselves sharpening swords, whittling arrows and practising horsemanship. This peaceful square, which was always so scrupulously kept clean, they have made literally into a stable. We do try every now and then to run out of shops and clear away at least the worst of the filth, but this happens less and less often, for the labour is in vain and brings us besides into danger of falling under the hoofs of the wild horses or of being crippled with lashes from the whips.

Speech with the nomads is impossible. They do not know our language, indeed they hardly have a language of their own. They communicate with each other much as jackdaws do. A screeching as of jackdaws is always in our ears. Our way of living and our institutions they neither understand nor care to understand. And so they are unwilling to make sense even out of our sign language. You can gesture at them till you dislocate your jaws and your wrists and still they will not have understood you and will never understand. They often make grimaces; then the whites of their eyes turn up and foam gathers on their lips, but they do not mean anything by that, not even a threat; they do it because it is their nature to do it. Whatever they need, they take. You cannot call it taking by force. They grab at something and you simply stand aside and leave them to it.

From my stock, too, they have taken many good articles. But I cannot complain when I see how the butcher, for instance, suffers over the way. As soon as he brings in any meat the nomads snatch it all from him and gobble it up. Even their horses devour flesh; often enough a horseman and his horse are lying side by side, both of them gnawing at the same joint, one at either end. The butcher is nervous and does not dare to stop his deliveries of meat. We understand that, however, and subscribe money to keep him going. If the nomads got no meat, who knows what they might think of doing; who knows anyhow what they may think of, even though they get meat every day?

Not long ago the butcher thought he might at least spare himself the trouble of slaughtering, and so one morning he brought along a live ox. But he will never dare to do that again. I lay for a whole hour flat on the floor at the back of my workshop with my head muffled in all the clothes and rugs and pillows I had, simply to keep from hearing the bellowing of that ox, which the nomads were leaping on from all sides, tearing morsels out of its living flesh with their teeth. It had been quiet for a long time before I risked coming out; they were lying overcome round the remains of the carcase like drunkards round a wine-cask.

This was the occasion when I fancied I actually saw the Emperor himself at a window of the palace; usually he never enters these outer rooms but spends all his time in the innermost garden; yet on this occasion he was standing, or so at least it seemed to me, at one of the windows, watching with bent head the ongoings before his residence.

'What is going to happen?' we all ask ourselves. 'How long can we endure this burden and torment? The Emperor's palace has drawn the nomads here but does not know how to drive them away again. The gate stays shut; the guards, who used to be always marching out and in with ceremony keep close behind barred windows. It is left to us artisans and tradesmen to save our country; but we are not equal to such a task; nor have we ever claimed to be capable of it. This is a misunderstanding of some kind; and it will be the ruin of us.'

Before the Law

Before the Law stands a door-keeper. To this door-keeper there comes a countryman and prays for admittance to the Law. But the door-keeper says that he cannot grant admittance at the moment. The man thinks it over and then asks if he will be allowed in later. 'It is possible,' says the door-keeper, 'but not at the moment.' Since the gate stands open, as usual, and the door-keeper steps to one side, the man stoops to peer through the gateway into the interior. Observing that, the door-keeper laughs and says: 'If you are so drawn to it, just try to go in despite my veto. But take note: I am powerful. And I am only the least of the door-keepers. From hall to hall there is one door-keeper after another, each more powerful than the last. The third door-keeper is already so terrible that even I cannot bear to look at him.' These are difficulties the countryman has not expected; the Law, he thinks, should surely be accessible at all times and to everyone, but as he now takes a closer look at the door-keeper in his fur coat, with his big sharp nose and long, thin, black Tartar beard, he decides that it is better to wait until he gets permission to enter. The door-keeper gives him a stool and lets him sit down at one side of the door. There he sits for days and years. He makes many attempts to be admitted, and wearies the door-keeper by his importunity. The door-keeper frequently has little interviews with him, asking him questions about his home and many other things, but the questions are put indifferently, as great lords put them, and always finish with the statement that he cannot be let in yet. The man, who has furnished himself with many things for his journey, sacrifices all he has, however valuable, to bribe the door-keeper. That official accepts everything, but always with the remark: 'I am only taking it to keep you from thinking you have omitted anything.' During these many years the man fixes his attention almost continuously on the door-keeper. He forgets the other door-keepers, and this first one seems to him the sole obstacle preventing access to the Law. He curses his bad luck, in his early years boldly and loudly, later, as he grows old, he only grumbles to himself. He becomes childish, and since in his year-long contemplation of the door-keeper he has come to know even the fleas in his fur collar, he begs the fleas as well to help him and to change the door-keeper's mind. At length his eyesight begins to fail, and he does not know whether the world is really darker or whether his eyes are only deceiving him. Yet in his darkness he is now aware of a radiance that streams inextinguishably from the gateway of the Law. Now he has not very long to live. Before he dies, all his experiences in these long years gather themselves in his head to one point, a question he has not yet asked the door-keeper. He waves him nearer, since he can no longer raise his stiffening body. The door-keeper has to bend low towards him, for the difference in height between them has altered much to the countryman's disadvantage. 'What do you want to know now?' asks the door-keeper. 'You are insatiable.' 'Everyone strives to reach the Law,' says the man, 'so how does it happen that for all these many years no one but myself has ever begged for admittance?' The door-keeper recognizes that the man has reached his end, and to let his failing senses catch the words roars in his ear: 'No one else could ever be admitted here, since this gate was made only for you. I am now going to shut it.'

Jackals and Arabs

We were camping in the oasis. My companions were asleep. The tall white figure of an Arab passed by; he had been seeing to the camels and was on his way to his own sleeping-place.

I threw myself on my back in the grass; I tried to fall asleep; I could not; a jackal howled in the distance; I sat up again. And what had been so far away was all at once quite near. Jackals were swarming round me, eyes gleaming dull gold and vanishing again, lithe bodies moving nimbly and rhythmically, as if at the crack of a whip.

One jackal came from behind me, nudging right under my arm, pressing against me, as if he needed my warmth, and then stood before me and spoke to me almost eye to eye.

'I am the oldest jackal far and wide. I am delighted to have met you here at last. I had almost given up hope, since we have been waiting endless years for you; my mother waited for you, and her mother, and all our foremothers right back to the first mother of all the jackals. It is true, believe me!'

'That is surprising,' said I, forgetting to kindle the pile of firewood which lay ready to smoke away jackals, 'that is very surprising for me to hear. It is by pure chance that I have come here from the far North, and I am making only a short tour of your country. What do you jackals want, then?'

As if emboldened by this perhaps too friendly inquiry the ring of jackals closed in on me; all were panting and open-mouthed.

'We know,' began the eldest, 'that you have come from the North, that is just what we base our hopes on. You Northerners have the kind of understanding that is not to be found among Arabs. Not a spark of understanding, let me tell you, can be struck from their cold arrogance. They kill animals for food, and carrion they despise.'

'Not so loud,' said I, 'there are Arabs sleeping near by.'

'You are indeed a stranger here,' said the jackal, 'or you would know that never in the history of the world has any jackal been afraid of an Arab. Why should we fear them? Is it not misfortune enough for us to be exiled among such creatures?'

'Maybe, maybe,' said I, 'matters so far outside my province I am not competent to judge; it seems to me a very old quarrel; I suppose it's in the blood, and perhaps will only end with it.'

'You are very clever,' said the old jackal; and they all began to pant more quickly; the air pumped out of their lungs although they were standing still; a rank smell which at times I had to set my teeth to endure streamed from their open jaws, 'you are very clever; what you have just said agrees with our old tradition. So we shall draw blood from them and the quarrel will be over.'

'Oh!' said I, more vehemently than I intended, 'they'll defend themselves; they'll shoot you down in dozens with their muskets.'

'You misunderstand us,' said he, 'a human failing which persists apparently even in the Far North. We're not proposing to kill them. All the water in the Nile couldn't cleanse us of that. Why, the mere sight of their living flesh makes us turn tail and flee into cleaner air, into the desert, which for that very reason is our home.'

And all the jackals around, including many newcomers from farther away, dropped their muzzles between their forelegs and wiped them with their paws; it was as if they were trying to conceal a disgust so overpowering that I felt like leaping over their heads to get away.

'Then what are you proposing to do?' I asked, trying to rise to my feet; but I could not get up; two young beasts behind me had locked their teeth through my coat and shirt; I had to go on sitting. 'These are your train-bearers,' explained the old jackal, quite seriously, 'a mark of honour.' 'They must let go!' I cried, turning now to the old jackal, now to the youngsters. 'They will, of course,' said the old one, 'since that is your wish. But it will take a little time, for they have got their teeth well in, as is our custom, and must first loosen their jaws bit by bit. Meanwhile, give ear to our petition.' 'Your conduct hasn't exactly inclined me to grant it,' said I. 'Don't hold it against us that we are clumsy,' said he, and now for the first time had recourse to the natural plaintiveness of his voice, 'we are poor creatures, we have nothing but our teeth; whatever we want to do, good or bad, we tackle it only with our teeth.' 'Well, what do you want?' I asked, not much mollified.

'Sir,' he cried, and all the jackals howled together; very remotely it seemed to resemble a melody. 'Sir, we want you to end this quarrel that divides the world. You are exactly the man whom our ancestors foretold as born to do it. We want to be troubled no more by Arabs; room to breathe; a sky-line cleansed of them; no more bleating of sheep knifed by an Arab; every beast to die a natural death; no interference till we have drained the carcase empty and picked its bones clean. A clean life, nothing but cleanliness is what we want' – and now they were all lamenting and sobbing – 'How can you bear to live in such a world, O noble heart and kindly bowels? Filth is their white; filth is their black; their beards are a horror; the very sight of their eye-sockets makes one want to spit; and when they lift an arm, the murk of hell yawns in the arm-pit. And so, sir, and so, dear sir, by means of your all-powerful hands slit their throats through with these scissors!' And in answer to a jerk of his head a jackal came trotting up with a small pair of sewing-scissors, covered in ancient rust, dangling from an eye-tooth.

'Well, here's the scissors at last, and high time to stop!' cried the Arab leader of our caravan who had crept up-wind towards us and now cracked his great whip.

The jackals fled in haste, but at some little distance rallied in a close huddle, all the brutes so tightly packed and rigid that they looked as if penned in a small fold girt by flickering will-o'-the-wisps.

'So you've been treated to this entertainment too, sir,' said the Arab, laughing as gaily as the reserve of his race permitted. 'You know, then, what the brutes are after?' I asked. 'Of course,' said he, 'it's common knowledge; so long as Arabs exist, that pair of scissors goes wandering through the desert and will wander with us to the end of our days. Every European is offered it for the great work; every European is just the man that Fate has chosen for them. They have the most lunatic hopes, these beasts; they're just fools, utter fools. That's why we like them; they are our dogs; finer dogs than any of yours. Watch this, now, a camel died last night and I have had it brought here.'

Four men came up with the heavy carcase and threw it down before us. It had hardly touched the ground before the jackals lifted up their voices. As if irresistibly drawn by cords each of them began to waver forward, crawling on his belly. They had forgotten the Arabs, forgotten their hatred, the all-obliterating immediate presence of the stinking carrion bewitched them. One was already at the camel's throat, sinking his teeth straight into an artery. Like a vehement small pump endeavouring with as much determination as hopefulness to extinguish some raging fire, every muscle in his body twitched and laboured at the task. In a trice they were all on top of the carcase, labouring in common, piled mountain-high.

And now the caravan-leader lashed his cutting whip criss-cross over their backs. They lifted their heads; half swooning in ecstasy; saw the Arabs standing before them; felt the sting of the whip on their muzzles; leaped and ran backwards a stretch. But the camel's blood was already lying in pools, reeking to heaven, the carcase was torn wide open in many places. They could not resist it; they were back again; once more the leader lifted his whip; I stayed his arm.

'You are right, sir,' said he, 'we'll leave them to their business; besides, it's time to break camp. Well, you've seen them. Marvellous creatures, aren't they? And how they hate us!'

A Visit to a Mine

Today the chief engineers have been down to our part of the mine. The management has issued some instruction or other about boring new galleries, and so the engineers arrived to make the initial survey. How young these men are and yet how different from each other! They have all grown up in freedom and show clearly defined characters without self-consciousness even in their youth.

One, a lively man with black hair, has eyes that take in everything.

A second with a scribbling-pad makes jottings as he goes, looks round him, compares, notes down.

A third, his hands in his coat pockets, so that everything about him is taut, walks very upright; maintains his dignity; only the fact that he keeps biting his lips betrays his impatient, irrepressible youth.

A fourth showers explanations on the third, who does not ask for them; smaller than the other, trotting beside him like a familiar, his index finger always in the air, he seems to be making a running commentary on everything he sees.

A fifth, perhaps the senior in rank, suffers no one to accompany him; now he is in front, now behind; the group accommodates its pace to him; he is pallid and frail; responsibility has made his eyes hollow; he often presses his hand to his forehead in thought.

The sixth and seventh walk leaning forward a little, their heads close together, arm in arm, in confidential talk; if this were not unmistakably our coal-mine and our working-station in the deepest gallery, one could easily believe that these bony, clean-shaven, knobbly-nosed gentlemen were young clerics. One of them laughs mostly to himself with a cat-like purring; the other, smiling too, leads the conversation and beats some kind of time to it with his free hand. How sure these two must be of their position; yes, what services must they have already rendered to our mine in spite of their youth, to be able here, on such an important survey, under the eyes of their chief, to devote themselves so unwaveringly to their own affairs, or at least to affairs that have nothing to do with the immediate task? Or might it be possible that, in spite of their laughter and apparent inattention, they are very well aware of whatever is needful? One scarcely ventures to pass a decisive judgement on gentlemen like these.

On the other hand, there is no doubt at all that the eighth man, for instance, is incomparably more intent on his work than these two, indeed more than all the other gentlemen. He has to touch everything and tap it with a little hammer which he keeps taking out of his pocket and putting back again. He often goes down on his knees in the dirt, despite his elegant attire, and taps the ground, then again taps the walls as he walks along or the roof over his head. Once he stretched himself out at full length and lay still; we were beginning to think something had gone wrong with him; then with a sudden recoil of his lithe body he sprang to his feet. He had only been making another investigation. We fancy that we know our mine and its rock formations, but what this engineer can be sounding all the time in such a manner lies beyond our comprehension.

A ninth man pushes a kind of perambulator in front of him with the surveying instruments. Extremely expensive apparatus, deeply embedded in the softest cotton wool. The office porter ought really to be pushing this vehicle, but he is not trusted with it; an engineer has to do it, and one can see that he does it with goodwill. He is probably the youngest, perhaps he doesn't even understand all the apparatus yet, but he keeps his eye on the instruments all the time, which brings him often into danger of running his vehicle into the wall.

But there is another engineer walking alongside who prevents that from happening. Obviously he understands the apparatus thoroughly and seems to be really the man in charge of it. From time to time, without stopping the vehicle, he takes up a part of some instrument, peers through it, screws it open or shut, shakes it and taps it, holds it to his ear and listens; and finally, while the man pushing the instruments usually stands still, he lays the small thing, which one can scarcely discern at a distance, back into its packing with great care. This engineer is a little domineering, but only in the service of his instruments. Ten paces ahead of the perambulator we have to give way to it at a wordless sign of his finger, even where there is no room for us to make way.

Behind these two gentlemen stalks the office porter, with nothing to do. The gentlemen, as is to be expected from men of their great knowledge, have long dropped any arrogance they ever had, but the porter seems to have picked it all up and kept it. With one hand tucked behind him, the other in front fingering the gilt buttons or fine face-cloth of his uniform, he keeps bowing to right and left as if we had saluted him and he were answering, or rather as if he assumed that we had saluted him, he being too high and mighty to see any salutes. Of course we do not salute him, yet one could almost believe, to look at him, that it is a great distinction to be a porter at the head office of the mine. Behind his back, to be sure, we burst out laughing, but as not even a thunderbolt could make him look round, he remains an unsolved riddle for us to respect.

Today we shall not do much work; the interruption has been too interesting; such a visitation draws away with it all thoughts of work. It is too tempting to stand gazing after the gentlemen as they vanish into the darkness of the trial gallery. Besides, our shift will soon come to an end; we shall not be here to see them coming back.

The Next Village

My grandfather used to say: 'Life is astoundingly short. To me, looking back over it, life seems so fore-shortened that I scarcely understand, for instance, how a young man can decide to ride over to the next village without being afraid that — not to mention accidents — even the span of a normal happy life may fall far short of the time needed for such a journey.'

A Message from the Emperor

The Emperor – so the story goes – has sent a message to you, the lone individual, the meanest of his subjects, the shadow that has fled before the Imperial sun until it is microscopic in the remotest distance, just to you has the Emperor sent a message from his death-bed. He made the messenger kneel by his bed and whispered the message into his ear; he felt it to be so important that he made the man repeat it into his own ear. With a nod of the head he confirmed that the repetition was accurate. And then, before the whole retinue gathered to witness his death – all the walls blocking the view had been broken down and on the wide high curve of the open stairway stood the notables of the Empire in a circle – before them all he empowered the messenger to go. The messenger set off at once; a robust, an indefatigable man; thrusting out now one arm, now the other, he forces his way through the crowd; where he finds obstacles he points to the sign of the sun on his breast; he gets through easily, too, as no one else could. Yet the throng is so numerous; there is no end to their dwelling-places. If he only had a free field before him, how he would run, and soon enough you would hear the glorious tattoo of his fists on your door. But instead of that, how vain are his efforts; he is still forcing his way through the chambers of the innermost palace; he will never get to the end of them; and even if he did, he would be no better off; he would have to fight his way down the stairs; and even if he did that, he would be no better off; he would still have to get through the courtyards; and after the courtyards, the second outer palace enclosing the first; and more stairways and more courtyards; and still another palace; and so on for thousands of years; and did he finally dash through the outermost gate – but that will never, never happen – he would still have the capital city before him, the centre of the world, overflowing with the dregs of humanity. No one can force a way through that, least of all with a message from a dead man. But you sit by your window and dream it all true, when evening falls.

Troubles of a Householder

Some say the word Odradek* is of Slavonic origin, and try to account for it on that basis. Others again believe it to be of German origin, only influenced by Slavonic. The uncertainty of both interpretations allows one to assume with justice that neither is accurate, especially as neither of them provides an intelligent meaning of the word.

No one, of course, would occupy himself with such studies if there were not a creature called Odradek. At first glance it looks like a flat star-shaped spool for thread, and indeed it does seem to have thread wound upon it; to be sure, only old, broken-off bits of thread are eligible, not merely knotted but tangled together, of the most varied sorts and colours. But it is not only a spool, for a small wooden cross-bar sticks out of the middle of the star, and another small rod is joined to that at a right angle. By means of this latter rod on one side and one of the points of the star on the other, the whole thing can stand upright as if on two legs.

One is tempted to believe that the creature once had some sort of intelligible shape and is now only a broken-down remnant. Yet this does not seem to be the case; at least there is no sign of it; nowhere is there an unfinished or unbroken surface to suggest anything of the kind; the whole thing looks senseless enough but in its own way perfectly finished. In any case, closer scrutiny is impossible, since Odradek is extraordinarily nimble and can never be laid hold of.

He lurks by turns in the garret, the stairway, the lobbies, the entrance hall. Often for months on end he is not to be seen; then he has presumably moved into other houses; but he always comes faithfully back to our house again. Many a time when you go out of the door and he happens just to be leaning directly beneath you against the banisters, you feel inclined to speak to him. Of course, you put no difficult questions to him, you treat him — he is so diminutive that you cannot help it — rather like a child. 'Well,

*Odradek means in Czech something like 'outside the law' — *Editor's note.*

what's your name?' you ask him. 'Odradek,' he says. 'And where do you live?' 'No fixed abode,' he says, and laughs; but it is only the kind of laughter that has no lungs behind it. It sounds rather like the rustling of fallen leaves. And that is usually the end of the conversation. Even these answers are not always forthcoming; often he stays mute for a long time, as wooden as his appearance.

I ask myself, to no purpose, what is likely to happen to him? Can he possibly die? Anything that dies has had some kind of aim in life, some kind of activity, which has worn out; but that does not apply to Odradek. Am I to suppose, then, that some time or other he will be rolling down the stairs, with ends of thread trailing after him, before the feet of my children, and my children's children? He does no harm to anyone that one can see; but the idea that he is likely to survive me I find almost painful.

Eleven Sons

I have eleven sons.

The first is outwardly rather insignificant, but serious and clever; yet, although I love him as I love all my children, I do not rate him very highly. His mental processes seem to me to be too simple. He looks neither to right nor left, nor into the distance; he is for ever running round and round, or rather turns about, within his own little circle of thoughts.

The second is handsome, slim, well-made; one draws one's breath with delight to watch him with a fencing foil. He is clever too, but has experience of the world as well; he has seen much, and therefore even our native country seems to yield more secrets to him than to the stay-at-home. Yet I am sure that this advantage is not only and not even essentially due to his travels, it is rather an attribute of his own inimitable nature, which is acknowledged for instance by everyone who has ever tried to copy him in, let us say, the fancy high-dive he does into the water, somersaulting several times over, yet with almost violent self-control. To the very end of the spring-board the emulator keeps up his courage and his desire to follow; but at that point, instead of leaping into the air, he sits down suddenly and lifts his arms in excuse. And despite all this (I ought really to feel blessed with such a son), my attachment to him is not untroubled. His left eye is a little smaller than his right and blinks a good deal; only a small fault, certainly, and one which even lends more audacity to his face than it would otherwise have, nor, considering that he is such an incomparably finished product, would anyone think of noticing and finding fault with this smaller eye and the way it blinks. Yet I, his father, do so. Of course, it is not the physical blemish that worries me, but a small irregularity of the spirit that somehow corresponds to it, a kind of stray poison in the blood, a kind of inability to develop to the full the potentialities of his nature which I alone can see. On the other hand, this is just what makes him again my own true son, for this fault of his is a fault of our whole family and in him it is only too apparent.

My third son is handsome, but not in a way that I appreciate. He has the good looks of a singer; the curving lips; the dreaming eye; the kind of head that asks for drapery behind it to make it effective; the deeply arched chest; hands that are quick to fly up and much too quick to fall limp; legs that move delicately because they cannot support a burden. And besides: the tone of his voice is not round and full; it takes you in for a moment; the connoisseur pricks up his ears; but almost at once its breath gives out. Although, in general, everything tempts me to bring this son of mine into the limelight, I prefer to keep him in the background; he himself is not insistent, yet not because he is aware of his defects but out of innocence. Moreover, he does not feel at home in our age; as if he admitted belonging to our family, yet knew that he belonged also to another which he has lost for ever, he is often melancholy and nothing can cheer him.

My fourth son is perhaps the most companionable of all. A true child of his age, he is understood by everyone, he stands on what is common ground to all men and everyone feels inclined to give him a nod. Perhaps this universal appreciation is what makes his nature rather light, his movements rather free, his judgements rather unthinking. Many of his remarks are worth quoting over and over again, but by no means all of them, for by and large his extreme facility becomes irritating. He is like a man who makes a wonderful take-off from the ground, cleaves the air like a swallow and after all comes down helplessly in a desert waste — a nothing. Such reflections gall me when I look at him.

My fifth son is kind and good; promised less than he performed; used to be so inconsiderable that one really felt alone in his presence; but has achieved a certain reputation. If I 'were asked how this came about, I could hardly tell you. Perhaps innocence makes its way easiest through the elemental chaos of this world, and innocent he certainly is. Perhaps too innocent; friendly to everyone. Perhaps too friendly. I confess: it makes me sick to hear his praises. It seems to make praise rather too cheap to bestow it on anyone so obviously praiseworthy as this son of mine.

My sixth son seems, at first glance anyhow, the most thoughtful of all. He is given to hanging his head, and yet he is a great talker. So he is not easy to get at. If he is on the down-grade, he falls into impenetrable melancholy; if he is in the ascendant, he maintains his advantage by sheer talk. Yet I grant him a certain self-forgetful passionate absorption; in the full light of day he often fights his way through a tangle of thoughts as if in a dream. Without being ill — his health on the contrary is very good — he sometimes staggers, especially in the twilight, but he needs no help, he never falls. Perhaps his physical growth is the cause of this phenomenon, he is much too tall for his age. That makes him look ugly in general, although he has remarkable beauty in detail, in hands and feet, for instance. His forehead, too, is ugly; both its skin and its bone-formation are somehow arrested in their development.

The seventh son belongs to me perhaps more than all the others. The world would not know how to appreciate him; it does not understand his peculiar brand of wit. I do not over-value him; I know he is of little enough importance; if the world had no other fault than that of not appreciating him, it would still be blameless. But within the family circle I should not care to be without this son of mine. He contributes a certain restlessness as well as a reverence for tradition, and combines them both, at least that is how I feel it, into an incontestable whole. True, he knows less than anyone what to do with this achievement; the wheel of the future will never be started rolling by him; but his disposition is so stimulating, so rich in hope; I wish that he had children and children's children. Unfortunately he does not seem inclined to fulfil my wish. With a self-satisfaction that I understand as much as I deplore, and which stands in marked contrast to the verdict of his neighbours, he goes everywhere alone, pays no attention to girls and yet will never lose his good humour.

My eighth son is my child of sorrow, and I do not really know why. He keeps me at a distance and yet I feel a close paternal tie binding me to him. Time has done much to lessen the pain; but once I used often to tremble at the mere thought of him. He goes his own way; he has broken off all communication with me; and certainly with his hard head, his small athletic body – only his legs were rather frail when he was a boy, but perhaps that has meanwhile righted itself – he will make a success of anything he chooses. Many a time I used to want to call him back, to ask him how things really were with him, why he cut himself off so completely from his father and what his fundamental purpose was in life, but now he is so far away and so much time has passed that things had better stay as they are. I hear that he is the only one of my sons to grow a full beard; that cannot look well, of course, on a man so small as he is.

My ninth son is very elegant and has what women consider a definitely melting eye. So melting that there are occasions when he can cajole even me, although I know that a wet sponge is literally enough to wipe away all that unearthly brilliance. But the curious thing about the boy is that he makes no attempt to be seductive; he would be content to spend his life lying on the sofa and wasting his glances on the ceiling, or still better, keeping them to himself under his eyelids. When he is lying in this favourite position, he enjoys talking and talks quite well; concisely and pithily; but still only within narrow limits; once he oversteps these, which he cannot avoid doing since they are so narrow, what he says is quite empty. One would sign him to step back again, if one had any hope that such slumbrous eyes were even aware of the gesture.

My tenth son is supposed to be an insincere character. I shall not entirely deny or confirm this supposition. Certainly anyone who sees him approaching with the pomposity of a man twice his age, in a frock-coat always tightly buttoned, an old but meticulously brushed black hat, with an expressionless face, slightly jutting chin, cavernous eyelids that mask the light behind them, two fingers very often at his lips – anyone seeing him thus is bound to think: What an utter hypocrite. But then, just listen to his talking! With understanding, thoughtfully, brusquely; cutting across questions with satirical vivacity; in complete accord with the universe, an accord that is wonderful, natural, and gay; an accord that of necessity straightens the neck and makes the body proud. Many who think themselves very clever and for this reason, as they fancied, felt a dislike for his outward appearance, have become strongly attached to him because of his conversation. There are other people, again, who are unaffected by his appearance but who find his conversation hypocritical. I, being his father, will not pronounce a verdict, but I must admit that the latter critics are at least to be taken more seriously than the former.

My eleventh son is delicate, probably the frailest of my sons; but deceptive in his weakness; for at times he can be strong and resolute, though even then there is somehow always an underlying weakness. Yet it is not a weakness to be ashamed of, merely something that appears as weakness only on this solid earth of ours. For instance, is not a readiness for flight a kind of weakness too, since it consists in a wavering, an unsteadiness, a fluttering? Something of that nature characterizes my son. These are not, of course, the characteristics to rejoice a father; they tend obviously to destroy a family. Sometimes he looks at me as if he would say: 'I shall take you with me, Father.' Then I think: 'You are the last person I would trust myself to.' And again his look seems to say: 'Then let me be at least the last.'

These are my eleven sons.

A Brother's Murder

The evidence shows that the murder was committed in the following manner:

Schmar, the murderer, took up his post about nine o'clock one night in clear moonlight by the corner where Wese, his victim, had to turn from the street where his office was into the street he lived in.

The night air was shivering cold. Yet Schmar was wearing only a thin blue suit; the jacket was unbuttoned, too. He felt no cold; besides, he was moving about all the time. His weapon, half a bayonet and half a kitchen knife, he kept firmly in his grasp, quite naked. He looked at the knife against the light of the moon; the blade glittered; not enough for Schmar; he struck it against the bricks of the pavement till the sparks flew; regretted that, perhaps; and to repair the damage drew it like a violin-bow across his boot-sole while he bent forward, standing on one leg, and listened both to the whetting of the knife on his boot, and for any sound out of the fateful side-street.

Why did Pallas, the private citizen, who was watching it all from his window near by in the second storey, permit it to happen? Unriddle the mysteries of human nature! With his collar turned up, his dressing-gown girt round his portly body, he stood looking down, shaking his head.

And five houses farther along, on the opposite side of the street, Mrs Wese, with a fox-fur coat over her night-gown, peered out to look for her husband who was lingering unusually late tonight.

At last there rang out the sound of the door-bell before Wese's office, too loud for a door-bell, right over the town and up to heaven, and Wese, the industrious night-worker, issued from the building, still invisible in that street, only heralded by the sound of the bell; at once the pavement registered his quiet footsteps.

Pallas bent far forward; he dared not miss anything. Mrs Wese, reassured by the bell, shut her window with a clatter. But Schmar knelt down; since he had no other parts of his body bare, he pressed only his face and his hands against the pavement; where everything else was freezing, Schmar was glowing hot.

At the very corner dividing the two streets Wese paused, only his walking-stick came round into the other street to support him. A sudden whim. The night sky invited him, with its dark blue and its gold. Unthinking he gazed up at it, unknowing he lifted his hat and stroked his hair; nothing up there drew together in a pattern to interpret the immediate future for him; everything remained in its meaningless, inscrutable place. In itself it was a highly reasonable action that Wese should walk on, but he walked on to Schmar's knife.

'Wese!' shrieked Schmar, standing on tip-toe, his arm out-stretched, the knife sharply lowered, 'Wese! You will never see Julia again!' And right into the throat and left into the throat and a third time deep into the belly stabbed Schmar's knife. Water-rats, slit open, give out such a sound as came from Wese.

'Done,' said Schmar, and pitched the knife, now superfluous blood-stained ballast, against the nearest house-front. 'The bliss of murder! The relief, the soaring ecstasy from the shedding of an-other's blood! Wese, old night-bird, friend, ale-house crony, you are oozing away into the dark earth below the street. Why aren't you simply a bladder of blood so that I could stamp on you and make you vanish into nothingness? Not quite all we want comes true, not all the dreams that blossomed have borne fruit, your solid remains lie here, already indifferent to every kick. What's the good of the dumb question they are asking?'

Pallas, choking down the muddle of horror in his body, stood at the double-leafed door of his house as it flew open. 'Schmar! Schmar! I saw it all, I missed nothing.' Pallas and Schmar scruti-nized each other. The result of the scrutiny satisfied Pallas, Schmar came to no conclusion.

Mrs Wese, with a crowd of people on either side, came rushing up, her face grown quite old with the shock. Her fur coat swung open, she collapsed on top of Wese, the night-gowned body belonged to Wese, the fur coat spreading over the couple like the smooth turf of a grave belonged to the crowd.

Schmar, fighting down with difficulty the last of his nausea, pressed his mouth against the shoulder of the policeman who, step-ping lightly, led him away.

A Dream

Josef K. was dreaming.

It was a beautiful day and K. felt like going for a walk. But hardly had he taken a couple of steps, when he was already at the cemetery. The paths there were very winding, ingeniously made and unpractical, but he glided along one of them as if on a rushing stream with unshaken poise and balance. From a long way off his eye was caught by a freshly-heaped grave-mound which he wanted to pause beside. This grave-mound exerted almost a fascination over him and he felt he could not reach it fast enough. But he often nearly lost sight of it, for his view was obscured by banners which veered and flapped against each other with great force; one could not see the standard bearers, but there seemed to be a very joyous celebration going on.

While he was still peering into the distance, he suddenly saw the grave-mound quite near his path, indeed he was almost leaving it behind him. He made a hasty spring on to the grass. But since the path went rushing on under his shifting foot, he tottered and fell on his knees just in front of the grave-mound. Two men were standing behind the grave and were holding a grave-stone between them in the air; scarcely had K. arrived when they thrust the stone into the earth and it stood as if cemented there. Out of some bushes there came at once a third man, whom K. recognized immediately as an artist. He was clad only in trousers and a badly-buttoned shirt; on his head was a velvet cap; in his hand he held an ordinary pencil with which he was already drawing figures in the air as he approached.

With his pencil he now addressed himself to the top end of the grave-stone; the stone was very tall, he did not have to bend down, though he had to bend forward, since the grave-mound, on which he shrank from setting foot, came between him and the stone. So he stood on tip-toe and steadied himself with his left hand on the stone's flat surface. With an astonishing turn of skill he managed to produce golden letters from his ordinary pencil; he wrote: 'HERE LIES'. Every letter was clear and beautifully made, deeply incised and of the purest gold. When he had inscribed these two words he looked at K. over his shoulder; K., who was very eager to know how the inscription would go, paid hardly any attention to the man, but was intent only on the stone. And in fact the man turned again to continue writing, but he could not go on, something was hindering him, he let the pencil sink and once more turned towards K. This time K. looked back at him and noted that he was deeply embarrassed and yet unable to explain himself. All his earlier vivacity had vanished. That made K. feel embarrassed too; they exchanged helpless glances; there was some dreadful misunderstanding between them which neither could resolve. An untimely little bell now began to ring from the cemetery chapel, but the artist made a sign with uplifted hand and the bell stopped. In a little while it began again; this time quite softly and without any insistence, breaking off again at once, as if it were only testing its own tone. K. felt miserable because of the artist's predicament, he began to cry and sobbed for a long time into his cupped hands. The artist waited until K. had calmed down and then decided, since there was no help for it, just to go on with the inscription. The first small stroke that he made was a relief to K., but the artist obviously achieved it only with the greatest reluctance; the work, too, was no longer beautifully finished, above all there seemed to be a lack of gold-leaf, pale and uncertain the stroke straggled down, only it turned into a very big letter. It was a J, it was almost finished, and at that moment the artist stamped angrily on the grave-mound with one foot so that the soil all around flew up in the air. At long last K. understood him; it was too late to start apologizing now; with all his fingers he dug into the earth which offered almost no resistance; everything seemed prepared beforehand; a thin crust of earth had been constructed only for the look of the thing; immediately beneath it a great hole opened out, with steep sides, into which K. sank, wafted on to his back by a gentle current. And while he was already being received into impenetrable depths, his head still straining upwards on his neck, his own name raced across the stone above him in great flourishes.

Enchanted by the sight he woke up.

A Report to an Academy

Honoured Members of the Academy!

You have done me the honour of inviting me to give your Academy an account of the life I formerly led as an ape.

I regret that I cannot comply with your request to the extent you desire. It is now nearly five years since I was an ape, a short space of time, perhaps, according to the calendar, but an infinitely long time to gallop through at full speed, as I have done, more or less accompanied by excellent mentors, good advice, applause, and orchestral music, and yet essentially alone, since all my escorters kept well off the course so as not to spoil the picture. I could never have achieved what I have done had I been stubbornly set on clinging to my origins, to the remembrances of my youth. In fact, to give up being stubborn was the supreme commandment I laid upon myself; free ape as I was, I submitted myself to that yoke. In revenge, however, my memory of the past has closed the door against me more and more. I could have returned at first, had human beings allowed it, through an archway as wide as the span of heaven over the earth, but as I spurred myself on in my forced career, the opening narrowed and shrank behind me; I felt more comfortable in the world of men and fitted it better; the strong wind that blew after me out of my past began to slacken; today it is only a gentle puff of air that plays around my heels; and the opening in the distance, through which it comes and through which I once came myself, has grown so small that, even if my strength and my will-power sufficed to get me back to it, I should have to scrape the very skin from my body to crawl through. To put it plainly, much as I like expressing myself in images, to put it plainly: your life as apes, gentlemen, in so far as something of that kind lies behind you, cannot be farther removed from you than mine is from me. Yet everyone on earth feels a tickling at the heels; the small chimpanzee and the great Achilles alike.

But to a lesser extent I can perhaps meet your demand, and indeed I do so with the greatest pleasure. The first thing I learned was to give a handshake; a handshake betokens frankness; well, today, now that I stand at the very peak of my career, I hope to add frankness in words to the frankness of that first handshake. What I have to tell the academy will contribute nothing essentially new, and will fall far behind what you have asked of me and what with the best will in the world I cannot communicate – none the less, it should indicate the line an erstwhile ape has had to follow in entering and establishing himself in the world of men. Yet I could not risk putting into words even such insignificant information as I am going to give you if I were not quite sure of myself and if my position on all the great variety stages of the civilized world had not become quite unassailable.

I belong to the Gold Coast. For the story of my capture I must depend on the evidence of others. A hunting expedition sent out by the firm of Hagenbeck – by the way, I have drunk many a bottle of good red wine since then with the leader of that expedition – had taken up its position in the bushes by the shore when I came down for a drink at evening among a troop of apes. They shot at us; I was the only one that was hit; I was hit in two places.

Once in the cheek; a slight wound; but it left a large, naked, red scar which earned me the name of Red Peter, a horrible name, utterly inappropriate, which only some ape could have thought of, as if the only difference between me and the performing ape Peter, who died not so long ago and had some small local reputation, were the red mark on my cheek. This by the way.

The second shot hit me in the groin. It was a severe wound, it is the cause of my limping a little to this day. I read an article recently by one of the ten thousand wind-bags who vent themselves concerning me in the newspapers, saying: my ape-nature is not yet quite under control; the proof being that when visitors come to see me I have a predilection for taking down my trousers to show them where the shot went in. The hand which wrote that should have its fingers shot away one by one. As for me, I can take my trousers down before anyone if I like; you would find nothing but well-groomed fur and the scar made – let me be particular in the choice of a word for this particular purpose, to avoid misunderstanding – the scar made by a wanton shot. Everything is open and above board; there is nothing to conceal; when the plain truth is in question, great minds discard the niceties of refinement. But if the writer of the article were to take down his trousers before a visitor, that would be quite another story, and I will let it stand to his credit that he does not do it. In return, let him refrain from hanging his prudery around my neck!

After these two shots I came to myself — and this is where my own memories gradually begin — between decks in the Hagenbeck steamer, inside a cage. It was not a four-sided barred cage; it was only a three-sided cage nailed to a locker; the locker made the fourth side of it. The whole construction was too low for me to stand up in and too narrow to sit down in. So I had to squat with my knees bent and trembling all the time, and also, since it was likely that for a time I would wish to see no one, and to stay in the dark, my face was turned towards the locker while the bars of the cage cut into my flesh behind. Such a method of confining wild beasts is supposed to have its advantages during the first days of captivity, and out of my own experiences I cannot deny that from the human point of view this is really the case.

But that did not occur to me then. For the first time in my life I could see no way out; at least no direct way out; directly in front of me was the locker, board fitted close to board. True, there was a gap running right through the boards which I greeted with the blissful howl of ignorance when I first discovered it, but the hole was not even wide enough to stick one's tail through and not all the strength of an ape could enlarge it.

I am supposed to have made uncommonly little noise, as I was later informed, from which the conclusion was drawn that I would either soon die or if I managed to survive the first critical period would be very amenable to training. I did survive this period. Hopelessly sobbing, painfully hunting for fleas, apathetically licking a coconut, beating my skull against the locker, sticking out my tongue at anyone who came near me — that was how I filled in time at first in my new life. But over and above it all only the one feeling: no way out. Of course what I felt then as an ape I can represent now only in human terms, and therefore I misrepresent it, but although I cannot reach back to the truth of the old ape tradition, there is no doubt that it lies somewhere in the direction I have indicated.

Until then I had had so many ways out of everything, and now I had none. I was pinned down. Had I been nailed down, my sense of a right to free movement would not have been lessened. Why so? Scratch your flesh raw between your toes, but you won't find the answer. Press yourself against the bar behind you till it nearly cuts you in two, you won't find the answer. I had no way out but I had to devise one, for without it I could not live. All the time facing that locker – I should certainly have perished. Yet as far as Hagenbeck was concerned, the place for apes was in front of a locker – well then, I had to stop being an ape! A fine clear train of thought, which I must have constructed somehow with my belly, since apes think with their bellies.

I fear that perhaps you do not quite understand what I mean by 'way out'. I use the expression in its fullest and most popular sense. I deliberately do not use the word 'freedom'. I do not mean the spacious feeling of freedom on all sides. As an ape, perhaps, I knew that, and I have met men who yearn for it. But for my part I desired such freedom neither then nor now. In passing may I say that all too often men are betrayed by the word freedom. And as freedom is counted among the most sublime feelings, so the corresponding disillusionment can be also sublime. In variety theatres I have often watched, before my turn came on, a couple of acrobats performing on trapezes high in the roof. They swung themselves, they rocked to and fro, they sprang into the air, they floated into each other's arms, one hung by the hair from the teeth of the other. 'And that, too, is human freedom,' I thought, 'self-controlled movement.' What a mockery of holy Mother Nature! Were the apes to see such a spectacle, no theatre walls could stand the shock of their laughter.

No, freedom was not what I wanted. Only a way out; right or left, or in any direction; I made no other demand; even should the way out prove to be an illusion; the demand was a small one, the disappointment could be no bigger. To get out somewhere, to get out! Only not to stay motionless with raised arms, crushed against a wooden wall.

Today I can see it clearly; without the most profound inward calm I could never have found my way out. And indeed, perhaps I owe all that I have become to the calm that settled within me after my first few days in the ship. And again for that calmness it was the ship's crew I had to thank.

They were good creatures, in spite of everything. I find it still pleasant to remember the sound of their heavy footfalls which used to echo through my half-dreaming head. They had a habit of doing everything as slowly as possible. If one of them wanted to rub his eyes, he lifted a hand as if it were a drooping weight. Their jests were coarse, but hearty. Their laughter had always a gruff bark in it that sounded dangerous but meant nothing. They always had something in their mouths to spit out and did not care where they spat it. They always grumbled that they got fleas from me; yet they were not seriously angry about it; they knew that my fur fostered fleas, and that fleas jump; it was a simple matter of fact to them. When they were off duty some of them often used to sit down in a semi-circle round me; they hardly spoke but only grunted to each other; smoked their pipes, stretched out on lockers; smacked their knees as soon as I made the slightest movement; and now and then one of them would take a stick and tickle me where I liked being tickled. If I were to be invited today to take a cruise on that ship I should certainly refuse the invitation, but just as certainly the memories I could recall between its decks would not all be hateful.

The calmness I acquired among these people kept me above all from trying to escape. As I look back now, it seems to me I must have had at least an inkling that I had to find a way out or die, but that my way out could not be reached through flight. I cannot tell now whether escape was possible, but I believe it must have been; for an ape it must always be possible. With my teeth as they are today I have to be careful even in simply cracking nuts, but at that time I could certainly have managed by degrees to bite through the lock of my cage. I did not do it. What good would it have done me? As soon as I had poked out my head I should have been caught again and put in a worse cage; or I might have slipped among the other animals without remark, among the pythons, say, who were opposite me, and so breathed out my life in their embrace; or supposing I had actually succeeded in sneaking out as far as the deck and leaping overboard, I should have rocked for a little on the deep sea and then been drowned. Desperate remedies. I did not think it out in this human way, but under the influence of my surroundings I acted as if I had thought it out.

I did not think things out; but I observed everything quietly. I watched these men go to and fro, always the same faces, the same movements, often it seemed to me there was only the same man. So this man or these men walked about unimpeded. A lofty goal faintly dawned before me. No one promised me that if I became like them the bars of my cage would be taken away. Such promises for apparently impossible contingencies are not given. But if one achieves the impossible, the promises appear later retrospectively precisely where one had looked in vain for them before. Now, these men in themselves had no great attraction for me. Had I been devoted to the aforementioned idea of freedom, I should certainly have preferred the deep sea to the way out that suggested itself in the heavy faces of these men. At any rate, I watched them for a long time before I even thought of such things, indeed, it was the mass weight of my observations that first impelled me in the right direction.

It was so easy to imitate these people. I learned to spit in the very first days. We used to spit in each other's faces; the only difference was that I licked my face clean afterwards and they did not. I could soon smoke a pipe like an old hand; and if I also pressed my thumb into the bowl of the pipe, a roar of appreciation went up between decks; only it took me a very long time to understand the difference between a full pipe and an empty one.

My worst trouble came from the Schnapps bottle. The smell of it revolted me; I forced myself to it as best I could; but it took weeks for me to master my repulsion. This inward conflict, strangely enough, was taken more seriously by the crew than anything else about me. I cannot distinguish the men from each other in my recollection, but there was one of them who came again and again, alone or with friends, by day, by night, at all kinds of hours; he would post himself before me with the bottle and give me instructions. He could not understand me, he wanted to solve the enigma of my being. He would slowly uncork the bottle and then look at me to see if I had followed him; I admit that I always watched him with wildly eager, too eager, attention; such another pupil no human teacher ever found on earth. After the bottle was uncorked he lifted it to his mouth; I followed it with my eyes right up to his jaws; he would nod, pleased with me, and set the bottle to his lips; I, enchanted with my gradual enlightenment, squealed and scratched myself comprehensively wherever scratching was called for; he rejoiced, tilted the bottle and took a drink; I, impatient and desperate to emulate him, befouled myself in my cage, which again gave him great satisfaction; and then, holding the bottle at arm's length and bringing it up with a swing, he would empty it at one draught, leaning back at an exaggerated angle for my better instruction. I, exhausted by too much effort, could follow him no further and hung limply to the bars, while he ended his theoretical exposition by rubbing his belly and grinning.

After theory came practice. Was I not already quite exhausted by my theoretical instruction? Indeed I was; utterly exhausted. That was part of my destiny. And yet I would take hold of the proffered bottle as well as I was able; uncork it, trembling; this successful action would gradually inspire me with new energy; I would lift the bottle, already following my original model almost exactly; put it to my lips and – and then throw it down in disgust, utter disgust, although it was empty and filled only with the smell of the spirit – throw it down on the floor in disgust. To the sorrow of my teacher, to the great sorrow of myself; neither of us being really comforted by the fact that I did not forget, even though I had thrown away the bottle, to rub my belly most admirably and to grin.

Far too often my lesson ended in that way. And, to the credit of my teacher, he was not angry; sometimes indeed he would hold his burning pipe against my fur, until it began to smoulder in some place I could not easily reach, but then he would himself extinguish it with his own kind, enormous hand; he was not angry with me, he perceived that we were both fighting on the same side against the nature of apes and that I had the more difficult task.

What a triumph it was then both for him and for me, when one evening, before a large circle of spectators – perhaps there was a celebration of some kind, a gramophone was playing, an officer was circulating among the crew – when on this evening, just as no one was looking, I took hold of a Schnapps bottle that had been carelessly left standing before my cage, uncorked it in the best style, while the company began to watch me with mounting attention, set it to my lips without hesitation, with no grimace, like a professional drinker, with rolling eyes and full throat, actually and truly drank it empty; then threw the bottle away, not this time in despair but as an artistic performer; forgot, indeed, to rub my belly; but instead of that, because I could not help it, because my senses were reeling, called a brief and unmistakable 'Hallo!' — breaking into human speech, and with this outburst breaking into the human community, and felt its echo: 'Listen, he's talking!' like a caress over the whole of my sweat-drenched body.

I repeat: there was no attraction for me in imitating human beings; I imitated them because I needed a way out, and for no other reason. And even that triumph of mine did not achieve much. I lost my human voice again at once; it did not come back for months; my aversion for the Schnapps bottle returned again with even greater force. But the line I was to follow had in any case been decided, once for all.

When I was handed over to my first trainer in Hamburg I soon realized that there were two alternatives before me: the Zoological Gardens or the variety stage. I did not hesitate. I said to myself: 'Do your utmost to get on to the variety stage; the Zoological Gardens means only a new cage; once there, you are done for.'

And so I learned things, gentlemen. Ah, one learns when one has to; one learns when one needs a way out; one learns at all costs. One stands over oneself with a whip; one flays oneself at the slightest opposition. My ape nature fled out of me, head over heels and away, so that my first teacher was almost himself turned into an ape by it, had soon to give up teaching and was taken away to a mental hospital. Fortunately he was soon let out again.

But I used up many teachers, indeed, several teachers at once. As I became more confident of my abilities, as the public took an interest in my progress and my future began to look bright, I engaged teachers for myself, established them in five communicating rooms and took lessons from them all at once by dint of leaping from one room to the other.

That progress of mine! How the rays of knowledge penetrated from all sides into my awakening brain! I do not deny it: I found it exhilarating. But I must also confess: I did not overestimate it, not even then, much less now. With an effort which up'till now has never been repeated I managed to reach the cultural level of an average European. In itself that might be nothing to speak of, but it is something in so far as it has helped me out of my cage and opened a special way out for me, the way of humanity. There is an excellent idiom: to fight one's way through the thick of things; that is what I have done, I have fought through the thick of things. There was nothing else for me to do, provided always that freedom was not to be my choice.

As I look back over my development and survey what I have achieved so far, I do not complain, but I am not complacent either. With my hands in my trousers pockets, my bottle of wine on the table, I half lie and half sit in my rocking-chair and gaze out of the window: if a visitor arrives, I receive him with propriety. My manager sits in the ante-room; when I ring, he comes and listens to what I have to say. Nearly every evening I give a performance, and I have a success which could hardly be increased. When I come home late at night from banquets, from scientific receptions, from social gatherings, there sits waiting for me a half-trained little chimpanzee and I take comfort from her as apes do. By day I cannot bear to see her; for she has the insane look of the bewildered half-broken animal in her eye; no one else sees it, but I do, and I cannot bear it. On the whole, at any rate, I have achieved what I set out to achieve. But do not tell me that it was not worth the trouble. In any case, I am not appealing for any man's verdict, I am only imparting knowledge, I am only making a report. To you also, honoured Members of the Academy, I have only made a report.

Translated by Willa and Edwin Muir

A Hunger Artist

Four Stories

First Sorrow

A trapeze artist – this art, practised high in the vaulted domes of
the great variety theatres, is admittedly one of the most difficult
humanity can achieve – had so arranged his life that, as long as he
kept working in the same building, he never came down from his
trapeze by night or day, at first only from a desire to perfect his
skill, but later because custom was too strong for him. All his
needs, very modest needs at that, were supplied by relays of attendants who watched from below and sent up and hauled down again
in specially constructed containers whatever he required. This way
of living caused no particular inconvenience to the theatrical
people, except that, when other turns were on the stage, his being
still up aloft, which could not be dissembled, proved somewhat
distracting, as also the fact that, although at such times he mostly
kept very still, he drew a stray glance here and there from the
public. Yet the management overlooked this, because he was an
extraordinary and unique artist. And, of course, they recognized that
this mode of life was no mere prank, and that only in this way could
he really keep himself in constant practice and his art at the pitch of
its perfection.

Besides, it was quite healthy up there, and when in the warmer
seasons of the year the side windows all round the dome of the
theatre were thrown open and sun and fresh air came pouring
irresistibly into the dusky vault, it was even beautiful. True, his
social life was somewhat limited, only sometimes a fellow-acrobat
swarmed up the ladder to him, and then they both sat on the
trapeze, leaning left and right against the supporting ropes, and
chatted, or builders' workmen repairing the roof exchanged a few

words with him through an open window, or the fireman, inspecting the emergency lighting in the top gallery, called over to him something that sounded respectful but could hardly be made out. Otherwise nothing disturbed his seclusion; occasionally, perhaps, some theatre hand, straying through the empty theatre of an afternoon, gazed thoughtfully up into the great height of the roof, almost beyond eyeshot, where the trapeze artist, unaware that he was being observed, practised his art or rested.

The trapeze artist could have gone on living peacefully like that, had it not been for the inevitable journeys from place to place, which he found extremely trying. Of course his manager saw to it that his sufferings were not prolonged one moment more than necessary; for town travel, racing automobiles were used, which whirled him, by night if possible or in the earliest hours of the morning, through the empty streets at breakneck speed, too slow all the same for the trapeze artist's impatience; for railway journeys, a whole compartment was reserved, in which the trapeze artist, as a possible though wretched alternative to his usual way of living, could pass the time up on the luggage-rack; in the next town on their circuit, long before he arrived, the trapeze was already slung up in the theatre and all the doors leading to the stage were flung wide open, all corridors kept free – yet the manager never knew a happy moment until the trapeze artist set his foot on the rope ladder and in a twinkling, at long last, hung aloft on his trapeze.

Once when they were again travelling together, the trapeze artist lying on the luggage-rack dreaming, the manager leaning back in the opposite window seat reading a book, the trapeze artist addressed his companion in a low voice. The manager was immediately all attention. The trapeze artist, biting his lips, said that he must always in future have two trapezes for his performance instead of only one, two trapezes opposite each other. The manager at once agreed. But the trapeze artist, as if to show that the manager's consent counted for as little as his refusal, said that never again would he perform on only one trapeze, in no circumstances whatever. The very idea that it might happen at all seemed to make him shudder. The manager, watchfully feeling his way, once more emphasized his entire agreement, two trapezes were better than one, besides it would be an advantage to have a second bar, more variety could be introduced into the performance. At that the trapeze artist suddenly burst into tears. Deeply distressed, the manager sprang to his feet and asked what was the matter, then getting no answer climbed up on the seat and caressed him, cheek to cheek, so that his own face was bedabbled by the trapeze artist's tears. Yet it took much questioning and soothing endearment until the trapeze artist sobbed: 'Only the one bar in my hands – how can I go on living!' That made it somewhat easier for the manager to comfort him; he promised to wire from the very next station for a second trapeze to be installed in the first town on their circuit; reproached himself for having let the artist work so long on only one trapeze, and thanked and praised him warmly for having at last brought the mistake to his notice. And so he succeeded in reassuring the trapeze artist, little by little, and was able to go back to his corner. But he himself was far from reassured, with deep uneasiness he kept glancing secretly at the trapeze artist over the top of his book. Once such ideas began to torment him, would they ever quite leave him alone? Would they not rather increase in urgency? Would they not threaten his very existence? And indeed the manager believed he could see, during the apparently peaceful sleep which had succeeded the fit of tears, the first furrows of care engraving themselves upon the trapeze artist's smooth, child-like forehead.

A Little Woman

She is a little woman; naturally quite slim, she is tightly-laced as well; she is always in the same dress when I see her, it is made of greyish-yellow stuff something the colour of wood and is trimmed discreetly with bobbles or button-like hangings of the same colour; she never wears a hat, her dull fair hair is smooth and not untidy, but worn very loose. Although she is tightly-laced she is quick and light in her movements, actually she rather overdoes the quickness, she loves to put her hands on her hips and abruptly turn the upper part of her body sideways with a suddenness that is surprising. The impression her hand makes on me I can convey only by saying that I have never seen a hand with the separate fingers so sharply differentiated from each other as hers; and yet her hand has no anatomical peculiarities, it is an entirely normal hand.

This little woman, then, is very ill-pleased with me, she always finds something objectionable in me, I am always doing the wrong thing to her, I annoy her at every step; if a life could be cut into the smallest of small pieces and every scrap of it could be separately assessed, every scrap of my life would certainly be an offence to her. I have often wondered why I am such an offence to her; it may be that everything about me outrages her sense of beauty, her feeling for justice, her habits, her traditions, her hopes, there are such completely incompatible natures, but why does that upset her so much? There is no connection between us that could force her to suffer because of me. All she has to do is to regard me as an utter stranger, which I am, and which I do not object to being, indeed I should welcome it, she only needs to forget my existence, which I have never thrust upon her attention, nor ever would, and obviously her torments would be at an end. I am not thinking of myself, I am quite leaving out of account the fact that I find her attitude of course rather trying, leaving it out of account because I recognize that my discomfort is nothing to the suffering she endures. All the same I am well aware that hers is no affectionate suffering; she is not concerned to make any real improvement in me, besides whatever she finds objectionable in me is not of a nature to hinder my development. Yet she does not care about my development either, she cares only for her personal interest in the matter, which is to revenge herself for the torments I cause her now and to prevent any torments that threaten her from me in the future. I have already tried once to indicate the best way of putting a stop to this perpetual resentment of hers, but my very attempt wrought her up to such a pitch of fury that I shall never repeat it.

I feel, too, a certain responsibility laid upon me, if you like to put it that way, for, strangers as we are to each other, the little woman and myself, and however true it is that the sole connection between us is the vexation I cause her, or rather the vexation she lets me cause her, I ought not to feel indifferent to the visible physical suffering which this induces in her. Every now and then, and more frequently of late, information is brought to me that she has risen of a morning pale, unslept, oppressed by headache and almost unable to work; her family are worried about her, they wonder what can have caused her condition, and they have not yet found the answer. I am the only one who knows that, it is her settled and daily renewed vexation with me. True, I am not so worried about her as her family; she is hardy and tough; anyone who is capable of such strong feeling is likely also to be capable of surviving its effects; I have even a suspicion that her sufferings – or some of them, at least – are only a pretence put up to bring public suspicion on me. She is too proud to admit openly what a torment my very existence is to her; to make any appeal to others against me she would consider beneath her dignity; it is only disgust, persistent and active disgust, that drives her to be pre-occupied with me; to discuss in public this unclean affliction of hers would be too shameful. But to keep utterly silent about something that so persistently rankles would also be too much for her. So with feminine guile she steers a middle course; she keeps silent but betrays all the outward signs of a secret sorrow in order to draw public attention to the matter. Perhaps she even hopes that once public attention is fixed on me a general public rancour against me will rise up and use all its great powers to condemn me definitively much more effectively and quickly than her relatively feeble private rancour could do; she would then retire into the background, draw a breath of relief and turn her back on me. Well, if that is what her hopes are really set on, she is deluding herself. Public opinion will not take over her rôle; public opinion would never find me so infinitely objectionable, even under its most powerful magnifying glass. I am not so altogether useless a creature as she thinks; I don't want to boast and especially not in this connection; but if I am not conspicuous for specially useful qualities, I am certainly not conspicuous for the lack of them; only to her, only to her almost bleached eyes, do I appear so, she won't be able to convince anyone else. So in this respect I can feel quite reassured, can I? No, not at all; for if it becomes generally known that my behaviour is making her positively ill, which some observers, those who most industriously bring me information about her, for instance, are not far from perceiving, or at least look as if they perceived it, and the world should put questions to me: why am I tormenting the poor little woman with my incorrigibility, and do I mean to drive her to her death, and when am I going to show some sense and have enough decent human feeling to stop such goings-on – if the world were to ask me that, it would be difficult to find an answer. Should I admit frankly that I don't much believe in these symptoms of illness, and thus produce the unfavourable impression of being a man who blames others to avoid being blamed himself, and in such an ungallant manner? And how could I say quite openly that even if I did believe that she were really ill, I should not feel the slightest sympathy for her, since she is a complete stranger to me and any connection between us is her own invention and entirely one-sided. I don't say that people wouldn't believe me; they wouldn't be interested enough to get so far as belief; they would simply note the answer I gave concerning such a frail, sick woman, and that would be little in my favour. Any answer I made would inevitably come up against the world's incapacity to keep down the suspicion that there must be a love affair behind such a case like this, although it is as clear as daylight that such a relationship does not exist, and that if it did it would come from my side rather than hers, since I should be really capable of admiring the little woman for the decisive quickness of her judgement and her persistent vitality in leaping to conclusions, if these very qualities were not always turned as weapons against me. She, at any rate, shows not a trace of friendliness towards me; in that she is honest and true; therein lies my last hope; not even to help on her campaign would she so far forget herself as to let any such suspicion arise. But public opinion which is wholly insensitive in such matters would abide by its prejudices and always denounce me.

So the only thing left for me to do would be to change myself in time, before the world could intervene, just sufficiently to lessen the little woman's rancour, not to wean her from it altogether, which is unthinkable. And, indeed, I have often asked myself if I am so pleased with my present self as to be unwilling to change it, and whether I could not attempt some changes in myself, even although I should be doing so not because I found them needful but merely to propitiate the little woman. And I have honestly tried, taking some trouble and care, it even did me good, it was almost a diversion; some changes resulted which were visible a long way off, I did not need to draw her attention to them, she perceives all that kind of thing much sooner than I do, she can even perceive by my expression beforehand what I have in mind; but no success crowned my efforts. How could it possibly do so? Her objection to me, as I am now aware, is a fundamental one; nothing can remove it, not even the removal of myself; if she heard that I had committed suicide she would fall into transports of rage.

Now I cannot imagine that such a sharp-witted woman as she is does not understand as well as I do, both the hopelessness of her own course of action and the helplessness of mine, my inability, with the best will in the world, to conform to her requirements. Of course she understands it, but being a fighter by nature she forgets it in the lust of battle, and my unfortunate disposition, which I cannot help since it is mine by nature, conditions me to whisper gentle admonitions to anyone who flies into a violent passion. In this way, naturally, we shall never come to terms. I shall keep on leaving the house in the gay mood of early morning only to meet that countenance of hers, lowering at the sight of me, the contemptuous curl of her lips, the measuring glance, aware beforehand of what it is going to find, that sweeps over me and, however fleeting, misses nothing, the sarcastic smile furrowing her girlish cheek, the complaining lift of the eyes to Heaven, the planting of the hands on the hips, to fortify herself, and then the access of rage that brings pallor with it and trembling.

Not long ago I took occasion, for the very first time as I realized with some astonishment, to mention the matter to a very good friend of mine, just in passing, casually, in a word or two, reducing it to even less than its just proportions, trivial as it is in essence when looked at objectively. It was curious that my friend all the same did not ignore it, indeed of his own accord he even made more of it than I had done, would not be side-tracked and insisted on discussing it. But it was still more curious that in one important particular he underestimated it, for he advised me seriously to go away for a short time. No advice could be less understandable; the matter was simple enough, anyone who looked closely at it could see right through it, yet it was not so simple that my mere departure would set all of it right, or even the greater part of it. On the contrary, such a departure is just what I must avoid; if I am to follow a plan at all it must be that of keeping the affair within its present narrow limits which do not yet involve the outside world, that is to say, I must stay quietly where I am and not let it affect my behaviour as far as can be seen, and that includes mentioning it to no one, but not at all because it is a kind of dangerous mystery, merely because it is a trivial, purely personal matter and as such to be taken lightly, and to be kept on that level. So my friend's remarks were not profitless after all, they taught me nothing new yet they strengthened my original resolution.

And on closer reflection it appears that the developments which the affair seems to have undergone in the course of time are not developments in the affair itself, but only in my attitude to it, in so far as that has become more composed on the one hand, more manly, penetrating nearer the heart of the matter, while on the other hand, under the influence of the continued nervous strain which I cannot overcome, however slight, it has increased in irritability.

I am less upset by the affair now that I think I perceive how unlikely it is to come to any decisive crisis, imminent as that sometimes seems to be; one is easily disposed, especially when one is young, to exaggerate the speed with which decisive moments arrive; whenever my small critic, grown faint at the very sight of me, sank sideways into a chair, holding on to the back of it with one hand and plucking at her bodice-strings with the other, while tears of rage and despair rolled down her cheeks, I used to think that now the moment had come and I was just on the point of being summoned to answer for myself. Yet there was no decisive moment, no summons, women faint easily, the world has no time to notice all their doings. And what has really happened in all these years? Nothing except that such occasions have repeated themselves, sometimes more and sometimes less violently, and that their sum total has increased accordingly. And that people are hanging around in the offing and would like to interfere if they could find some way of doing it; but they can find none, so up till now they have had to rely on what they could smell out, and although that by itself is fully qualified to keep the owners of the noses busy it can't do anything more. Yet the situation was always like that, fundamentally, always provided with superfluous bystanders and nosy onlookers, who always justified their presence by some cunning excuse, for preference claiming to be relatives, always stretching their necks and sniffing trouble, but all they have achieved is to be still standing by. The only difference is that I have gradually come to recognize them and distinguish one face from another; once upon a time I believed that they had just gradually trickled in from outside, that the affair was having wider repercussions, which would themselves compel a crisis; today I think I know that these onlookers were always there from the beginning and have little or nothing to do with the imminence of a crisis. And the crisis itself, why should I dignify it by such a name? If it ever should happen – and certainly not tomorrow or the day after tomorrow, most likely never – that public opinion concerns itself with the affair, which, I must repeat, is beyond its competence, I certainly won't escape unharmed, but on the other hand people are bound to take into account that I am not unknown to the public, that I have lived for long in the full light of publicity, trustingly and trustworthily, and that this distressed little woman, this latecomer in my life, whom, let me remark in passing, another man might have brushed off like a burr and privately trodden underfoot without a sound, that this woman at the very worst could add only an ugly little flourish to the diploma in which public opinion long ago certified me to be a respectable member of society. That is how things stand today, little likely to cause me any uneasiness.

The fact that in the course of years I have all the same become somewhat uneasy has nothing to do with the real significance of this affair; a man simply cannot endure being a continual target for someone's spite, even when he knows well enough that the spite is gratuitous; he grows uneasy, he begins, in a kind of physical way only, to flinch from impending crises, even when like an honest man he does not much believe that they are coming. Partly, too, it is a symptom of increasing age; youth sheds a bloom over everything; awkward characteristics are lost to sight in the endless up-welling of youthful energy; if, as a youth, a man has a somewhat wary eye it is not counted against him, it is not noticed at all, even by himself; but the things that survive in old age are residues, each is necessary, none is renewed, each is under scrutiny, and the wary eye of an ageing man is clearly a wary eye and is not difficult to recognize. Only, as also in this case, it is not an actual degeneration of his condition.

So from whatever standpoint I consider this small affair, it appears – and this I will stick to – that if I keep my hand over it, even quite lightly, I shall quietly continue to live my own life for a long time to come, untroubled by the world, despite all the outbursts of the woman.

A Fasting Showman

During these last decades the interesting professional fasting has markedly diminished. It used to pay very well to stage such great performances under one's own management, but today that is quite impossible. We live in a different world now. At one time the whole town took a lively interest in the fasting showman; from day to day of his fast the excitement mounted; everybody wanted to see him at least once a day; there were people who bought season tickets for the last few days and sat from morning till night in front of his small barred cage; even in the night-time there were visiting hours, when the whole effect was heightened by torch flares; on fine days the cage was set out in the open air, and then it was the children's special treat to see the fasting showman; for their elders he was often just a joke that happened to be in fashion, but the children stood open-mouthed, holding each other's hands for greater security, marvelling at him as he sat there pallid in black tights, with his ribs sticking out so prominently, not even on a seat but down among straw on the ground, sometimes giving a courteous nod, answering questions with a constrained smile, or perhaps stretching an arm through the bars so that one might feel how thin it was, and then again withdrawing deep into himself, paying no attention to anyone or anything, not even to the striking of the clock that was the only piece of furniture in his cage, but merely staring into vacancy with half-shut eyes, now and then taking a sip from a tiny glass of water to moisten his lips.

Besides casual onlookers there were also relays of permanent watchers selected by the public, usually butchers, strangely enough, and it was their task to watch the fasting showman day and night, three of them at a time, in case he should have some secret recourse to nourishment. This was nothing but a formality, instituted to reassure the masses, for the initiates knew well enough that during his fast the artiste would never in any circumstances, not even under forcible compulsion, swallow the smallest morsel of food; the honour of his profession forbade it. Not every watcher, of course, was capable of understanding this, there were often groups of night watchers who were very lax in carrying out their duties and deliberately huddled together in a retired corner to play cards with great absorption, obviously intending to give the fasting show-man the chance of a little refreshment, which they supposed he could draw from some private hoard. Nothing annoyed the artiste more than such watchers; they made him miserable; they made his fast seem unendurable; sometimes he mastered his feebleness sufficiently to sing during their watch for as long as he could keep going, to show them how unjust their suspicions were. But that was of little use; they only wondered at his cleverness in being able to fill his mouth even while singing. Much more to his taste were the watchers who sat close up to the bars, who were not content with the dim night lighting of the hall but focused him in the full glare of the electric pocket-torch given them by the im-presario. The harsh light did not trouble him at all, in any case he could never sleep properly, and he could always drowse a little, whatever the light, at any hour, even when the hall was thronged with noisy onlookers. He was quite happy at the prospect of spending a sleepless night with such watchers; he was ready to exchange jokes with them, to tell them stories out of his nomadic life, anything at all to keep them awake and demonstrate to them again that he had no eatables in his cage and that he was fasting as not one of them could fast. But his happiest moment was when the morning came and an enormous breakfast was brought them, at his expense, on which they flung themselves with the keen appetites of healthy men after a weary night of wakefulness. Of course there were people who argued that this breakfast was an unfair attempt to bribe the watchers, but that was going rather too far, and when they were invited to take on a night's vigil without a breakfast, merely for the sake of the cause, they made themselves scarce, although they stuck stubbornly to their suspicions.

Such suspicions, anyhow, were a necessary accompaniment to the profession of fasting. No one could possibly watch the fasting showman continuously, day and night, and so no one could produce first hand evidence that the fast had really been rigorous and continuous; only the artiste himself could know that, he was, therefore, bound to be the sole completely satisfied spectator of his own fast. Yet for other reasons he was never satisfied; it was not perhaps mere fasting that had brought him to such skeleton thinness that many people had regretfully to keep away from his exhibitions because the sight of him was too much for them, perhaps it was dissatisfaction with himself that had worn him down. For he alone knew, what no other initiate knew, how easy it was to fast. It was the easiest thing in the world. He made no secret of this, yet people did not believe him, at the best they set him down as modest, most of them however thought he was out for publicity or else was some kind of cheat who found it easy to fast because he had discovered a way of getting round it, and then had the impudence to admit the fact, more or less. He had to put up with all that, and in the course of time had got used to it, but his inner dissatisfaction always rankled, and never yet, after any term of fasting – this must be granted to his credit – had he left the cage of his own free will. The longest time he could fast was fixed by his impresario at forty days, beyond that term he was not allowed to go – not even in great cities, and there was good reason for it, too. Experience had proved that for about forty days the interest of the public could be stimulated by steady pressure of advertisement, but after that the town began to lose interest, sympathetic support began notably to fall off; there were, of course, local variations as between one town and another or one country and another, but as a general rule forty days marked the limit. So on the fortieth day the flower-bedecked cage was opened, enthusiastic spectators filled the hall, a military band played, two doctors entered the cage to measure the results of the fast, which were announced through a megaphone, and finally two young ladies appeared, blissful at having been selected for the honour, to help the fasting showman down the few steps leading to a small table on which was spread a carefully chosen invalid repast. And at this very moment the artiste always turned stubborn. True, he would entrust his bony arms to the outstretched helping hands of the ladies bending over him, but stand up he would not. Why stop fasting at this particular moment, after forty days of it? He had held out for a long time, an illimitably long time; why stop now, when he was in his best fasting form, or rather, not yet quite in his best fasting form? Why should he be cheated of the fame he would get for fasting longer, for being not only the record fasting showman of all time — which presumably he was already — but for beating his own record by a performance beyond human imagination, since he felt that there were no limits to his capacity for fasting. His public pretended to admire him so much, why should it have so little patience with him; if he could endure fasting longer, why shouldn't the public endure it? Besides, he was tired, he was comfortable sitting in the straw, and now he was supposed to lift himself to his full height and go down to a meal the very thought of which gave him a nausea that only the presence of the ladies kept him from betraying, and even that with an effort. And he looked up into the eyes of the ladies who were apparently so friendly and in reality so cruel, and shook his head, which felt too heavy on its strengthless neck. But then there happened yet again what always happened. The impresario came forward, without a word — for the band made speech impossible — lifted his arms in the air above the artiste, as if inviting Heaven to look down upon its creature here in the straw, this suffering martyr, which indeed he was, although in quite another sense; grasped him round the emaciated waist, with exaggerated caution, so that the frail condition he was in might be appreciated; and committed him to the care of the blenching ladies, not without secretly giving him a shaking so that his legs and body tottered and swayed. The artiste now submitted completely; his head lolled on his breast as if it had landed there by chance, his body was hollowed out,[*] his legs in a spasm of self-preservation clung close to each other at the knees, yet scraped on the ground as if it were not really solid ground, as

if they were only trying to find solid ground; and the whole weight
of his body, a featherweight after all, relapsed on to one of the
ladies, who, looking round for help and panting a little – this post
of honour was not at all what she had expected it to be – first
stretched her neck as far as she could to keep her face at least free
from contact with the artiste, then finding this impossible, and her
more fortunate companion not coming to her aid but merely holding extended on her own trembling hand the little bunch of
knuckle bones that was the artiste's, to the great delight of the
spectators burst into tears and had to be replaced by an attendant
who had long been stationed in readiness. Then came the food, a
little of which the impresario managed to get between the artiste's
lips, while he sat in a kind of half-fainting trance, to the accompaniment of cheerful patter designed to distract the public's attention from the artiste's condition; after that, a toast was drunk to
the public, supposedly prompted by a whisper from the artiste in
the impresario's ear; the band confirmed it with a mighty flourish,
the spectators melted away, and no one had any cause to be dissatisfied with the proceedings, no one except the fasting showman
himself, he only, as always.

So he lived for many years, with small regular intervals of re-
cuperation, in visible glory, honoured by the world, yet in spite of
that troubled in spirit, and all the more troubled because no one
would take his trouble seriously. What comfort could he possibly
need? What more could he possibly wish for? And if some good-
natured person, feeling sorry for him, tried to console him by pointing out that his melancholy was probably caused by fasting, it
could happen, especially when he had been fasting for some time,
that he reacted with an outburst of fury and to the general alarm
began to shake the bars of his cage like a wild animal. Yet the
impresario had a way of punishing these outbreaks which he rather
enjoyed putting into operation. He would apologize publicly for
the artiste's behaviour, which was only to be excused, he admitted,
because of the irritability caused by fasting; a condition hardly to
be understood by well-fed people; then by natural transition he
went on to mention the artiste's equally incomprehensible boast
that he could fast for much longer than he was doing; he praised
the high ambition, the goodwill, the great self-denial undoubtedly

implicit in such a statement; and then quite simply countered it by bringing out photographs, which were also on sale to the public, showing the artiste on the fortieth day of a fast lying in bed almost dead from exhaustion. This perversion of the truth, familiar to the artiste though it was, always unnerved him afresh and proved too much for him. What was a consequence of the premature ending of his fast was here presented as the cause of it! To fight against this lack of understanding, against a whole world of non-understanding, was impossible. Time and again in good faith he stood by the bars listening to the impresario, but as soon as the photographs appeared he always let go and sank with a groan back on to his straw, and the reassured public could once more come close and gaze at him.

A few years later when the witnesses of such scenes called them to mind, they often failed to understand themselves at all. For meanwhile the aforementioned change in public interest had set in; it seemed to happen almost overnight; there may have been profound causes for it, but who was going to bother about that? At any rate the pampered fasting showman suddenly found himself deserted one fine day by the amusement seekers, who went streaming past him to other more favoured attractions. For the last time the impresario hurried him over half Europe to discover whether the old interest might still survive here and there; all in vain; everywhere, as if by secret agreement, a positive revulsion from professional fasting was in evidence. Of course it could not really have sprung up so suddenly as all that, and many premonitory symptoms which had not been sufficiently remarked or suppressed during the rush and glitter of success now came retrospectively to mind, but it was now too late to take any counter-measures. Fasting would surely come into fashion again at some future date, yet that was no comfort for those living in the present. What, then, was the fasting showman to do? He had been applauded by thousands in his time and could hardly come down to showing himself in a street booth at village fairs, and as for adopting another profession, he was not only too old for that but too fanatically devoted to fasting. So he took leave of the impresario, his partner in an unparalleled career, and hired himself to a large circus; in order to spare his own feelings he avoided reading the conditions of his contract.

A large circus with its enormous traffic in replacing and recruiting men, animals, and apparatus can always find a use for people at any time, even for a fasting showman, provided, of course, that he does not ask too much, and in this particular case anyhow it was not only the artiste who was taken on but his famous and long-known name as well, indeed, considering the peculiar nature of his performance, which was not impaired by advancing age, it could not be objected that here was an artiste past his prime, no longer at the height of his professional skill, seeking a refuge in some quiet corner of a circus; on the contrary, the fasting showman averred that he could fast as well as ever, which was entirely credible, he even alleged that if he were allowed to fast as he liked, and this was at once promised him without more ado, he could astound the world by establishing a record never yet achieved, a statement which certainly provoked a smile among the other professionals, since it left out of account the change in public opinion, which the fasting showman in his zeal conveniently forgot.

He had not, however, actually lost his sense of the real situation and took it as a matter of course that he and his cage should be stationed, not in the middle of the ring as a main attraction, but outside, near the animal cages, on a site that was after all easily accessible. Large and gaily painted placards made a frame for the cage and announced what was to be seen inside it. When the public came thronging out in the intervals to see the animals, they could hardly avoid passing the fasting showman's cage and stopping there for a moment, perhaps they might even have stayed longer had not those pressing behind them in the narrow gangway, who did not understand why they should be held up on their way towards the excitements of the menagerie, made it impossible for anyone to stand gazing quietly for any length of time. And that was the reason why the fasting showman, who had of course been looking forward to these visiting hours as the main achievement of his life, began instead to shrink from them. At first he could hardly wait for the intervals; it was exhilarating to watch the crowds come streaming his way, until only too soon – not even the most obstinate self-deception, clung to almost consciously, could hold out against the fact – the conviction was borne in upon him that these people, most of them, to judge from their actions, again and again, without exception, were all on their way to the menagerie. And the first sight of them from the distance remained the best. For when they reached his cage he was at once deafened by the storm of shouting and abuse that arose from the two contending factions, which renewed themselves continuously, of those who wanted to stop and stare at him – he soon began to hate them more than the others – not out of real interest but only out of obstinate self-assertiveness, and those who wanted to go straight on to the animals. When the first great rush was past, the stragglers came along, and these, whom nothing could have prevented from stopping to look at him as long as they had breath, raced past with long strides, hardly even glancing at him, in their haste to get to the menagerie in time. And all too rarely did it happen that he had a stroke of luck, when some father of a family fetched up before him with his children, pointed a finger at the fasting showman and explained at length what the phenomenon meant, telling stories of earlier years when he himself had watched similar but much more thrilling performances, and the children, still rather incomprehending, since neither inside nor outside school had they been sufficiently prepared for this lesson – fasting was a commonplace to them – yet showed by the brightness of their intent eyes that new and better times might be coming. Perhaps, said the fasting showman to himself many a time, things would be a little better if his cage were set not quite so near the menagerie. That made it too easy for people to make their choice – to say nothing of what he suffered from the stench of the menagerie, the animals' restlessness by night, the carrying past of raw lumps of flesh for the beasts of prey, the roaring at feeding times, which depressed him continually. But he did not dare to present himself in person to the management; after all, he had the animals to thank for the troops of people who passed his cage, among whom there might always be one here and there to take an interest in him, and who could tell where they might seclude him if he called attention to his existence and thereby to the fact that, strictly speaking, he was only an impediment on the way to the menagerie?

A small impediment, to be sure, one that grew steadily less. People grew familiar with the strange idea that they could be expected, in times like these, to take an interest in a fasting showman, and with this familiarity the verdict went out against him. He might fast as much as he could, and he did so; but nothing could save him now, people passed him by. Just try to explain to anyone the art of fasting! Anyone who has no feeling for it cannot be made to understand it. The fine placards grew dirty and illegible, they were torn down; the little notice-board telling the number of fast-days achieved, which at first was changed carefully every day, had long stayed at the same figure, for after the few weeks even this small task seemed pointless to the staff; and so the artiste simply fasted on and on, as he had once dreamed of doing, and it was no trouble to him, just as he had always foretold, but no one counted the days, no one, not even the artiste himself, knew what records he was already breaking, and his heart grew heavy. And when once in a time some leisurely passer-by stopped, made merry over the old figure on the board, and spoke of swindling, that was in its way the stupidest lie ever invented by indifference and inborn malice, since it was not the fasting showman who was cheating, he was working honestly, but the world was cheating him of his reward.

More days went by, however, and that too came to an end. An overseer's eye fell on the cage one day and he asked the attendants why this perfectly good cage should be left standing there unused with dirty straw inside it; nobody knew, until one man, helped out by the notice-board, remembered about the fasting showman. They poked into the straw with sticks and found him in it. 'Are you still fasting?' asked the overseer. 'When on earth do you mean to stop?' 'Forgive me, everybody,' whispered the fasting showman; only the overseer, who had his ear to the bars, understood him. 'Of course,' said the overseer and tapped his forehead with a finger to let the attendants know what state the man was in, 'we forgive you.' 'I always wanted you to admire my fasting,' said the fasting showman. 'We do admire it,' said the overseer, affably. 'But you shouldn't admire it,' said the fasting showman. 'Well then we don't admire it,' said the overseer, 'but why shouldn't we admire it?' 'Because I have to fast, I can't do anything else,' said the fasting showman. 'What a fellow you are,' said the overseer, 'and why can't you do anything else?' 'Because,' said the fasting showman, lifting his head a little and speaking with his lips pursed, as if for a kiss, right into the overseer's ear, so that no syllable might be lost, 'because I couldn't find any food I liked. If I had found any, believe me, I should have made no bones about it and stuffed myself like you or anyone else.' These were his last words, but in his dimming eyes remained the firm though no longer proud persuasion that he was still continuing to fast.

'Well, clear this out now!' said the overseer, and they buried the fasting showman, straw and all. Into the cage they put a young panther. Even the most insensitive felt it refreshing to see this wild creature leaping around the cage that had so long been dreary. The panther was all right. The food he liked was brought him without hesitation by the attendants; he seemed not even to miss his freedom; his noble body, furnished almost to bursting point with all that it needed, seemed to carry freedom around with it too; somewhere in his jaws it seemed to lurk; and the joy of life streamed with such ardent passion from his throat that for the onlookers it was not easy to stand the shock of it. But they braced themselves, crowded round the cage, and did not want ever to move away.

Josephine the Singer, or the Mouse-folk

Our singer is called Josephine. Anyone who has not heard her does not know the power of song. There is no one but is carried away by her singing, a tribute all the greater as we are not in general a music-loving race. Tranquil peace is the music we love best; our life is hard, we are no longer able, even on occasions when we have tried to shake off the cares of daily life, to rise to anything so high and remote from our usual routine as music. But we do not much lament that; we do not get even so far; a certain practical cunning, which admittedly we stand greatly in need of, we hold to be our greatest distinction, and with a smile born of much cunning we are wont to console ourselves for all shortcomings, even supposing – only it does not happen – that we were to yearn once in a way for the kind of bliss which music may provide. Josephine is the sole exception; she has a love for music and knows too how to transmit it; she is the only one; when she dies, music — who knows for how long — will vanish from our lives.

I have often thought about what this music of hers really means, for we are quite unmusical; how is it that we understand Josephine's singing or, since Josephine denies that, at least think we can understand it? The simplest answer would be that the beauty of her singing is so great that even the most insensitive cannot be deaf to it, but this answer is not satisfactory. If it were really so, her singing would have to give one an immediate and lasting feeling of being something out of the ordinary, a feeling that from her throat something is sounding which we have never heard before and which we are not even capable of hearing, something that Josephine alone and no one else can enable us to hear. But in my opinion that is just what does not happen, I do not feel this and have never observed that others feel anything of the kind. Among intimates we admit freely to one another that Josephine's singing, as singing, is nothing out of the ordinary.

Is it in fact singing at all? Although we are unmusical we have a tradition of singing; in the old days our people did sing; this is mentioned in legends and some songs have actually survived, which, it is true, no one can now sing. Thus we have an inkling of what singing is, and Josephine's art does not really correspond to it. So is it singing at all? Is it not perhaps just a piping? And piping is something we all know about, it is the real artistic accomplishment of our people, or rather no mere accomplishment but a characteristic expression of our life. We all pipe, but, of course, no one dreams of making out that our piping is an art, we pipe without thinking of it, indeed without noticing it, and there are even many among us who are quite unaware that piping is one of our characteristics. So if it were true that Josephine does not sing but only pipes, and perhaps, as it seems to me at least, hardly rises above the level of our usual piping — yet, perhaps her strength is not even quite equal to our usual piping, whereas an ordinary earth-worker can keep it up effortlessly all day long, besides doing his work — if that were all true, then, indeed, Josephine's alleged vocal skill might be disproved, but that would merely clear the ground for the real riddle which needs solving — the enormous influence she has.

After all, it is only a kind of piping that she produces. If you post yourself quite far away from her and listen, or, still better, put your judgement to the test, whenever she happens to be singing along with others, by trying to identify her voice, you will undoubtedly distinguish nothing but a quite ordinary piping tone, which at most differs a little from the others through being delicate or weak. Yet if you sit down before her, it is not merely a piping; to comprehend her art it is necessary not only to hear but to see her. Even if hers were only our usual work-a-day piping, there is first of all this peculiarity to consider, that here is someone making a ceremonial performance out of doing the usual thing. To crack a nut is truly no feat, so no one would ever dare to collect an audience in order to entertain it with nut-cracking. But if all the same one does do that and succeeds in entertaining the public, then it cannot be a matter of simple nut-cracking. Or it is a matter of nut-cracking, but it turns out that we have overlooked the art of cracking nuts because we were too skilled in it and that this newcomer to it first shows us its real nature, even finding it useful in making his effects to be rather less expert in nut-cracking than most of us.

Perhaps it is much the same with Josephine's singing; we admire in her what we do not at all admire in ourselves; in this respect, I may say, she is of one mind with us. I was once present when someone, as of course often happens, drew her attention to the folk-piping everywhere going on, making only a modest reference to it, yet for Josephine that was more than enough. A smile so sarcastic and arrogant as she then assumed I had never seen; she, who in appearance is delicacy itself, conspicuously so even among our people who are prolific in such feminine types, seemed at that moment actually vulgar; she was at once aware of it herself, by the way, with her extreme sensibility, and controlled herself. At any rate she denies any connection between her art and ordinary piping. For those who are of the contrary opinion she has only contempt and probably unacknowledged hatred. This is not simple vanity, for the opposition, with which I too am half in sympathy, certainly admires her no less than the crowd does, but Josephine does not want mere admiration, she wants to be admired exactly in the way she prescribes, mere admiration leaves her cold. And when you take a seat before her, you understand her; opposition is possible only at a distance, when you sit before her, you know: this piping of hers is no piping.

Since piping is one of our thoughtless habits, one might think that people would pipe up in Josephine's audience too; her art makes us feel happy, and when we are happy we pipe; but her audience never pipes, it sits in mouse-like stillness; as if we had become partakers in the peace we long for, from which our own piping at the very least holds us back, we make no sound. Is it her singing that enchants us or is it not rather the solemn stillness enclosing her frail little voice? Once it happened while Josephine was singing that some silly little thing in all innocence began to pipe up too. Now it was just the same as what we were hearing from Josephine; in front of us the piping sound that despite all rehearsal was still tentative, and here in the audience the unselfconscious piping of a child; it would have been impossible to define the difference; but yet at once we hissed and whistled the interrupter down, although it would not really have been necessary, for in any case she would certainly have crawled away in fear and shame, whereas Josephine struck up her most triumphal notes and was quite beyond herself, spreading her arms wide and stretching her throat as high as it could reach.

That is what she is like always, every trifle, every casual incident, every nuisance, a creaking in the parquet, a grinding of teeth, a failure in the lighting incites her to heighten the effectiveness of her song; she believes anyhow that she is singing to deaf ears; there is no lack of enthusiasm and applause, but she has long learned not to expect real understanding, as she conceives it. So all disturbance is very welcome to her; whatever intervenes from outside to hinder the purity of her song, to be overcome with a slight effort, even with no effort at all, merely by confronting it, can help to awaken the masses, to teach them not perhaps understanding but awed respect.

And if small events do her such service, how much more do great ones. Our life is very uneasy, every day brings surprises, apprehensions, hopes, and terrors, so that it would be impossible for a single individual to bear it all did he not always have by day and night the support of his fellows; but even so it often becomes very difficult; frequently as many as a thousand shoulders are trembling under a burden that was really meant only for one pair. Then

Josephine holds that her time has come. So there she stands, the
delicate creature, shaken by vibrations, especially below the breast-
bone, so that one feels anxious for her, it is as if she has concentrated all her strength on her song, as if from everything in her
that does not directly subserve her singing all strength has been
withdrawn, almost all power of life, as if she were laid bare,
abandoned, committed merely to the care of good angels, as if
while she is so wholly withdrawn and living only in her song a cold
breath blowing upon her might kill her. But just when she makes
such an appearance, we who are supposed to be her opponents are
in the habit of saying: 'She can't even pipe; she has to put such
a terrible strain on herself to force out not a song – we can't call it
song – but some approximation to our usual customary piping.' So
it seems to us, but this impression, although, as I said, inevitable, is
yet fleeting and transient. We, too, are soon sunk in the feeling of
the mass, that, warmly pressed body to body, listens with indrawn
breath.

And to gather around her this mass of our people who are almost
always on the run and scurrying hither and thither for reasons that
are often not very clear, Josephine mostly needs to do nothing else
than take up her stand, head thrown back, mouth half-open, eyes
turned upwards, in the position that indicates her intention to sing.
She can do this where she likes, it need not be a place visible a long
way off, any secluded corner pitched on in a moment's caprice will
serve as well. The news that she is going to sing flies round at once
and soon whole processions are on the way there. Now, sometimes,
all the same, obstacles intervene, Josephine likes best to sing just
when things are most upset, many worries and dangers force us
then to take devious ways, with the best will in the world we cannot assemble ourselves as quickly as Josephine wants, and on occasion she stands there in ceremonial state for quite a time without
a sufficient audience – then indeed she turns furious, then she
stamps her feet, swearing in most unmaidenly fashion; she actually
bites. But even such behaviour does no harm to her reputation; instead of curbing a little her excessive demands, people exert themselves to meet them; messengers are sent out to summon fresh
hearers; she is kept in ignorance of the fact that this is being done;
on the roads all around sentries can be seen posted who wave on

newcomers and urge them to hurry; this goes on until at last a tolerably large audience is gathered.

What drives the people to make such exertions for Josephine's sake? This is no easier to answer than the first question about Josephine's singing, with which it is closely connected. One could eliminate that and combine them both in the second question, if it were possible to assert that because of her singing our people are unconditionally devoted to Josephine. But this is simply not the case; unconditional devotion is hardly known among us; ours are people who love slyness beyond everything, without any malice, to be sure, and childish whispering and chatter, innocent, superficial chatter, to be sure; but people of such a kind cannot go in for unconditional devotion, and that Josephine herself certainly feels is what she is fighting against with all the force of her feeble throat.

In making such generalized pronouncements, of course, one should not go too far, our people are all the same devoted to Josephine, only not unconditionally. For instance, they would not be capable of laughing at Josephine. It can be admitted: in Josephine there is much to make one laugh; and laughter for its own sake is never far away from us; in spite of all the misery of our lives quiet laughter is always, so to speak, at our elbows; but we do not laugh at Josephine. Many a time I have had the impression that our people interpret their relationship to Josephine in this way, that she, this frail creature, needing protection and in some way remarkable, in her own opinion remarkable for her gift of song, is entrusted to their care and they must look after her; the reason for this is not clear to anyone, only the fact seems to be established. But what is entrusted to one's care one does not laugh at; to laugh would be a breach of duty; the utmost malice which the most malicious of us wreak on Josephine is to say now and then: 'The sight of Josephine is enough to make one stop laughing.'

So the people look after Josephine much as a father takes into his care a child whose little hand — one cannot tell whether in appeal or command — is stretched out to him. One might think that our people are not fitted to exercise such paternal duties, but in reality they discharge them, at least in this case, admirably; no single individual could do what in this respect the people as a whole are capable of doing. To be sure, the difference in strength between the people and the individual is so enormous that it is enough for the nursling to be drawn into the warmth of their nearness and he is sufficiently protected. To Josephine, certainly, one does not dare mention such ideas. 'Your protection isn't worth an old song,' she says then. Yes, yes, the same old song, we think. And besides her protest is no real contradiction, it is rather a thoroughly childish way of doing, and childish gratitude, while a father's way of doing is to pay no attention to it.

Yet there is something else behind it which is not so easy to explain by this relationship between the people and Josephine. Josephine, that is to say, thinks just the opposite, she believes it is she who protects the people. When we are in a bad way politically or economically, her singing is supposed to save us, nothing less than that, and if it does not drive away the evil, at least gives us the strength to bear it. She does not put it in these words or in any other, she says very little anyhow, she is silent among the chatterers, but it flashes from her eyes, on her closed lips – few among us can keep their lips closed, but she can – it is plainly legible. Whenever we get bad news – and on many days bad news comes thick and fast at once, lies and half-truths included – she rises up at once, whereas usually she sits listlessly on the ground, she rises up and stretches her neck and tries to see over the heads of her flock like a shepherd before a thunderstorm. It is certainly a habit of children, in their wild, impulsive fashion, to make such claims, but Josephine's are not quite so unfounded as children's. True, she does not save us and she gives us no strength; it is easy to stage oneself as a saviour of our people, inured as they are to suffering, not sparing themselves, swift in decision, well acquainted with death, timorous only to the eye in the atmosphere of reckless daring which they constantly breathe, and as prolific besides as they are bold – it is easy, I say, to stage oneself after the event as the saviour of our people, who have always somehow managed to save themselves, although at the cost of sacrifices which make research historians – generally speaking we ignore historical research entirely – quite horror-struck. And yet it is true that just in emergencies we hearken better than at other times to Josephine's voice. The menaces that loom over us make us quieter, more humble, more submissive to Josephine's domination; we like to come together, we like to huddle close to each other, especially on an occasion set apart from the troubles preoccupying us; it is as if we were drinking in all haste – yes, haste is necessary, Josephine too often forgets that – from a cup of peace in common before the battle. It is not so much a performance of songs as a folk-assembly, and an assembly where, except for the small piping voice in front, there is complete stillness; the hour is much too grave for us to waste it in chatter.

A relationship of this kind, of course, would never content Josephine. Despite all the nervous uneasiness that fills Josephine because her position has never been quite defined, there is still much that she does not see, blinded by her self-conceit, and she can be brought fairly easily to overlook much more, a swarm of flatterers is always busy about her to this end, thus really doing a public service – and yet to be only an incidental, unnoticed performer in a corner of a folk-assembly, for that, although in itself it would be no small thing, she would certainly not make us a gift of her singing.

Still, she does not need to, for her art does not go unnoticed. Although we are at bottom preoccupied with quite other things and it is by no means only for the sake of her singing that stillness prevails and many a listener does not even look up but buries his face in his neighbour's fur, so that Josephine up in front seems to be exerting herself to no purpose, there is yet something – it cannot be denied – that irresistibly makes its way into us from Josephine's piping. This piping, which rises up where everyone else is pledged to silence, comes almost like a message from the whole people to each individual; Josephine's thin piping among grave decisions is almost like our people's precarious existence among the tumult of a hostile world. Josephine exerts herself, a mere nothing in voice, a mere nothing in execution, she asserts herself and gets across to us; it does us good to think of that. A really trained singer, if ever such a one should be found among us, we could certainly not endure at such a time and we should unanimously turn away from the senselessness of any such performance. May Josephine be spared from perceiving that the mere fact of our listening to her is proof that she is no singer. An intuition of it she must have, else why does she so passionately deny that we do listen, only she keeps on singing and piping her intuition away.

But there are other things she could take comfort from: we do really listen to her in a sense, probably much as one listens to a trained singer; she gets effects which a trained singer would try in vain to achieve among us and which are only produced precisely because her means are so inadequate. For this, doubtless, our way of life is mainly responsible.

Among our people there is no age of youth, scarcely the briefest childhood. Regularly, it is true, demands are put forward that the children should be granted a special freedom, a special protection, that their right to be a little carefree, to have a little senseless giddiness, a little play, that this right should be respected and the exercise of it encouraged; such demands are put forward and nearly everyone approves them, there is nothing one could approve more, but there is also nothing, in the reality of our daily life, that is less likely to be granted; one approves these demands, one makes attempts to meet them, but soon all the old ways are back again. Our life happens to be such that a child, as soon as it can run about a little and a little distinguish one thing from another, must look after itself just like an adult; the areas on which, for economic reasons, we have to settle sparsely are too wide, our enemies too numerous, the dangers lying everywhere in wait for us too incalculable – we cannot shelter our children from the struggle for existence, if we did so, it would bring them to an early grave. These depressing considerations are reinforced by another, which is not depressing: the fertility of our race. One generation – and each is numerous – treads on the heels of another, the children have no time to be children. Other races may foster their children carefully, schools may be erected for their little ones, out of these schools the children may come pouring daily, the future of the race, yet among them it is always the same children that come out day after day for a long time. We have no schools, but from our race come pouring at the briefest intervals the innumerable swarms of our children, merrily lisping or chirping so long as they cannot yet pipe, rolling or tumbling along by sheer impetus so long as they cannot yet run, clumsily carrying everything before them by mass weight so long as they cannot yet see, our children! And not the same children, as in those schools, no, always new children again and again, without end, without a break, hardly does a child appear than it is no more a child, while behind it new childish faces are already crowding so fast and so thick that they are indistinguishable, rosy with happiness. Truly, however delightful this may be and however much others may envy us for it, and rightly, we simply cannot give a real childhood to our children. And that has its consequences. A kind of unexpended, ineradicable childishness pervades our people; in direct opposition to what is best in us, our infallible practical common sense, we often behave with the utmost foolishness, with exactly the same foolishness as children, senselessly, wastefully, grandiosely, irresponsibly, and all that often for the sake of some trivial amusement. And although our enjoyment of it cannot of course be so wholehearted as a child's enjoyment, something of this survives in it without a doubt. From this childishness of our people Josephine, too, has profited since the beginning.

Yet our people are not only childish, we are also in a sense prematurely old, childhood and age come upon us not as upon others. We have no youth, we are all at once grown up, and then we stay grown up far too long, a certain weariness and hopelessness spreading from that leaves a broad trail through our people's nature, tough and strong in hope that it is in general. Our lack of musical gifts has surely some connection with this; we are too old for music, its excitement, its rapture does not suit our heaviness, wearily we wave it away; we content ourselves with piping; a little piping here and there, that is enough for us. Who knows, there may be talents for music among us; but if there were, the character of our people would suppress them before they could unfold. Josephine, on the other hand, can pipe as much as she will, or sing or whatever she likes to call it, that does not disturb us, that suits us, that we can well put up with; any music there may be in it is reduced to the least possible trace; a certain tradition of music is preserved, yet without making the slightest demand upon us.

But our people, being what they are, get still more than this from Josephine. At her concerts, especially in times of stress, it is only the very young who are interested in her singing as singing, they alone gaze in astonishment as she purses her lips, expels the air between her pretty front teeth, swoons in sheer wonderment at the sounds she herself is producing and after such a dying away swells her performance to new and more incredible heights, whereas the real mass of the people – this is plain to see – are quite withdrawn into themselves. Here in the brief intervals between their struggles our people dream, it is as if the limbs of each were loosened, as if the harried individual once in a while could relax and stretch himself at ease in the great warm bed of the community. And into these dreams Josephine's piping drops note by note; she calls it pearl-like, we call it staccato; but at any rate here it is in its right place, as nowhere else, finding the moment wait for it as music scarcely ever does. Something of our poor brief childhood is in it, something of lost happiness that can never be found again, but also something of active daily life, of its small gaieties, unaccountable and yet springing up and not to be obliterated. And indeed this is all expressed not in full round tones but softly, in whispers, confidentially, sometimes a little hoarsely. Of course it is a kind of piping. Why not? Piping is our people's daily speech, only many a one pipes his whole life long and does not know it, where here piping is set free from the fetters of daily life and it sets us free too for a little while. We certainly should not want to do without these performances.

But from that point it is a long, long way to Josephine's claim that she gives us new strength and so on and so forth. For ordinary people, at least, not for her train of flatterers. 'What other explanation could there be?' – they say with quite shameless sauciness – 'How else could you explain the great audiences, especially when danger is most imminent, which have even often enough hindered proper precautions being taken in time to avert danger.' Now, this last statement is unfortunately true, but can hardly be counted as one of Josephine's titles to fame, especially considering that when such large gatherings have been unexpectedly flushed by the enemy and many of our people left lying for dead, Josephine, who was responsible for it all, and, indeed, perhaps attracted the enemy by her piping, has always occupied the safest place and was always the first to whisk away quietly and speedily under cover of her escort. Still, everyone really knows that, and yet people keep running to whatever place Josephine decides on next, at whatever time she rises up to sing. One could argue from this that Josephine stands almost beyond the law, that she can do what she pleases, at the risk of actually endangering the community, and will be forgiven for everything. If this were so, even Josephine's claims would be entirely comprehensible, yes, in this freedom to be allowed her, this extraordinary gift granted to her and to no one else in direct contravention of the laws, one could see an admission of the fact that the people do not understand Josephine, just as she alleges, that they marvel helplessly at her art, feel themselves unworthy of it, try to assuage the pity she rouses in them by making really desperate sacrifices for her and, to the same extent that her art is beyond their comprehension, consider her personality and her wishes to lie beyond their jurisdiction. Well, that is simply not true at all, perhaps as individuals the people may surrender too easily to Josephine, but as a whole they surrender unconditionally to no one, and not to her either.

For a long time back, perhaps since the very beginning of her artistic career, Josephine has been fighting for exemption from all daily work on account of her singing; she should be relieved of all responsibility for earning her daily bread and being involved in the general struggle for existence, which – apparently – should be transferred on her behalf to the people as a whole. A facile enthusiast – and there have been such – might argue from the mere unusualness of this demand, from the spiritual attitude needed to frame such a demand, that it has an inner justification. But our people draw other conclusions and quietly refuse it. Nor do they trouble much about disproving the assumptions on which it is based. Josephine argues, for instance, that the strain of working is bad for her voice, that the strain of working is, of course, nothing to the strain of singing, but it prevents her from being able to rest sufficiently after singing and to recuperate for more singing, she has to exhaust her strength completely and yet, in these circumstances, can never rise to the peak of her abilities. The people listen to her arguments and pay no attention. Our people, so easily moved, sometimes cannot be moved at all. Their refusal is sometimes so decided that even Josephine is taken aback, she appears to submit, does her proper share of work, sings as best she can, but all only for a time, then with renewed strength – for this purpose her strength seems inexhaustible – she takes up the fight again.

Now it is clear that what Josephine really wants is not what she puts into words. She is honourable, she is not work-shy, shirking in any case is quite unknown among us, if her petition were granted she would certainly live the same life as before, her work would not at all get in the way of her singing nor would her singing grow any better — what she wants is public, unambiguous, permanent recognition of her art, going far beyond any precedent so far known. But while almost everything else seems within her reach, this eludes her persistently. Perhaps she should have taken a different line of attack from the beginning, perhaps she herself sees that her approach was wrong, but now she cannot draw back, retreat would be self-betrayal, now she must stand or fall by her petition.

If she really had enemies, as she avers, they could get much amusement from watching this struggle, without having to lift a finger. But she has no enemies, and even though she is often criticized here and there, no one finds this struggle of hers amusing. Just because of the fact that the people show themselves here in their cold, judicial aspect, which is otherwise rarely seen among us. And, however one may approve it in this case, the very idea that such an aspect might be turned upon oneself some day prevents amusement from breaking in. The important thing, both in the people's refusal and in Josephine's petition, is not the action itself, but the fact that the people are capable of presenting a stony, impenetrable front to one of their own comrades, and that it is all the more impenetrable because in other respects they show an anxious paternal care, and more than paternal care, for this very comrade.

Suppose that instead of the people one had an individual to deal with: one might imagine that this man had been giving in to Josephine all the time while nursing a wild desire to put an end to his submissiveness one fine day; that he had made superhuman sacrifices for Josephine in the firm belief that there was a natural limit to his capacity for sacrifice; yes, that he had sacrificed more than was needful merely to hasten the process, merely to spoil Josephine and encourage her to ask for more and more until she did indeed reach the limit with this last petition of hers; and that he then cut her off with a final refusal which was curt because long held in reserve. Now, this is certainly not how the matter stands, the people have no need of such guile, besides, their respect for Josephine is well tried and genuine, and Josephine's demands are after all so far-reaching that any simple child could have told her what the outcome would be; yet it may be that such considerations enter into Josephine's way of taking the matter and so add a certain bitterness to the pain of being refused.

But whatever her ideas on the subject, she does not let them deter her from pursuing the campaign. Recently she has even intensified her attack; hitherto she has used only words as her weapons but now she is beginning to have recourse to other means, which she thinks will prove more efficacious but which we think will run herself into greater dangers.

Many believe that Josephine is becoming so insistent because she feels herself growing old and her voice falling off, and so she thinks it high time to wage the last battle for recognition. I do not believe it. Josephine would not be Josephine if that were true. For her there is no growing old and no falling off in her voice. If she makes demands it is not because of outward circumstances but because of an inner logic. She reaches for the highest garland not because it is momentarily hanging a little lower but because it is the highest; if she had any say in the matter she would have it still higher.

This contempt for external difficulties, to be sure, does not hinder her from using the most unworthy methods. Her rights seem beyond question to her; so what does it matter how she secures them? especially since in this world, as she sees it, honest methods are bound to fail. Perhaps that is why she has transferred the battle for her rights from the field of song to another which she cares little about. Her supporters have let it be known that, according to herself, she feels quite capable of singing in such a way that all levels of the populace, even to the remotest corners of the opposition, would find it a real delight, a real delight not by popular standards, for the people affirm that they have always delighted in her singing, but a delight by her own standards. However, she adds, since she cannot falsify the highest standards nor pander to the lowest, her singing will have to stay as it is. But when it comes to her campaign for exemption from work, we get a different story; it is, of course, also a campaign on behalf of her singing, yet she is not fighting directly with the priceless weapon of her song, so any instrument she uses is good enough. Thus, for instance, the rumour went round that Josephine meant to cut short her grace-notes if her petition were not granted. I know nothing about grace-notes, and have never noticed any in Josephine's singing. But Josephine is going to cut short her grace-notes, not, for the present, to cut them out entirely, only to cut them short. Presumably she has carried out her threat, although I for one have observed no difference in her performance. The people as a whole listened in the usual way without making any pronouncement on the grace-notes, nor did their response to her petition vary by a jot. It must be admitted, however, that Josephine's way of thinking, like her figure, is often very charming. And so, for instance, after that performance, just as if her decision about the grace-notes had been too severe or too sudden a move against the people, she announced that next time she would put in all the grace-notes again. Yet after the next concert she changed her mind once more, there was to be definitely an end of these great arias with the grace-notes, and until her petition was favourably regarded they would never recur. Well, the people let all these announcements, decisions and counter-decisions go in at one ear and out at the other, like a grown-up person deep in thought turning a deaf ear to a child's babble, fundamentally well-disposed but not accessible.

Josephine, however, does not give in. The other day, for instance, she claimed that she had hurt her foot at work, so that it was difficult for her to stand up to sing; but since she could not sing except standing up, her songs would now have to be cut short. Although she limps and leans on her supporters, no one believes that she is really crippled. Granted that her frail body is extra sensitive, she is yet one of us and we are a race of workers; if we were to start limping every time we got a scratch, the whole people would never be done limping. Yet though she lets herself be led about like a lameter, though she shows herself in this pathetic condition oftener than usual, the people all the same listen to her singing thankfully and appreciatively as before, but do not bother much about the shortening of her songs.

Since she cannot very well go on limping for ever, she thinks of something else, she pleads that she is tired, not in the mood for singing, feeling faint. And so we get a theatrical performance as well as a concert. We see Josephine's supporters in the background begging and imploring her to sing. She would be glad to oblige, but she cannot. They comfort and caress her with flatteries, they almost carry her to the selected spot where she is supposed to sing. At last, bursting inexplicably into tears, she gives way, but when she stands up to sing, obviously at the end of her resources, weary, her arms not widespread as usual but hanging lifelessly down, so that one gets the impression that they are perhaps a little too short — just as she is about to strike up, there, she cannot do it after all, an unwilling shake of the head tells us so and she breaks down before our eyes. To be sure, she pulls herself together again and sings, I fancy, much as usual; perhaps, if one has an ear for the finer shades of expression, one can hear that she is singing with unusual feeling, which is, however, all to the good. And in the end she is actually less tired than before, with a firm tread, if one can use such a term for her tripping gait, she moves off, refusing all help from her supporters and measuring with cold eyes the crowd which respectfully makes way for her.

That happened a day or two ago; but the latest is that she has disappeared, just at a time when she was supposed to sing. It is not only her supporters who are looking for her, many are devoting themselves to the search, but all in vain; Josephine has vanished, she will not sing, she will not even be cajoled into song, this time she has deserted us entirely.

Curious, how mistaken she is in her calculations, the clever creature, so mistaken that one might fancy she has made no calculations at all but is only being driven on by her destiny, which in our world cannot be anything but a sad one. Of her own accord she abandons her singing, of her own accord she destroys the power she has gained over people's hearts. How could she ever have gained that power, since she knows so little about these hearts of ours? She hides herself and does not sing, but our people, quietly, without visible disappointment, a self-confident mass in perfect equilibrium, so constituted, even although appearances are misleading, that they can only bestow gifts and not receive them, even from Josephine, our people continue on their way.

Josephine's road, however, must go downhill. The time will soon come when her last notes sound and die into silence. She is a small episode in the eternal history of our people, and the people will get over the loss of her. Not that it will be easy for us; how can our gatherings take place in utter silence? Still, were they not silent even when Josephine was present? Was her actual piping notably louder and more alive than the memory of it will be? Was it even in her lifetime more than a simple memory? Was it not rather because Josephine's singing was already past losing in this way that our people in their wisdom prized it so highly?

So perhaps we shall not miss so very much after all, while Josephine, redeemed from the earthly sorrows which to her thinking lay in wait for all chosen spirits, will happily lose herself in the numberless throng of the heroes of our people, and soon, since we are no historians, will rise to the heights of redemption and be forgotten like all her brothers.

Translated by Willa and Edwin Muir

FOR THE BEST IN PAPERBACKS, LOOK FOR THE

In every corner of the world, on every subject under the sun, Penguin represents quality and variety – the very best in publishing today.

For complete information about books available from Penguin – including Puffins, Penguin Classics and Arkana – and how to order them, write to us at the appropriate address below. Please note that for copyright reasons the selection of books varies from country to country.

In the United Kingdom: Please write to *Dept E.P., Penguin Books Ltd, Harmondsworth, Middlesex, UB7 0DA.*

If you have any difficulty in obtaining a title, please send your order with the correct money, plus ten per cent for postage and packaging, to *PO Box No 11, West Drayton, Middlesex*

In the United States: Please write to *Dept BA, Penguin, 299 Murray Hill Parkway, East Rutherford, New Jersey 07073*

In Canada: Please write to *Penguin Books Canada Ltd, 2801 John Street, Markham, Ontario L3R 1B4*

In Australia: Please write to the *Marketing Department, Penguin Books Australia Ltd, P.O. Box 257, Ringwood, Victoria 3134*

In New Zealand: Please write to the *Marketing Department, Penguin Books (NZ) Ltd, Private Bag, Takapuna, Auckland 9*

In India: Please write to *Penguin Overseas Ltd, 706 Eros Apartments, 56 Nehru Place, New Delhi, 110019*

In the Netherlands: Please write to *Penguin Books Netherlands B.V., Postbus 195, NL–1380AD Weesp*

In West Germany: Please write to *Penguin Books Ltd, Friedrichstrasse 10–12, D–6000 Frankfurt/Main 1*

In Spain: Please write to *Longman Penguin España, Calle San Nicolas 15, E–28013 Madrid*

In Italy: Please write to *Penguin Italia s.r.l., Via Como 4, I-20096 Pioltello (Milano)*

In France: Please write to *Penguin Books Ltd, 39 Rue de Montmorency, F-75003 Paris*

In Japan: Please write to *Longman Penguin Japan Co Ltd, Yamaguchi Building, 2–12–9 Kanda Jimbocho, Chiyoda-Ku, Tokyo 101*